I'm a young transgender woman who came out in 2018, just a week before I turned 18! Since then, I have been living happily and proudly as a woman. For me, writing has been an escape from my own worries while I wait for the next steps of my transition. I am lucky that I am accepted and supported by my friends and family and can now live my life the way I want to.

(M)Ollie

Eilidh Chambers

(M)Ollie

VANGUARD PAPERBACK

© Copyright 2023
Eilidh Chambers

The right of Eilidh Chambers to be identified as author of
this work has been asserted by them in accordance with the
Copyright, Designs and Patents Act 1988.

A CIP catalogue record for this title is
available from the British Library.

ISBN 978 1 80016 876 3

This is a work of fiction. Names, characters, businesses, places, events and incidents are either the
product of the author's imagination or used in a fictitious manner. Any resemblance to actual
persons, living or dead, or actual events is purely coincidental.

Vanguard Press is an imprint of
Pegasus Elliot Mackenzie Publishers Ltd.
www.pegasuspublishers.com

First Published in 2023

Vanguard Press
Sheraton House Castle Park
Cambridge England

Printed & Bound in Great Britain

Contents

Eight Years Ago

The bell sounded to bring the school day to an end as I was tying the laces on my black trainers. As an eight-year-old child, the weekend was one of the best occasions around. I raced home through the narrow, snaking, concrete path which slithered its way from the school up to the street where my home was. A mass of grey slate, no grass to play on except the small patch by the main road which was obviously a no-go zone. Not that I minded that all too much — there was a park nearby and I didn't tend to be the outgoing or sociable type. At least, not the me that I was then.

I trudged up the cracking steps of my front garden and up to the house's pristine, white front door. Mum did always like to keep a clean house, especially ever since we were left alone in the same house after the settlements. It was peaceful and my life was the simple and typical eight-year-old boy's. *Was.*

I inserted the small silver key into the goldish lock and turned until I heard the satisfying little click which signified that access was permitted. It always felt like I was in a spy film whenever I did that. I was Tom Cruise in the *Mission Impossible* movies, an unstoppable secret agent with unlimited access. In reality, my mum often worked until an hour or so after the school day finished so she trusted me to just let myself in. Babysitters weren't expensive, she just didn't have much trust in them. It meant I felt like I was in MI5 every single weekday, so I didn't complain. I often thought I could be a spy when I was younger and… different.

Once I opened the door, I stood on the black welcome mat in the hall and wiped my feet, hearing little squeaks of the residual mud which remained on my shoes after another day of wandering around the playground alone in my own little world. I kicked off the Adidas trainers and rushed upstairs to change into something less bland and dull. Grey sweatshirt, grey trousers, black shoes, grey coat — it was almost as if the school was training us how to blend into the concrete landscape of the local area which permeated throughout the small community of Pitton, named after its rich and storied coal-mining history.

I unbuttoned and removed my polo shirt, revealing my then pudgy body to the hidden cameras of the Russian agents who were observing my every move in my fantasy world of missions and going undercover. I realised this was a dreadful move — they could have been on their way, and I may have compromised myself on this top-secret task. I couldn't ever seem to escape this imaginary high-stakes universe I had created in my mind when I was a small, overweight boy. I had to find a disguise, and quick.

I slid my back up against the red walls of my bedroom, hoping that I had escaped the digital eyes of the enemy technology. I looked up and down consistently as I escaped from my room, keeping a close look out for any gadgets and gizmos the opposition could be using to ensure I failed my mission. As I entered the upstairs hall which had one sole function of connecting the two floors of the house together — there was no other purpose for this room — I noticed something which could be used as the perfect cover-up. Hanging over the white banister was an object made of baby pink fabric. I picked it up and held it in front of my face to discover that it was one of my mum's T-shirts. Perfect; those spies weren't looking for a girl

I quickly grabbed the top and threw it on over my head. I was a very small boy for my age, so this T-shirt actually stretched down to about knee-height. Even better for hiding my identity from the spies. I was curious so I went through to my mum's room to look in her wide, full-length mirror which took up a whole wall on its own. It wasn't that huge a waste of space though, since her wardrobe was behind this reflective wall when you slid it a certain way.

Her whole room was arranged as though she was a spy too. Her drawers all had locks on them and on the purple and white floral walls were just plaques of inspirational quotes and simple pictures of summer days and daisies. There were a few photos from her past, including her wedding, but mostly this room could have been the ideal secret hideout, even if you removed the high-tech reflecting wall of glass on the far side.

Reading my new disguise, I saw that it said 'Hope.' I sure hoped the enemies wouldn't catch me, so this was very fitting. I was feeling the breeze on my chubby legs, so I decided that I needed something to fix that. There was nothing else lying loose in her room but returning to the hall, I saw the washing basket from just inside the bathroom, the room that was an immediate right turn from my mum's. I took a peek inside the white washing basket and pulled out a pair of my own black jogging bottoms. I slipped them on, and it was time to return downstairs to the retreat of the living room, safe from the Russian spies yet again. Ollie Clarke had nailed the mission yet again, an undeniable success. He had never been caught!

Unfortunately, in my excitement, I lost track of time, and my mum was due to come home any minute. I realised that I needed to hurry and take her shirt off my body. As I stood up and left the living room, I heard the door opening and the familiar sound off my mum's low-heeled boots thumping off the laminate flooring in the hall. I was in plain sight, I was caught.

"Ollie, I'm ho — what on earth are you wearing?"

"Oh this? This is my disguise. The enemies almost had me compromised."

"You shouldn't be wearing my things, they're not for boys."

My mum's tone was serious this time, unlike previous occasions where she had laughed at my silly spy fantasies.

"Sorry Mum, it's just a game I like to play."

"I know that, honey. But boys don't wear tops like this. If you wear my things, I'll think you want to be my daughter instead. Girls wear tops like that one so if you want to be a girl, we can make that happen."

I was stunned, this was a very unexpected reaction to one of my antics. I felt my heart accelerating with no obvious cause and strange dryness creep into my throat.

"Sorry Mum, I won't do it again. I promise."

"Good. Now go and change into your *own* top and we can forget about this over dinner."

I was shaking as I took my mum's top off and draped it over the banister once more, just as I found it. Why did that annoy her? Why was

I so nervous? I assumed it was because I didn't ask but she did say that boys aren't meant to be wearing their mum's stuff. Either way, it was a pretty clear warning. One which I made sure I followed. I didn't bother disguising myself any more, or so I thought.

Eight Years Later

I was just home from school and straight into a bit of social time Shawn, my friend from a nearby town sometimes comes around in the evening, he has done since we were in different primary schools. We met all those years ago because my next-door neighbour is his auntie, and he would spend the weekends there since his mum and dad work nights or even whole weekends sometimes. He would also come through to see his aunt when his parents were working late, or when he just wanted some space. It wasn't a long walk. We had the same typical boy interests — sports, video games and sometimes mischief.

After what feels like our 973rd game of FIFA for the day on my white 30-inch TV, Shawn is clearly fed up with losing.

"I'm bored."

I look out of my bedroom window, not that I have to speculate on the weather since we can hear the rain pelting off the slates on the roof.

"Well, we can't exactly go outside and play footie."

"I know what we can do though. We can play truth or dare."

I snigger. "Truth or dare? What are we, ten?"

"Do you have a better suggestion?"

I shrug my weak shoulders and reluctantly agree to play. Shawn wants to go first so I ask the three fateful words.

"Truth or dare?"

Shawn clearly ponders this for a moment then declares "Truth."

This is an easy one.

"Is it true that you have a crush on Sarah Stewart?"

His face turns red, and he blushes intensely.

"N-no…"

I am not buying that for a second, so I remind him of the game.

"Tell the truth."

I feel like I am interrogating him at this point with the bright lights shining directly in his face, which would explain the burnt-looking red face he is currently sporting.

"OK, yes it is. But come on man, she is so fit in her football stuff."

It is tough to argue, she is fairly attractive. Sarah sometimes comes to the cage with us to play football and is often the centre of attention when she does. Perhaps this is a result of her being the only girl there when we play. She more than holds her own in our games, although a few of the guys are reluctant to admit it. Not Shawn though, he has no problem complementing his crush.

I laugh regardless. It's one of those trump cards you can hold in a game of masculinity poker, knowing exactly who your best mate wants to go out with. At sixteen years old, it's a classic bit of banter to use, especially when you're the smallest and least athletic of the guys in the group, which I most certainly am at five-foot-four and with my size six feet which just won't seem to grow nor learn how to play football well. Anyway, Shawn is quite annoyed by my teasing, so he wants to move on to my turn.

"Fine, let's stop talking about your crush and play. Give me one."

Shawn composes himself and asks me the same question.

"Truth or dare?"

"Truth as well."

Shawn takes a bit more time to think of his question, but it is a good one to be fair to him.

"Who was your first girlfriend?"

"I-uh-I don't have one. I've never had one."

Shawn is in hysterics as he more than exacts his revenge with this stinging truth. While all the girls my age are growing and their bodies are changing, I remain short, pudgy and with not even a single hair on my face and truly little on my body — so little that it's hard to see any until you're right up close. Now I am the one turning red and desperate to move on.

"Right, whatever. Truth or dare?"

He pauses and ponders then decides to bring the game's intensity up a notch or two.

"Dare."

Once again, my dare is too easy not to choose.

"I dare you to ask Sarah out. Right now, over Messenger."

"Mate, come on! That's not right, I can't jus—"

I cut him off with my best chicken impression and mock him.

"Come on man, giving up already?"

He is visibly ticked off as he takes his phone from his pocket. I demand that I see his every letter that he types to the girl of his adolescent dreams. The message itself is sweet but like I am ever going to admit that. This is Truth or Dare, the very goal of this is to humiliate and embarrass your friends!

'Hey Sarah, we've been close pals for a long time and I was wondering if you wanted to go for a walk sometime. just the two of us?'

"Aw, cute little lovebird. That's so cringey lad, I can't believe you just did that."

"You dared me! I had no choice!"

"Well anyways, my turn I guess." I try to hide my laughter, but it is just too funny sometimes.

Shawn tries to calm himself as his once clearly embarrassed face paled with worry and regret over what he just said. He runs his hands through his gelled black hair and says those three words I have been waiting for, albeit in a weaker and less confident manner than the usual.

"Truth or dare?"

"Truth."

Shawn is now the one sniggering.

"Again? Really? You're such a chicken, you won't even take a dare."

"Fine, dare. You can't embarrass me as much as that."

Shawn takes an abnormal length of time to think of a dare for me. Since I have no girlfriend and no known crush, he can't ask me to do the same thing as he just did. The minutes tick by as I hear the clock on the wall of the upstairs hall confirming my suspicion. Finally, he speaks up.

"I've got one, it's based on what I just saw on my Facebook feed."

"Aye, go ahead. What's the task then? Drink a raw egg? Eat some ridiculously sour sweet?"

Shawn's ideas are never usually what you would call 'outside the box', so I expect something fairly predictable and typical of this strange

15

game. Unfortunately for him, his phone has just vibrated.

"That's my mum texting that I need to go home. You were lucky this time."

I go downstairs with Shawn to see him out. Mum raised me to always do that whenever I have a guest.

"See you soon, mate."

"Will do, thanks for coming."

With the door closing behind him, it is now time for me to do the second thing I've been waiting for the chance to try every Sunday since Mum started going out with the girls from her work on weekends. I peer out of the glass window on the front door to make sure no one is watching, then head upstairs to activate Operation Hidden Princess.

I start by raking through the washing basket at the foot of her double bed, hoping for a full outfit to be lying loose. I grab the first bra and panties I can find as well as something which looks like a dress. I unravel it to reveal it is only a strange towel, no luck. I instead find a denim skirt and a T-shirt of hers and decide that it's close enough. I can't risk needing to take something out of her wardrobe, not with how neat and proper she likes to keep everything.

I strip myself naked and start with the panties. They are so constricting and tight on my mid-section as I try hopelessly to make them a little more comfortable where it counts. Giving up on this quickly, I decide to move on to the bra. I can't even begin to figure out how to fasten a bra, so I simply drape it over my shoulders in the most obvious way possible and move on to the easiest item — the long-sleeve T-shirt. I throw it on as I would any of my own tops and notice that it's not a bad fit, which is encouraging. I now know that I have to dress in this black, denim skirt which was crumpled messily in the bottom of the basket before I pulled it out in my desperate, excited and deeply anxious raking.

I start by putting it on upside-down but soon realise the error and remove it to put it on the proper way. Honestly, how do the girls at school do all this? It's so tight as it wraps its way around my legs, imprisoning me in a cage of downright femininity. I try to button the top of the skirt and eventually succeed, much to the despair of both my brain and my oversized gut. I can't tell whether the nausea building in my digestive system is a result of the squeezing of the high-waisted skirt or the anticipation of what comes next. Heels. Mum always keeps a pair of heels under her wooden bed frame, so I at least know where to go for them. Her reasoning? Well, she likes to have a quick change available immediately when she is getting ready and often puts those heels into her handbag as an alternative option. Imagine caring that much about your outfit all the time. Guys have it simple; they wear what they wear and that's that. No make-up, no impractical footwear, no itchy material, just clean and simple clothes. And I hate it.

I sit on the edge of my mum's bed, on her fluffy white throw, and shove and push and crush my feet into these alien, black, pointy shoes. My mum actually has size 7 feet, but it's the triangle shape of these shoes which make them so awkward. Well, not just that. Once I have them on, I look in the mirror at the hellscape I have become. I look like a total sissy. I'm just about ready to try to leave the room but then I recall the last part of my plan. Lipstick, every girl needs her lipstick. I steadily wobble my way over to my mum's make-up case as on top of it sits her favourite lipstick. It has a pinkish colour without being too bright or noticeable. You would know it was lipstick but not from miles away. I stand right in front of the mirror and go all tingly as I lift the lid off the container and close my eyes. I can feel my small hands shaking as I move the stick closer to my closed mouth until I feel the cold contact. Then, as I have seen my mum do many times, I open my eyes and roughly trace my lips with it. I feel so faint as I sway uneasily back and forth and wobble in the black heels but manage to avoid fainting and close the lipstick again, being extra careful to put it back exactly where it goes and gripping the dresser with all my might as the shoes try to feed my awkward, constricted frame to the bedroom carpet much like a sea lion is fed tuna at the shows you see on holiday.

But that's it, I'm done. As I'm shuffling my way back through, I can read on the clock that this whole ordeal took me nearly an hour to do.

Just as I'm returning to my room, practising walking baby steps in the heels, the front door opens with a frighteningly sharp pull on the handle.

"Ollie, that's me back!"

My vocal cords are pulled from my throat at this point; I'm in shock. She isn't meant to be back so soon, she isn't usually.

"Ollie! Come and see me; I didn't raise you to be rude. Pause your game!"

I try slip the heels off, I'm trying to do anything to make this less of a disaster, but I can hear her footsteps coming up the subtly creaking stairs. I have no choice, I am compromised.

"Sorry, I just wasn't expecting you to be home so soon."

As I emerge from my bedroom, Mum looks at my face in a weird way, but she goes back down the stairs and into the kitchen then summons me to join her.

"Ollie Kat Clarke, we need to talk."

Kat is my middle name. I took it from my mum after the whole settlement with my dad, whom I'm too young to really remember since he left when I was two. When I'm summoned by that call, I know I'm in trouble and I know not to make her angry by delaying the inevitable.

I swallow my fear and my pride and accept that this is going to be a horrible conversation to have. Once I face that fact, I head down the stairs as quickly as possible while still in the tight skirt. And every step just increases my hopeless feelings. When I reach the bottom of the stairs and turn the corner, my mum is stood at the kitchen door.

"So this is why you were hiding, huh?"

"Mum, I can explain. You see—"

She cuts me off, totally expectedly.

"No, it's my turn to talk and your turn to listen. I have warned you before about wearing my clothes and instead of keeping your promise, you dress head-to-toe in my things? I know you had my heels on too, I could hear you in them thumping around up there!"

"Mum, please hear me out. I-I…"

"You want to be a girl."

I freeze. How did she know that? Boys will be boys and all that, so I thought she'd just take it as me messing around. She continued as my heart raced intensely.

"I know that boys will be boys when it comes to their mum's lingerie, but this is something different. You dressed this way on purpose because you want this. You didn't do it by half, you're wearing a skirt and make-up. If this is what you want, we can make it happen."

Tears are forming in my eyes as I try to explain myself again but to no avail, the words just stop forming.

"So here is the script. You want to be a girl? That's totally OK, honey. I'll make sure you experience everything a girl should. We'll have to buy you your own clothes but that will have to wait. I can't have my daughter wearing my things; you need clothes that fit you better. And clothes that are way more feminine."

I try my best to smile and stop my tears as she explains this all to me. She is accepting who I want to be, this is huge. My mind is on an endless rollercoaster of shifting emotions. Fear, joy, relief and shame all hurtling through my confused teenage head. I nod and give my best attempt at looking less humiliated.

"At school, you will be Ollie for now. But when I come home every night, you will be transformed into the mummy's girl you want to be. I will teach you everything you need to know to bring out the real you."

I'm finally starting to smile now. My salty tears are clogging my throat, making talking absolutely impossible so I just keep nodding as she continues to outline my next steps. I can finally feel words coming out again, they're back from their quarantine in the back of my throat.

"Thanks Mum. I need this, you're right."

"Mother knows best, my baby girl. Always. Now, you best go and fetch those heels again. We'll see how you cope as a girl while we eat at the table."

She hugs me closer than ever before, and I grip the banister tightly as I walk each step back up to pick up the same black high heels.

Dinner is an awkward affair, made more so by the fact that Mum insists I stay dressed as a girl. She calls it my first night as a girl, a new beginning for me.

I sit on a chair at the dinner table and crush my feet back into the uncomfortable yet irresistible footwear while Mum watches. It's so frustrating when the heels slide off the hard flooring.

"Wipe your last few tears away, honey. You'll get the hang of all of this and become my beautiful daughter. It will just take time and practice, but we have lots of time to work on the new real you. Besides, carpet is a lot easier for putting heels on, trust me."

Her words are like a warm, comforting blanket to settle my insecurities about who I really am. I do my best to smile as we talk about anything else to distract ourselves for a few minutes.

"So how are your work pals?"

"Eh? Oh they're good yeah. We had a lovely lunch in town today at the new Italian café. Honestly, we will have to go at some point."

"You want to have lunch with me? That's rare!"

We laugh, we smile, and this may be the closest I have ever felt to my mum.

"Well, I'll need to show my darling daughter off somewhere on her big debut! But we have time before that, you don't need to worry. Also, mother and daughter time is so common; every mum goes places with their girls. That's what we'll be able to do soon."

The events of the last hour are like a sparkling, bright pink elephant. No matter where we try to take the conversation, it always comes back to the big plans for my future.

"Now tonight, you can go relax with your games. But please can you keep the full outfit on? It will help you adjust the more often you wear girly clothes. I also want to take a photo of you, just to have, so we can remember where you're starting."

"OK, do you want to take that now?"

Mum nods so I stand up, then immediately fall back into my chair which sends us both into hysterics.

Finally settling down, and wiping away a different kind of tears, I steadily stand up and gingerly shuffle over to the plain duck-egg-blue wall by the back door of the house.

"Smile for me, my lovely girl."

I can finally feel my happiness coming back in waves of emotional glee as I stand proudly and have my photo taken.

"Mum, I've been thinking. What are we going to call me? Ollie doesn't really fit any more."

Mum shrugs and looks at me. "What do you want your name to be?"

"I uh, I don't know. I've called myself many."

This is true. I've probably used around a hundred different names for this side of myself in the past. Now though, I have to pick just one to carry into this new life I am going to lead.

"We'll look online tonight before you go to bed. You can go play now, honey."

20

"Awesome, thanks."

"Girls don't use that word — we'll work on it. It's all going to take time."

"Seriously? Even my vocabulary has to change?"

"Oh sweetie, if you want to do this properly then just about everything has to change."

I'm a little taken aback by this but I still smile as I carefully leave the kitchen. My feet are already starting to hurt from being squeezed into these high heels, so much so that I go up the stairs on my hands and knees which leaves carpet marks on my bare skin. As I return to my room and sit in my gaming chair, I take a moment to let it all sink in. 'Everything has to change.' That's what she said. New friends, new clothes, new name, new hobbies — this is going to be eventful to say the least.

The games happen, it doesn't so much feel like I played them. My mind spins around, doing pirouettes and twirls as I reflect on the events of this whole evening. I finally have exactly what I want, my mum understands, accepts and is even prepared to support my journey into womanhood. I mean, I'm wearing a skirt and heels and lipstick while I sit and play my Xbox. Life is turning around! So why am I so nervous, so scared, so unsure? I guess it's that line from the woman herself. 'Everything has to change.'

And she clearly means it. I'm off the football squad which is not much of a loss since I am not exactly Kieran Tierney or Andrew Robertson. I play left back as in usually left back on the subs bench!

I'd usually be in a game chat with a couple of the lads from school, but I remember what else Mum said. 'No boys.' I go through to her room to ask what she meant by that rule and if it meant I can't chat to them while playing. She pauses her ironing to reassure me.

"Honey, you can talk to them in games! It's not that you're not allowed to talk to boys, it's that a girl like you can't be bringing boys back here anymore! Who knows what we would end up with then? Would my little girl have a boyfriend?"

"Mum! That's weird, don't say that!" Then we both giggle, and everything is all right again. I turn around and slowly leave her room, forgetting that I'm wearing heels which is why walking feels so awkward. After far too long, I'm back in my gaming chair and I set up a game chat, being extra careful not to do anything which shows a video chat. Imagine if the guys saw me like this.

Then it dawns on me. They *will* eventually see just that. If everything goes to plan, Ollie is going to be a relic in very little time, and I'll finally be able to be myself. All the time, not just when I'm alone or even when I'm at home. School, family gatherings, shopping trips, holidays... prom...

"Ollie, you all right? Something up with your mic? You've barely made a sound!"

"Yeah, you're usually telling us shitty jokes all night. Might need to unplug it and try again."

I take a deep breath and try to ditch the thoughts for at least a little while. I do as the lads instructed so that it doesn't seem so weird.

"Sorry guys, I'm back. Damn mic issues, eh?"

"That's all right, let's try win a few games now we're all sorted."

I should probably explain. I didn't have many friends. I never have had lots of friends but it's the few quality ones that I kept close. Chris, Stephen and Darius are just that. Three people who didn't exclude me right away, they gave me a chance and now they are my closest friends. We spend every break and lunch at school together, chatting the usual boy stuff. Football, girls, gaming. I am always more of a contributor to a conversation than a starter, chipping in with *hilarious* jokes and sometimes, even knowing what I am talking about.

I don't know how they'll take this news though. I'm nowhere near ready to tell them anyway so again I attempt to ditch the thoughts. While I sit cross-legged. In a skirt and heels, still tasting the lipstick that was applied a few hours ago.

As we reach the final battle, it is a now or never — well, not tonight — situation. We do our best and for one of the few occasions, our best is good enough. The final opposition team crumbles as their sniper is taken out by a well-thrown grenade from Stephen and Darius and I storm the base with aggressive fire. Chris is already dead and spectating our historic victory.

"Yes!"

"Get in!"

"Come on!"

"Wooo!"

That right there is the sound of victory. Four different cries of success and achievement.

"Great way to end the night!"

"And maybe next time Chris, you'll be alive for the victory!"

We have a final joke about how bad we all are at respective things, and I realise the time. Mum wants to talk about names, so I know I have to go.

"Right guys, I'll catch you later."

"See ya."

"Bye Ollie."

"Laters!"

I switch off the console and stand up, shivering once more. No idea this time if the shivering is from nerves or the fact that I'm not used to wearing a skirt and having so much skin showing while not sat in the cosiest room.

No more confident in my heels, I walk(?) back through to my mum's room. Her favourite chore finished and the result in the favourite white ironing basket; she's lying on her bed watching who knows what. She's into so many shows, it's tough to keep up with what she's watching this time. Sometimes re-runs, sometimes something totally new and random. This time it seems to be an old film, the colour saturation isn't exactly up to scratch with the latest Blu-ray releases.

"Ah, there's my girl! How was your gaming? I heard some cheering."

"Oh, it was good. We managed to win that last game just there."

"See? Girls can play games just as well as boys! But I do want you to spend your time doing some girlier activities too in future. With me, by yourself, or even with some friends!"

"Hmm, the guys don't exactly seem like the manicures and shopping type. I'm guessing you mean I should meet some new friends."

"I know it won't be easy for you, but we'll try different ways of making that possible. I have been looking at support groups, but they all seem to be aimed at younger children. I've found a few after-school clubs like dancing, cheer and netball for us — well, you to try. Not all right away though!"

The relief is physically there in my lower abdomen. "Yeah, was going to say that's a lot."

"I'm getting more carried away about this than you son — eh, hon. Sorry, it's all new. I'll get used to it."

"I will too. And I'll have to adjust to a new name."

Mum's eyes light up with inspiration as if candles have been placed in her brain.

"Ah! I've already sorted that. I've got two options for you that will work perfectly. I have no preference so it's totally up to you but for ease and similarity, I narrowed it down to two."

"What are they?"

"Hey, one minute! I wrote them down here so you could see how it looks on paper instead of just hearing it."

Mum reaches over to her bedside unit and takes an old envelope from the surface.

"Hope you like them."

I graciously accept the envelope from her hand.

"Thanks."

I look on the front of the white paper but there are just phone numbers and random shapes doodled on there. No doubt a result of Mum being bored while on hold to the company that sent the letter. Always a bill seemingly. Adulthood does not look fun!

"On the back, honey. Turn it over. Your name isn't the phone number!" she says with a smile. She often laughs at my little mistakes, but it makes me feel more human. It makes me feel loved even when I'm being a bit dopey and not using my brain.

"Honestly, all that intelligence and no common sense at all!"

"That's me!" I proudly reply, turning the envelope over to reveal just four words. Two names, two spellings.

"I'm sorry, I just love your name so much that I had to keep it involved in your new one. At least you have a name that fits into girly ones!"

The envelope reads:

Hollie? Holly?

Mollie? Molly?

"It's the sound that I love, so you can change the spelling if you like.

Practise writing them all, see which one you like most."

I start following that instruction, beginning with Hollie. The name is easy enough to write but it feels very weird. Then I do the same with Mollie, and something clicks. Then I try writing 'Molly' with the y, and it feels a bit better still. I try 'Holly' for the sake of it, but I can only think of Christmas time when I do.

"You could also have Polly, but that's too much like a parrot for me."

That cracks me up, I must admit. Mum just has a way of making everything fun, even a serious decision like this.

"I think I like Molly, spelled M-O-L-L-Y."

"Molly is a beautiful name. It's also a drug but just don't take any or even raise that point and you'll be fine!"

And again, I'm cracking up. It's no wonder where I gained my sense of humour from. Mum has always been able to put a smile on my face, even when times were tough all those years ago and up to now.

"Great, so Molly Kat Clarke?" I ask, looking for a final answer.

"Well, not quite. See, you know you have the middle name Kat because I'm Katherine. But now that you're going to become my daughter, you can take the full 'Katherine' middle name now too. Molly Katherine Clarke. And you can carry that until you are married to a nice man, and you take his surname!"

"Mum! Come on, don't make jokes like that! It's weird enough to think about so soon!"

"Well, teen girls often want to see teen boys. That's sort of how you came about after all! Don't worry, we'll find out if you actually like boys. I'm not going to arrange a marriage for you or force you to be with a guy even through all this. It's an ever-changing world, you can fall in love with whomever you want. It's fine so long as they love you back and it's all legal."

"Ha, ha, ha, yeah I guess you're right. Mother knows best I suppose."

"Quoting princess movies already are we? I knew I had a girl all this time!"

"I have no idea what that's from, I've just heard it said."

"Part of your education and another reason to find girly pals. They'll fill you in on everything you've missed, honey."

I nod in agreement.

"Now, Molly," she says, throwing a dramatic wink my way as if to say 'see, I did it'. "It's time for you to go settle down, take all that stuff off and drift off to sleep."

"Yeah, it's been a long day."

"Well, you go get sorted in the bathroom and I'll put something nice for you to sleep in on your bed. I have a few things I was getting rid of anyways, no reason to waste it when I can give you some nightshirts."

I head off to the bathroom and sit on the toilet to take my heels off. My feet are red and sport a few blisters from the strain of being four inches taller and at an angle. I stand to remove my skirt, my top and the underwear, except the panties. Can't be going out there totally naked."

When I return to my room, now walking normally, I pick up the long black T-shirt that has been left on my bed. It stretches down to just above the knee. There is also a make-up wipe left on my chest of drawers so I can remove the lipstick. The white wipe is quickly tinted by the pink hue of the lipstick, and I feel my normal lips come back. I look down at the nightshirt once more to see it has a typical cheesy slogan on it. This one says 'dream bigger' in white writing. I say goodnight to my mum as she asks me to put out her bedroom light for her. I go through and flick the switch.

"Night Mum, see you in the morning."

"Goodnight Molly, sleep well."

I lie in bed, watching some YouTube and before long, I drift off to sleep. My first sleep since the secret escaped. And somehow, no dreams, no nightmares and no disruption. I slept right through the night, unexpectedly to say the least.

No one tells us what we get to be. We decide who we are and what we can do.

Molly's journey is just beginning, but she must go away while Ollie goes to school. Or must she?

First Day as Mum's Girl

As daylight breaks and the light intrudes through the not completely covered window on a cool Monday morning, I awake with my mind in a thick haze. Was last night all real? Did it really happen? Have I been reading too much fiction about transgender people and somehow imagined I'm now living one of their lives?

One quick glance down at my body once I kicked the duvet off my body confirms that it was all real. I'm still wearing the black nightshirt. What confirms it even more is Mum gently opening my door to greet me.

"Morning Molly!"

"Good morning, Mum. You're in a bright mood this morning."

"Well, it's my daughter's first full day!"

I am perplexed to say the least. I am sure she said it wouldn't be so fast.

"Mum, I have school today."

"That's what you think. But no. You actually have the day off, dear."

I go to speak but all I can muster is a confused stare.

"I've been reflecting on last night so much since it happened. I think you've waited long enough, the last thing I want to do is make this wait to be yourself any longer and more agonising."

"Right, but school is still pretty important. I don't know if they'll be too thrilled about me skipping it."

"I'm going to call them and arrange a meeting for the end of this week. Molly will be there to show them exactly who she is. Until then, all I have to say is that we are visiting family."

"If the meeting is for Friday, why am I taking the whole week off?" I ask foolishly, still not quite connecting all of the dots on this one. My pencil can't be found to start connecting them, but I put that down to it being so early in the morning.

"Well, honey, we have work. To. Do. My daughter is going to look fabulous and undeniably feminine for this meeting. Treat it as your first big test for passing as a sixteen-year-old girl."

"Oh, all right then. So what's the plans then?"

"You go and grab your breakfast while I wait to call the school and arrange a few other things. We are going to be remarkably busy this week, lots of people to see and things to do."

"OK, going now."

I'm used to Mum being all happy and bright and motivational in the morning. She often brings a pearl of wisdom with her to my bedroom door when the time comes to check that I'm awake. But this morning, it is as though she has had coffee laced with Adderall. She never drinks a coffee and I doubt she's even heard of the latter drug, but it feels like she has it hooked to her veins this morning.

I venture downstairs in a far-from-dainty fashion. Our stairs are not the most solid and creak often but the thuds and bangs from my flat size 7 feet all echo clearly throughout the house. I enter the duck-egg blue kitchen and start preparing breakfast. 'Cereal or toast?'

I opt for cereal; I love a bit of milk in the morning — has to be the green lid though. Semi-skimmed milk is the only acceptable kind. Full-fat is too heavy like cream and skimmed milk tastes like sour water to me. Cereal is also dead quick to prepare. With toast, it feels like waiting for it to be ready to spread slows the entire morning down, so I tend to save that for weekends when I'm less pushed for time. I'm not the best timekeeper there is.

I usually have breakfast upstairs, but I can hear Mum on the phone to somebody and I don't want the volume of my TV to interrupt her, so I just turn on the main TV in the living room and sit on the brown leather sofa.

Curiously, my hands are unsteady while I eat breakfast. The spoon shakes around in my hand while I try to scoop a mouthful of cereal and a small drop of milk hits my nightshirt. Good thing it is black!

This comfort still doesn't explain *why* I'm shaking. I guess I'm coming to terms with the reality I have just formed. It's really happening. It's going to actually happen. I'm coming out as a girl. In *high school* of all places I could have said something. Primary school would've been more straightforward, no one honestly cares at that young age. Those spy missions should've failed more regularly back then, I would already be out the other side of this mystery tunnel and instead I'm only just descending in the lift before the crossing starts.

Don't overthink it, Molly. Just put on your favourite YouTube content and it will all be fine. Except for the fact that I scroll through the trending section, actively *seeking* girly videos. I settle for one of those 'try-on haul' videos. You know the ones. Women with far more money than sense buy hundreds of pounds' worth of clothing and show us all of it within ten minutes. Something which seemed so silly yesterday is something I now can't ignore.

I finish eating just as the woman is showing off a white tulle skirt. It looks incredibly soft and feminine, but also like it would shrivel up after even a single drop of rain graced its delicate surface. 'Some day, I'll own a skirt like that.'

The shaking doesn't settle so I go through to the kitchen again to put the bowl in the sink and grab a cold drink of water. Water is the answer for everything from anxiety to asthma, or so it seems based on what I see on social media. I return to the couch and take little sips, as if I'm unwell.

I feel healthy, but also uneasy about what's coming. Anticipation is a drug much like Adderall, but you don't always have to pay for it. Just say something which alters your entire path in life, and it will make you feel like you've consumed a whole jar of pills.

The woman on the screen is now squeezing her way into this very tight bodycon dress that is bright to say the least. A neon yellow minidress that's barely enough to cover her rear end, never mind make it any distance down her legs. And she stands there puckering up and pouting and shaking and possibly even dancing around, her matching neon yellow heels fixed to the floor as her hips move like Shakira's. And the song in the background of the video is oddly similar to that of the Brazilian superstar.

I find myself noticing the smaller details, details guys wouldn't pick up on or care enough to point out. Her lips have been injected several times, probably with collagen. A couple of the girls in my class have had that done recently with it being sixth year and all that. I don't think I want that done. Her eyelashes are a lot longer than any natural ones, I'm more interested in that process. I love the idea of being able to bat my eyelashes and create the illusion that I can summon storms with them, especially if I pair that with having totally artificial eyebrows. But her nails seem too long to be even slightly practical. I bet all these cuts between outfits are actually because she has a team helping her into these cute clothes. There is no way she is dealing with those awkward zips, buttons and laces on everything she's showing off.

And just as the video cuts again to a beachwear outfit, that is exactly when my mum joins me in the living room. Her voice startles me.

"Ah, I guess you are still into girls then!"

"Mum! I'm just getting ideas for what I could look like someday."

"You won't be wearing anything like that for a while yet! That's more skin than clothes!"

"It's beachwear. Surely that's acceptable!"

"Hmm I'm not sure actually. You'll need a beach body first for that, hon."

"Yeah, it's so much effort. Seems so far away."

Mum looks at me with her caring eyes, sits down beside me and puts her arm around my shoulder then flicks my hair gently.

"It is a long road. It will take a while; it won't always be perfect and there will be bumps along the way. But step one is always the hardest one to take. And we have to do that first before we can get anywhere towards who you truly are, Molly."

I make eye contact and smile as Mum wraps me in a hug. The conversation shifts to today's plans as I forget that school is not happening for me today.

"I really need to get ready for school."

"Honey, I already told you no school this week. We have to start your preparation for your debut next week, my beautiful daughter-to-be."

"Oh yeah!" I reply, laughing excitedly. "So, what's the plan?"

"I decided you should be in the room when I call the school." And then she dials the number. Each little beep as she keys it in on her smartphone's touch screen is like the build up to a rousing crescendo which is the ringing itself in this case. Then the familiar voice through the phone.

"Good morning, Grafton High School. Miss Lidell speaking, how may I help you?"

Ah good old Miss Lidell. The kids all joke that her name is really pronounced LIDL like the budget yet brilliant supermarket. When you reach my age and you reach the last year of high school, that joke has been around so long that it is just part of school life. None of the senior pupils laugh at it any more but we all never say her name properly either. She's a nice woman though, mid-thirties and willing to go the extra mile in a seemingly depressing job.

"Hi there, Miss Lidell; it's Katherine Clarke, Olly's mum," my mum politely says in her 'phone voice'. We all have a phone voice, a voice we just throw on as an act to sound cheerier and more formal when speaking to people without them seeing that you haven't even bothered to change out of your nightshirt yet. She continues.

"I'm afraid Mo — eh, Olly has to miss this week of school. We have plans to see family, something has come up." Nice save, admittedly.

"That's OK Ms Clarke, I'll inform his teachers. Will he be back next week?"

"Actually, I was hoping to have a meeting on Friday with the headteacher. It's quite an important topic, hence all the family gatherings and such."

Hence? And such? Mum is almost speaking Shakespearean at this point compared to her usual East-Central Scottish dialect.

"I can arrange that; I'll give you a call later today and let you know if that's possible."

"Brilliant, thanks. Have a nice day."

"You too, bye!" Miss Lidell's upbeat yet blunt farewell ends the call.

"Friday, huh?" I ask nervously.

"Oh my girl, we have a lot of work to do. But it will be a lot of fun too I hope."

"What's first then?"

"We are doing home-schooling today. Make-up, mannerisms, speech. We need some practice at all of this before we even try to go outside tomorrow."

Her words drop the stick of dynamite into my mind. I'm holding back my panic and fear at the overwhelming nature of this whole upcoming week.

"Go clear your head with a nice long, feminine bath. I'll have everything set up for your make-up lesson and a little outfit for you as well."

She kisses me on the forehead before I leave the room and climb the stairs to start my prep. I pick up my phone from my bed and see a notification. A new message? From Mum? What is this?

> *Hi honey, here is what you'll need to do in the bathroom.*
> 1. *Run a warm bath that's plenty full*
> 2. *Use plenty of bubble bath and add a scented bath bomb*
> 3. *Shave your whole body from the face down*
> 4. *Wash your hair thoroughly with soap and conditioner*
> 5. *Moisturise after you've shaved fully*

She has clearly copy and pasted it from somewhere. This is again all too formal for Mum's own words.

I open my bedroom's double-door cupboard and arm myself with a large pink towel, ready for the war I am about to wage on my own body.

The steps seem so simple yet so incredibly complex that I imagine there are black flash cards appearing between each one. And as such, I'll describe and explain what happens next in this manner.

Run a warm bath that's plenty full

Well this one seems fairly obvious, run a bath. I've been doing this for years, though sporadically. I turn the 'H' tap to the right and the water begins to flow into the pristine white bath. I leave the room for five minutes since a watched bath never fills or something like that.

Whenever you run a bath, do you ever do a temperature check by throwing caution to the wind and just sticking a hand in there, even when it is producing more steam than an old-fashioned locomotive? It's a standard bath technique for me and it takes not even a second of self-scalding to realise that yes, that bath is way too hot. Time to run the cold tap for a few minutes and balance it out.

Those few minutes pass and it is considerably less scorching. I turn the hot tap back on along with the cold and wait another two minutes for the water to stop just under the fill line, which I have always judged as the bit the plug chain rests on when not in use. Of course, it is in use right now or I would just be wasting a lot of water.

OK, hand back in and… yes, that's a hot bath. Maybe not quite 'nice' as the instructions say but adding more water would threaten to turn my mum's lovely bathroom into SeaWorld. Unless I pull the shower curtain out but that just doesn't seem right. I'm now in the bath. Next step.

Use plenty of bubble bath and add a scented bath bomb

I know what those words mean since I have heard most of them before. Granted, not specifically in that order nor this context but let's look for some clues.

Bubble bath? See, I'm used to just using shower gel in the bath since the soap isn't sentient. It doesn't know I'm not in the shower. But this is a very specific instruction, bubble bath. There is a small orange bottle on the side of the bath against the wall that could easily be mistaken for bleach or some other toilet cleaner or drain unblocker. This shade of orange does not seem suitable for human use, especially not on delicate skin.

But one turn of the bottle reveals all, it is 'Perfectly Imperfect Orange Overload Bubble Bath.' That name opens up so many questions, too many to dwell on but seriously, what sort of brand name is 'Perfectly Imperfect'? Why would you ever buy something with such low self-esteem?

I unscrew the top of the neon bottle eventually, resisting the mad urge to confuse it for an energy drink. This is such a struggle because my hands are already soaked, and the bottle is slippery. I drop the bottle in the bath and that isn't what they mean by use it, so I recover it and squirt a generous dollop of bright orange bubble bath into the water. The smell hits immediately, it's like an orange grove inside the Fanta factory. It's not unpleasant, just a little too pungent.

And if this is a foreign object to me, you can imagine how I feel about scented bath bombs. Luckily, the packaging for this one is less misleading. 'Beautiful Bath Bombs — only £2.99'. Well, that's a bargain. I think it is, anyway. The instruction says 'a scented bath bomb' so I add one and it is done. The chemicals start to fizz up and dilute the orange oversaturation with a floral fuse.

I am in awe at the colour of this water, orange with a purple fizzy substance working its way through. I wonder which of those colours I will emerge as — spray-tan or jam? Anyway, what now?

Shave your whole body from the face down

Great, razor blades! A pink one and a white one lie on the side — one intended for the face and the other for the body. It's important not to use one for everything, bad for the skin generally. I start with the pink one on my face, but I need to wet it first. Reach in, pull out some bubbles, apply them to the face and shave! I have done this before, it always sucks! Maybe one day in the future, I won't have to shave my face because nothing will grow on it. Wouldn't that be nice?

It's always a few minutes and I always scrape the same spot just under my chin. Could be worse though, and now my face is smooth and soft like Mum needs it to be.

Now for the new experience — shaving my body hair. I'm hardly a gorilla when it comes to hair, but I have a lot more than I would like. I've just learned to deal with it over the years but not any more. Today, I take my body back from the puberty witch!

Ow! Ow, ow! Mother— ow that stings. And that is just one leg. A lot of cursing, shaving, cursing, rubbing and cursing later, I have done a standard job. It's not perfect but it will do.

The pubic hair is by far the strangest to shave. It's so thick and curly and horrible and it strips away like cheap plasterboard. Make a cut and the whole thing comes away with it. I can't put it down the bath's drain without blocking it, so I have to resort to leaving it on the side. Once out, I'll clear it up with some toilets roll and toss it in the bin.

The backside is a tricky shave as well. How am I meant to see if it's done? And why is this so important? Less asking, more shaving. This takes ten minutes alone before I'm satisfied with the job, I can't do much better. My back, torso and arms are much easier by comparison and I'm eventually feeling smooth all over.

Wash your hair thoroughly with soap and conditioner

Not sure if I need to explain this one. I wash my hair every time I shower.

Not with conditioner though, that was always something that I thought best not to touch. But today it is an order so after the usual shampoo wash in the bath with Mum's floral stuff, I use the matching conditioner. The bottle says 'leave to soak in for five minutes' so I lose myself in my playlist for a few minutes and inspect my handiwork with the razors once more. Always a perfectionist!

I wash it out and my hair doesn't feel much different. It's still wet and still a fair way off my shoulders. It also has a whiff of orange about it but maybe that's just because I've been lying in orange liquid for over half an hour, and it feels like I'm trapped in a Lucozade bottle.

Moisturise after you've shaved fully

The coconut oil and moisturising creams are all kept on the windowsill, so I know that this step takes place out of the water. While it is still so warm in the bath, I resist the urge to transform into a tangerine and slowly stand up. The water tries to flee up my newly shaved body and pull me back in, but I refuse and pull out the plug once I'm safely on the large bathmat. My skin is somehow a normal colour, but I smell so citrusy!

Wrapping the towel around my now shivering frame, I feel so sensitive. My skin is catching fire and the towel is hardly flame retardant. I need some of that moisturiser stuff, so I let the towel drop to one side.

Starting with coconut oil since it seems like the coldest one, I take big clumps out of the jar and rub them all over my scratched skin. I use the face cream on my face, surprisingly enough! After a few minutes, I redress myself with the towel and summon the courage to unlock the old door and step out to show Mum the result of her daughter's first bath!

Then I turn back around to grab my phone and pause the music while Eminem was typically tearing up a track on my playlist. And then I report to Mum.

A soft knock on her bedroom door is enough to catch her attention. She has clearly been waiting for this moment as eagerly as I have anticipated it all.

"So eh, how did I do?"

"Well your music choice needs some girly changes, but the actual pampering seems to have gone perfectly! My girl is so smooth now!"

"Yeah! I love it!"

She gives me a weird look and the next thing she says explains why.

"Drop the towel, let's see if you did all of what your mummy asked."

"Oh eh, I don't think you should see that," I reply, laughing nervously.

"Nonsense! Girls have nothing to hide from their mothers!" she replies with a little titter.

"OK, here goes."

I close my eyes and drop the towel once more.

"Oh yes! Now **that's** what I call feminine foundations. We can build on this!"

"Can I cover up again? This feels weird."

She yells "Oh of course you can! I'm **so proud** of you already Molly!"

Mum grabs a carrier bag and pulls out all manner of clothing to find a pair of pink panties. "Now, I hope you don't mind the colour. I'm maybe just getting used to you being a girl so you're my little girl. At least it's only the underwear though!"

The panties are a baby pink with a famous girly logo printed all over them in hot pink. I don't know whether this is her way of checking if I am a serious girly girl or just a girl, but I honestly love them! True, they are probably designed for younger teen girls, but I am technically a very young girl, so it works in my messed-up head.

I slide the panties on with my back turned, letting the towel fall away once more but only showing off my rear. When I turn back around, I'm greeted with a matching training bra.

"Eh… I don't actually have tits."

"Breasts, dear. Or boobs; try not to say tits. Tits is a filthy man's word. Boobs is cutesy, breasts is proper. Adjust accordingly based on the situation."

"Oh yeah, sorry." I then continue to make the point clear. "I don't actually have breasts, Mum."

"Not yet, but you are going to. And you need to know how a bra feels if that's the direction you are heading. Plus, I couldn't resist buying the matching set. I even have socks for you as well, but you won't need them today."

"Sweet, a lazy day."

Mum smirks. "Nope, we will be very busy. Now hurry up and put your bra on, princess."

I jokingly sigh and then gleefully do as instructed. The training bra has no straps at the back, so it is essentially just a cropped vest top. Still feels nice on, even with my not very shapely figure. Curves in all the wrong places but I try to stay upbeat about it. I am just a beginner after all, everything improves with time.

"OK, now you're probably noticing a theme, but your dressing gown is also Barbie. I thought you'd like to wear what you missed out on!"

No problems with that at all! I **do** want to wear everything Barbie or Bratz... well I don't even know if that's a thing any more. A lot of it isn't in my size, of this I'm well aware. All the more reason to cherish any moment where I can sport a capitalist brand that makes kids' entertainment. I wrap myself in the soft, comforting, pink robe and fasten it tightly with a tie, even double knotting to ensure it stays on.

"Now *there's* a girl! A short-haired girl with a deep voice, but a girl, nonetheless. And we can fix the imperfections, iron out the creases. That's what a lot of our work will be."

"Excited to keep going! What next? I'm guessing this is all I need to wear for now?"

"Yes and no, sweetheart. Go down to the kitchen and wait for me there, I'm just grabbing the materials for your next lesson."

"Will do!"

"Oh, and Molly? Try to be more light-footed when going down the stairs from now on, OK? I'm sure one of the extra-curriculars you can join will be perfect for that. I can see you doing dance class just out of being girly enough to love it!"

Guys can like dance too, of course. But Mum has always viewed such men as fruity, flamboyant, even sometimes just flat out homosexual. There is nothing wrong with that at all, just funny how she always assumes male dancers are gay. Patrick Swayze isn't enough to convince her.

I'm slower than usual to reach the kitchen on account of taking my time to be as quiet and reserved and dainty as possible when heading downstairs and even on the laminate flooring in the hall.

Another few minutes of waiting, Mum enters the room with a pink carrier bag choc-full of stuff.

"Did somebody say manicure?"

"A maniwhat?" I've never heard of this before, and I'm sixteen!

"Nails, darling. You're having your nails done. Fingernails and your toes as well. Then we'll see what else we can do today. Sound good?"

I nod and agree without even saying a word. I'm already presenting her my hands over our solid-oak dining table.

"Now, nails are about more than just chucking colour on. You need to do several steps in preparation for that fun part. Much like everything feminine, you need to work hard to reap the rewards of being fabulous."

I have no words to respond to this, I barely understand what she is talking about.

"We need to file and shape those nails, scrape back those poor cuticles and buff those babies up. Once they're all neat and shiny, it's time for colour."

"Sure, I'll let you lead on this one."

"Well, you still have to pay attention. There will come a day where you will have to do your own nails. Or you will do what I do and pay someone to do them well! You are starting here because I want you to learn how it works. You should do your next set."

Mum takes a file and starts shaping my nails to be perfectly rounded. She then picks up a devilish little tool which scrapes back the white bit at the base of the nail — I understand this to be the cuticle. All I know for sure is that it really wasn't pleasant to have that metal thing driven into my fingers for five excruciating minutes. Once that's done, a small pink sponge which feels more like rubber is rubbed on each nail, seemingly aiming to start a fire. However, once Mum finishes buffing, I can see exactly what she means.

"Oh wow! These look great, Mum!"

"And that's before colour! See? All these years, you've been joking that you don't care about your appearance, but it was never true. We have a lot of lost time to make up for and this is just the start! Now, guess what colour we are going for on your nails?"

"Oh I don't know. Pink by any chance?" I ask the pointless question with as much sass as a morning news presenter.

"My girly girl is finally getting it. Pretty in pink, just like the really old film you've likely never even heard of." She called it, to be fair.

The odour of the nail polish pots is so strong. I would compare it to paint but that's just obvious. I'm also curious as to why there are two pots. One has a clear liquid in it, the other with the promised pink.

"Your nails always need a base coat and always need a top coat of this magic stuff," Mum explains, holding up the clear gel. "It keeps those nails beds nice and healthy, keeps the chemicals from going into anywhere they shouldn't be as well."

The cold liquid is carefully brushed on to my newly-refreshed nail beds, adding an extra glare. The light from the large window in the kitchen — which overlooks the back garden — allows for a lot of natural light to break through into the room. It isn't long before all ten nails are shining.

"Now for your nails to match the rest of your cosy clothes! The shade is so you. I took one look at it and thought of Molly."

It doesn't take much to cause a hot flush in me today, even just hearing my new name causes my heart to skip a beat or two.

"Barbie pink?" I read aloud the shade on the bottle. "Yes, I can see why you thought of me with all the Barbie stuff."

"You're loving this, aren't you?"

"Hell yeah!"

Mum clears her throat in disapproval. "Excuse me, young lady?"

"Sorry, I mean, yes Mum I love my new look."

"That's better," she smirks again. I can't honestly tell at this point whether she has chosen Barbie out of trying to humiliate and embarrass me or if she genuinely thinks I love it. If it's the latter, she has nailed it. I can't even think of any other girl my age who would wear such seemingly childish clothes. Anyway, I have the perfect excuse and no one else can see us. Yet.

"OK, while they dry, let's paint your toes too."

I won't go into the details of how she paints my toes the same colour, we've covered the steps of the process already. I do however feel the need to ask something as they dry.

"Will anyone see my toes anyway?"

"You never know princess! A woman must always be ready and

groom herself to perfection for every day."

A rather outdated rule there since freedom of expression has never meant so much in the world. Who cares how well-kept you are these days? I suppose my main issue is I do. I want to be the perfect lingerie model, the star on the cover of those magazines, the pop star princess everyone fawns over. Even just one of those ridiculous yet popular streamers who play games live while wearing very unique and feminine costumes. Come to think of it, some of them aren't even girls. That goal might be achievable.

"Mum? What's the plans for the rest of the week?"

"Well, girly stuff." The vague nature of her answer prompts me to dig deeper.

"What needs done before we see the headteacher on Friday? And when is it all happening?"

"My child, you sound worried. Let Mum take care of the details, you just enjoy this first experience of everything. I have many more surprises for you."

"OK, you can keep your secrets. Can you at least tell me what's next?"

"I want you to experience a face mask. And while you do that, you will watch a video all about feminine speech. You should be able to listen along while the cucumber slices are over your eyes."

"Right. A different type of school, then."

"A better school! Way more fun!"

If she says so. Mum applies a generous handful of clay to my face. This looks nothing like all those Hollywood movies where the woman has the green face. Mine looks a lot more like I've been living in the woods for a week. Maybe even the type of thing you see on survival shows, these woodland warriors draw war paint on with their fingers and some dirt. More Amazon Rainforest chic than a cliché mum-in-sitcom look

Mum reassures me that this is the right stuff and then escorts me to the living room where my video waits. She places two thinly-cut slices of cucumber over my eyes and then starts the video titled 'Male-To-Female Speech Therapy — Why?' Sounds more like a book title or something you would see written in a paper than the title of some random

YouTube video.

I sit there with my sight obscured by vegetables and listen carefully. I wonder if this is part of that effect where blind people have sharpened hearing or something like that because this video starts to touch my soul.

'Quite simply," begins the truly incredibly American voice, "you are tired of being heard as someone you are not. I mean, that's why any of us, myself included, choose this path of transitioning. We aren't seen or heard as who we are but as who nature decided that we must present. Science has come a long way, and we can now treat many of the inconsistencies we have between our physical sex, and our gender identity."

I think I understood about 30% of what she just said but it rocks my insides like a ship on choppy waters. I keep listening.

"A voice says a lot. Quite literally, it says stuff. That's what a voice does and if yours doesn't sounds like you, it can be a huge contributor to that dysphoria us transgender people usually feel. Every time you speak, it feels like it is someone else. I'm hopefully going to help you deal with this and change it for the better."

Is this what a trance feels like? I'm hooked on this woman's every word. Not out of being attracted to her but out of agreeing with her. She is making total sense with every word that I hear. And her own voice sounds so naturally feminine and beautiful that it is genuinely hard to believe she is transgender. Maybe she's lying so she has that false sense of sympathy, but I really do doubt it. She seems too personally touched by the issue for that to be the case.

As the video continues, the mystery woman tells me all about the goals of her training. By following her free tutorials available on YouTube, I should be able to adjust my voice into being totally feminine and as sweet as any sixteen-year-old girl's. I'm determined to make that happen.

I'm listening so intently that I don't even hear Mum come into the room. It's only as she removes the cucumber slices from my eyes that I even notice her presence.

"These can come off now, but you seem to be enjoying your lessons! Now, I want you to try to use only your sweetest girly voice from now on. Follow all those tutorials and never give up on it. It sure won't be easy, but I know my little girl can do anything. I'm going to run to the shops really quick, you stay here and study up, buttercup!"

"Happily, but can I cover my eyes again?"

Mum hands me a pink sleep mask with a weird look on her face. She doesn't understand how soothing it is just to listen to these videos. I can't let my eyes distract my ears, not for this. This is more important than any test I've ever done, my voice needs to be perfect.

"I'll be back soon. Enjoy yourself."

I hardly move a muscle, except the ones in my throat. Trying to perfect the pitch is a rocky start but everything gets there with time. That's what the instructor says with every new little exercise she shares for practising. It's similar to those done by singers and stage performers moments before the show to make sure their voices are perfectly clear and sound as they should. I'd love for Molly to make the stage one day. Any stage would do really, just to have eyes on the real me would be enough.

There is the odd sentence I recite where I feel as though I have really nailed the voice but then the very next is straight back to rough and grisly teen-boy tones. It is only the beginning, but I'll need to put a lot of time into this. Not that I'm complaining, these videos are almost euphoric.

To ensure I'm not losing focus completely, I watch another 3 videos, each 10 minutes long, then remove the sleep mask, rub my eyes and put on a video from my suggestions called 'MTF Makeover on My Brother — HE LOOKS LIKE ME?!'

Classic clickbait title with the blurred face of the brother in question, but it breaks up the learning nicely and to be fair, the girl does make quite the effort in attempting to make her brother into her sister for the day.

Unfortunately, the video then turns into a brand deal and then some weird deal where they decide to see if they can fool the girl's boyfriend. It's just totally cringy and feels wrong to me. I suppose it would since I have never been in a relationship that way. I don't even know if I'm more attracted to the girl or the boys in this video, I'm just fixated on the make-up and clothing more than anything. Jeez, I might end up being one of those crazy cat ladies at this stage.

The video finally ends and it's back to learning. I cover my eyes once more and throw myself right back into practice and reciting. It's tough, but I'm enjoying the grind.

That is until Mum comes back with those supplies she went searching for. I remove my blindfold and see a drug store carrier bag in her left hand. It can mean only one thing — make-up.

We Have Movement

"What have you been up to then, hon?" Mum asks inquisitively.

"Just list—"

"Voice, baby girl."

Oops, I forget to adjust my voice into its girly pitch. I clear my throat and use the vocal exercises the mysterious woman has been teaching me for the past who knows how many minutes, hours even! After a few goes at a scale, I take another deep breath and then answer Mum's question.

"Just listening to the voice coaching and practising it. What do you think?"

"It's not perfect but it's very good for a beginner. Now, I don't want to hear it drop below that. It's tough but you need to get used to it. Can't have you slipping up, especially not in school on Friday."

"That would be really embarrassing."

"Exactly, honey. And equally embarrassing would be if my little girl can't do her own make-up. So I'll teach you just once — right now — then you can use YouTube and get practising on the cosmetic side of being a girl as well as the vocal work."

"Lots to do; can we get it all done by Friday?"

"I believe we can, yeah. You really want this and it's all there for you but being a woman is no joke. You have to **want** it and show that you want it in everything you do."

I nod in agreement; unsure what words Mum wants to hear in response.

"So," she continues. "We need to work on movement and mannerisms. I'm going to watch you walk up the stairs to my room where we are doing the make-up lesson but try to move like a girl, OK?"

"What do you mean?"

"You know, sway the hips, make your wrists go limp, move with a bit of a skip and a swing about you like you're just the prettiest daughter a mother could have."

"O-OK." I'm still not quite sure.

"Oh and please, smile more! It makes your voice sound better too, remember?"

There is so much to remember. It's all fantastic when I get it right but then a million more steps are added to what never seems easy but certainly didn't appear as hard as this. I guess Mum has high standards, knowing that she's going to be talked about a lot in friend circles for having a transgender child. Even more 'outrageous', a visibly 'strong, sturdy, fierce son' longing to become a 'pretty, sissy girl.' That's what everyone is going to say, that's going to be my tagline from now on. Not that I have ever been popular but is it better to be forgotten about than to be the burning topic in town? I don't have much of a choice, I'm so eager to be feminine that even potential bullying and backlash isn't going to deter me.

Anyway, I walk as femininely as possible to the bottom of the stairs with Mum watching my every move like an owl. I try to drop one hip and shift the weight with each step while also trying to swing my limp wrists modestly with each dainty stride. This results in me almost falling forward but I manage to keep enough control to reach the top.

"Very good, that's the way I need to see you moving from now on. Hip movement is key to moving like a lady, it's all in those hips!"

I smile, that felt amazing!

"Now, take a seat in front of my dressing table, Molly. I'm about to show you how to make yourself gorgeous."

Make-up Tutorial — Make Me Gorgeous?

That is my confusion as I take a seat in front of Mum's vanity. I've played about with make-up many times, even as recently as yesterday, but I would never ever say that it can make me look pretty. It's an improvement, sure, but that's not saying a whole lot. Maybe the nails and all the pink everywhere else on my body will help the make-up work its magic, and Mum is the magician today.

"So as I said, you must pay attention very closely. Once I've shown you how to do it this once, the next time someone else will do your make-up will be if you pay them to."

This was usually only for when Mum would go to a make-up artist before a wedding but I'm guessing she's alluding to prom.

"I'll follow along, don't worry."

"Good girl. Now, before we start adding the shiny stuff, we need to prime your face."

Primer? Now I know it's serious. I only ever went as far as toying with mascara before, and even then I washed it off immediately out of fear it would be so obvious if it was left on for even five minutes. My usual go-to was lipstick. It's so easy to apply and remove, you can try a new shade in about a minute and wipe all the evidence away once you're done. But now it's all serious, and I'm learning serious make-up.

Mum squeezes some pale liquid out of its tube on to her index finger and delicately dots it all around my face while explaining exactly what she's doing. I'm just paraphrasing her.

"These dots will now blend nicely into your foundation, which I bought in your skin tone. Or at least close enough to it for it to be acceptable. You're a warm vanilla, I reckon."

I don't know quite how to react to that, so I just observe the next step. The foundation is applied to a beauty blender — a little pink sponge in the shape of a teardrop — and again, dotted all around the face but this time with far more dots. Mum then turns the blender side on and starts dabbing it on my face again to spread the make-up around without actually rubbing it on.

"Already looking beautiful, Molly! And this is before we add colour!"

Mum then goes on to explain that for school, it's not going to be necessary to do proper dramatic contouring like you see on TikTok. Apparently, just a nice mix of blusher and bronzer will do the trick. She also explains that having different shades of blush is important but never to go too far with using any particular colour.

"You don't want to go into school, or anywhere, looking sunburnt so light and little with the blush. The shine will come through along with the bronzer, which should be a used a little more. In both cases though, put it on your cheeks, under the eyes and sometimes, a bit on the nose. Nowhere else, OK?"

Another rapid tutorial, but this is pretty easy to remember. Not to mention, it should be easy to tell if I have overdone the blush at any point.

As the bronze and the blush is added to my ensemble, I start to see it all coming together in the mirror. A little artificial shine on my face but more importantly, those unsightly scars of acne and puberty have mostly disappeared.

"Today, we go for pink eyes and pink lips. But choosing your eyeshadow and lipstick each day can be a lot of fun. Experiment! You have a whole palette to explore for the eyes, and a couple of lipsticks there so you don't need to keep borrowing mine!"

"Yay, more pink!"

My girl voice somehow isn't retreating! This is fantastic! Mum gives me a warm smile as she starts doing the mascara. The black brush is followed by a different black brush, this one for eyeshadow. She brushes the shade 'Strawberry Dream' on to my eyelids.

"Perfect! Now, you can finish it off. I know you know how to use this."

She hands me my very own first lipstick — a baby pink one of course! I close my eyes as I go to apply it.

"You can look, there's no shame in girls wearing lipstick!"

"Oh yeah! I'm so used to feeling bad about it all."

"Well don't! The secret is out, and soon everyone will know about my lovely daughter. So relax and be yourself! Show me how a confident young lady puts lipstick on."

I open my eyes and do as I have done many times before.

"That's good, yeah. Needs a little work on technique and finesse, but you clearly know how to use a lippy!"

I smile, a mix of pride and still a little shame.

"Lastly, setting spray. Close your eyes."

A quick skoosh of very watery chemicals and the make-up session is over.

"And that's everything?"

"Well, it's an everyday make-up tutorial. You can go more dramatic with it as you learn more about it. But a look you can put together in 15 minutes is perfect for school."

"Yeah, nice and quick. I hope the other girls are impressed when they do finally see me."

"The other girls may not like you when you show up, honey. Just the way some women are, you've got to be strong. It may be tough for them to accept that you're prettier than them!"

"Yeah right, some of the girls in my year at school are stunning."

"And you will join them soon. They'll be clinging tightly to their boyfriends hoping you don't cause the breakup!"

"Mum! That's weird!"

"I'm just saying you may now feel differently about love than you did even a day ago. There's no need to rush it, just find who you are and love yourself first."

My heart thuds away at a scary speed, was it the mention of the other girls or the mention of boyfriends? Not worth dwelling on, for now.

"Well, that about does us for girly school today. You've got plenty to be practising. Voice, movement, make-up — all three will be needed tomorrow. And please, stay in your adorable Barbie loungewear, princess! You look so precious as my little girl."

All of this stuff has to be perfect for tomorrow, or at least good enough to pass the initial test — the first outing of Molly.

Where to start? Do I work on movement, do I practise the voice, or do I launch myself straight into make-up? What a dilemma! I settle for mincing around my room while quietly and girlishly talking then take a breather by watching a make-up tutorial titled 'Back to School Looks to Impress Everyone'.

That would be the dream, to just *impress* everyone. I've never been beautiful enough nor anywhere near fast enough to turn a single head before. My friend wasn't joking when he said I was a virgin, it's true. And Ollie will always be a virgin — it's Molly's time to shine.

You Sit Like a Girl

"Oh Molly, dear! Come take a break from your feminisation homework, dinner is ready!"

"OK, Mum. Do you want me to change or—"

"No need to change, it's just us, doll!"

"OK, coming!"

I score my voice here about a 6/10, it was pretty androgynous and can be a lot better (I hope it will be) but it is a strong start to the whole girly presentation.

The movement, on the other hand, is about a 9/10. I'm swaying and swinging and flailing everything at just the right time, the one aspect I'm not quite nailing is smiling. I've always been self-conscious and hated my smile so it's weird trying to make it a habit.

And I know exactly the mistake I'm making. This is day one of the process and I am already holding myself to such high standards. I don't expect it to come overnight but if all it takes is effort, I'm willing to exhaust myself to make it as soon as possible.

"You look great, oh daughter of mine. However, you will have to wear actual clothes at the dinner table usually. I just love the look you currently have. So innocent and childish!"

"Ah, I did ask if you wanted me to change."

"Tonight is different but usually, yes. In from school, and unless you need to be somewhere quickly, changed into something more comfortable but still dressed."

I decide to switch the topic of conversation because (ironically based on this diary) I hate talking about myself. I ask Mum about her day, but she just recounts another unremarkable day of keeping the house running. She then says she expects Molly to be of more help around the house as well, something I'm unsure about with my general lack of common sense.

"I'll teach you cooking, ironing, washing and all sorts! You won't just be on dishes any more, I may finally be able to relax in the evenings and leave the housework to you!"

"Fat chance, Mum!"

I'm glad a sense of humour isn't outlawed in this home-school crash-course of femininity.

"I'm impressed by your posture already, but you did always tend to sit like a girl. Maybe it was a sign."

"I did?"

"Oh yes, other people we've had visit even commented on it once or twice, but you just shrugged it off. Your friends sat with their legs spread but you always cross yours over at the thigh. Does anyone at school say anything about that?"

"Nah, a few taunts about being 'gay' but that's about it. A lot of people have matured since first year of high school. The kids don't tend to care about much outside their own circles at this point."

"Trust me, all of your peers will have something to say about this. They may also not all be so welcoming. I am worried for you, sweetie."

"I'll be fine, Mum. I'm not popular as it is, Molly might have more luck making friends! She may be a social butterfly!"

"Fat chance, honey!"

I hope these dinner table conversations are around forever. Something so wholesome about just chatting nonsense with the woman who raised you.

"That was delicious. Thanks, Mum."

"You're welcome. Now, a bit more training for you then you best come see me to see how best to remove that make-up. You can't sleep with a powdered face — it's hell on the skin!"

Can't argue with it.

Clean-up

'What do you want to do today?'

The video speaks to me, and with covered eyes, I pause it and repeat the statement.

"What do you want to do today? Nah, too low." I clear my throat and try again

"What do you want to doo —"my vocal chords crack on that long o vowel.

"What do you want to do today?" Not perfect, but better. And that's all that matters. Again.

"What do you want to do today? What do you want to do today? What do you want to do today?"

During the third attempt, there is a subtle knock on my door.

"Sounding good, honey. Do you want to come through and wash your make-up off?"

"Coming, Mum."

Much like I did hours earlier, I sit in front of Mum's mirror. This time not for make-up, but for make down. Make down? Did I just make that term up? What do you call it when you wash make-up off? There has to be a term for it surely. I'll call it a make down for now, someone can let me know later what the actual term is.

"So, what do you think we need to do to take make-up off?" Mum asks, knowing I don't know.

"OK, I know wipes are involved somewhere. Do you need to have a shower then wipe your face down?"

"No need for the shower, but yes, you do wipe your face with a baby wipe. Now, do it gently but make sure not to miss any of it. Showering is good to make sure you don't miss any spots but if you shower too often, you'll dry the skin out. Try to stick to just one in the morning."

I never thought I would hear that it's bad to shower twice a day, not even convinced that's the case to be honest! Still, what is that line from earlier? Mother knows best.

"OK, so just like this?"

I start rubbing the wipe back and forth, but Mum quickly corrects my technique.

"Not so hard, baby girl. You need to be gentle on your skin, especially while you've got your youth! Just a gentle wipe, you're not trying to remove the skin!"

Her warning is serious but delivered in a humorous tone, almost patronising. I am a beginner though, so hearing her talk to me like I'm a child is actually strangely comforting.

Much gentler this time, I wipe my face all over.

"Don't forget to wipe those lashes! Mascara's tricky to take off completely but you need to get the worst of it."

"Yes, Mum."

Today has probably been the most often I've ever just obeyed and complied with whatever Mum says. I usually have some comment to make, but maybe that was just Ollie. Maybe I'm now polite or something. Or I'm just so unsure, that's probably it.

I take the wipe to the lashes on each eye just the once, so I don't remove them!

"Not bad for a newbie! Now, you need to moisturise before you go to bed. We'll figure out which brand and formula works best for your face but for now, here's a standard tea tree gel. It soothes irritation and redness on the face."

She could tell me it was a potion that let you breathe fire, and I would have taken her word for it. I suppose part of the education is that (eventually) I will be an expert on all this stuff, from movement and make-up to moisturising and mastering the much more feminine voice. It's tough to see it going that way from this point but remember, this is only the beginning. I have to remind myself of this constantly, so you have to unfortunately bear through all those reminders as well. Proper broken record style.

Anyway, I rub the green stuff gently into my cheeks, under my nose and on to my chin, then massage it all the way up and across my forehead.

In the mirror, I resemble a princess, but that princess is Fiona! It is also definitely tea tree. It smells like that one Japanese Kit Kat!

"Good girl, you are now ready for bed!"

"Don't I need to wash this tea tree stuff off first?"

"Nope, it all soaks into your pores naturally. Leave it on at all costs."

Bit confusing, but I roll with it and head through to my room with the ogre face still in full effect. Just as I'm about to climb into bed, I realise that I'm still wearing today's 'clothes.'

"Mum, do I change or not?"

"Nah, you're pretty much in jammies already! I'd remove the housecoat though!"

I loosen the knot in the robe and untie it from my waist, then let it slip from my shoulders. I imagine it like one of those bedroom scenes in those cheesy Netflix dramas, however, it's likely more like a deleted scene from Shrek. Ah well, bed time!

I run down to grab a glass of water for through the night, and upon my return, I put YouTube on to fall asleep to as usual. It's only a few minutes before I resemble the sleeping beauty.

He's Dead

"*O*llie, what's the answer to number 2?"

"Oh um, that would be 17.38, Miss?"

"Spot on!"

This is how maths tends to go. I'm in a pretty good class. See, by age sixteen (and going on seventeen), most of the kids who can't be bothered have left school or are in the lower sets if they did stay. This leaves the nerds like me in good classes where we can get a lot of work done.

You can tell I am one of those nerds as my dreams almost exclusively take place in school or school-like settings. And just as I turn the page to see the next question and follow along with Mike, the boy tasked with answering the next one, the fire alarm sounds, and we have to leave the room right away!

As we leave the room, there is a real sense of panic as the fire is in the hall and blocking the stairwell! The only option is the window which the kids start climbing out of one by one. I'm at the back of the queue as the fire creeps its way into the room, and just as it seems as though it will be too late for me to escape the fiery demise and the flames catch my left shoulder, my eyes open.

Yeah, my dreams can be pretty messed up. I don't think there is a single person who doesn't fear dying in a fire, so it's not strange that I awake in a state of panic. A quick drink from the glass of water on my bedside table and I return to my senses. The duvet lifted from my body, I see what I am wearing, and the events of the previous day all flood back to me. Ollie was in that maths class, but Ollie isn't around any more. This is Molly's life.

With it being just ten minutes before my usual wake-up time, I start thinking that it's not worth trying to go back to sleep. Mum did say there was a lot to do today. In fact, she did say that today was my first outing.

To settle my nerves, I switch to the usual coping mechanism — YouTube on my TV. In my suggestions is an eclectic mix of girl videos and the typical gaming content. From last night's playlist, nothing seems so appealing. I choose to browse another try-on haul instead, from the same channel as yesterday.

The content creator's blonde hair is a source of mild envy within me. It's so golden and beautiful, and just the perfect length for all the conventional and all the flirty styles. Curse my brunette genes! I suppose I could fix it with dye, but the length still wouldn't be there.

And her hair isn't all that I'm jealous of. Obviously, her body looks one million times more appealing than my own rigid and sturdy frame. I like that she looks as though she would blow over in a strong wind. And all this energy of liking this woman is not at all sexually charged. It's all more of an admiration than it ever is a lust over her body or a desire for her love. No, if I could trade bodies with her, I would in an instant. Then again, I think I have had that thought about just about every girl in my year, and every girl and woman I have ever seen since I first realised how much of a girl I truly am.

And if my friends knew what I was really thinking every time I agreed with them that a girl was 'proper fit' or would 'get it', I was really wondering where she got her top and if I could ever wear heels like that without falling over. I suppose they'll know it soon enough.

My impending thought spiral is mercifully interrupted by the sudden appearance of my mother. She's wrapped a towel in her wet hair, and is already dressed in a purple knitted jumper, black jeans and white socks. She hasn't reached the make-up stage yet. Not that I can criticise from where I am — still in bed, still in Barbie underwear with bedhead to match.

"Good morning honey, today's a big day for you! How are you feeling?"

I scramble for the controller to pause the video and respond:

"I'm all right, yeah. Ahem, sorry, need to prep my voice. I just woke up if you couldn't tell."

"At least you noticed it yourself, already on your way to feminine greatness," Mum replies with a smile. "Now, sort your voice, grab some breakfast and have a quick shower. I got you a shower cap; you can't be washing your hair every day any more, it'll stop it growing as long as we need it to be! And if you don't believe me, wait until you hear what Sharon has planned for you today!"

I can't reply since I'm in the throes of 'sorting my voice' which involves all sorts of vocal exercises. Mum just leaves me to it, knowing that Molly will listen to whatever she says and do what she is told. I really am becoming such a goody two-shoes as a girl. And so long as those shoes are cute, I really don't mind that character change. I'm sure Mum agrees that she prefers an obedient daughter over an untrustworthy son any day!

Game Face ON

I should take this moment to explain exactly what Mum meant when she said that Sharon has plans for me. Sharon is Mum's hairdresser and has been for years. I've always been going to her salon for my haircuts, but it has been Joe, the barber, who dealt with my short back and sides. Now though, Sharon will have her first crack at whatever she can do with a short-haired boy longing to look like and be a girl in every way possible. It can't just work like it does in video games, it's not possible to actually leave with physically more hair. If life worked that way, I would have just picked a female character from the menu screen.

It would be much easier, but I need to stay grounded in the reality I'm facing. It's tougher than any game I've ever played, and it isn't even a game in itself. My identity is my life, it's literally who I am. I **need** to make every little detail perfect.

Breakfast is as routine as ever with the new added staple of browsing girly videos while munching on my cereal. Another boy-to-girl makeover video appears in my suggestions, although this one does not seem to be played for laughs. There are cute little title cards which say, 'Girl for a Day' and explain how these boys — all around my age or a little older (so young men) — decide to explore their inner girl and seek the services of this special makeover studio.

The guys are given the works! Everything from make-up, acrylic nails and false eyelashes to long, elegant gowns, adorable high heels and luxurious flowing wigs. By the time they are done in the chair, they look almost indistinguishable from real women. A heavy pulse reaches my heart — a mix of the pressure to be just like them and the reality that I don't have those resources available to ever make it happen, or at least any time soon.

Mum, curious as ever, pops in to see what I'm watching.

"Wow, that's a guy?!" Mum sounds almost as excited and bewildered as me about the situation.

"Yeah, this channel seems dedicated to turning everyday guys into stunning young ladies with make-up and all the good stuff."

"Well, just think, that may be you come prom time! Maybe even without all the assistance if you master make-up well enough!"

"Ah, I don't think I'd handle the pressure of doing my own make-up on prom night!"

"Hmm, well we'll see if you have anyone to impress by then! Your voice sounds good, but just soften it up a little more before we go out. Keep talking to yourself, bring your inner monologue out with you so you can start hearing Molly's thoughts in Molly's voice."

I nod as I drink the last of the milk in my bowl. It's tough to do that and still look feminine in any way but I do my best by slowing down more than anything else. I also let out a girlish sigh once I'm done and set the bowl aside.

"Now, pop into the shower real quick with your new shower cap. I put it on the towel rack. I'll have your clothes for today all laid out on your bed for you to wear once you have dried off."

Mum is quite calm all things considered. I mean, this can't be easy for her either. She probably knows a lot of the regulars at the salon who have heard stories about her son in the past. And now her youngest son is gone, and she has a daughter-in-training in her place. I suppose that makes it less uncomfortable, knowing that we are both in the thick of it and that we will both be subject to much speculation.

The shower is nowhere near as eventful, relaxing or productive as yesterday's long bath but it's not like that can be an everyday thing. While my rock music blares from my mobile phone, I shave my face carefully in the shower, making sure I'm as smooth as possible where it counts most. I manage not to cut myself too badly, just a little scrape on the chin which is barely visible and dries up after a few seconds of pressure.

No bath bomb today (obviously) so it's just some floral shower gel instead. It smells like a lovely spring garden with the strongest scent being lavender. That is also the colour of the slightly shiny, slightly slimy gel that I scrub my whole body with.

I take a few minutes to psych myself up for the day by standing under the shower on its coldest setting. Not only a cruel wake-up, but it is also a good way of hyping myself into smashing through any obstacle I may face today. And I'm sure there will be no shortage of obstacles on this day, my first outing as my real self.

From the bathroom window, even with it steaming up, I can see that the weather is hardly welcoming. The rain is pouring down to its usual beat, following the monotonous Scottish weather metronome in perfect sync. Bar the four days of summer weather, our options are rain, more rain or the most rain. The clouds sport an ominous shade of grey, almost foreshadowing the tricky feelings surrounding this whole day.

My train of negative or uncertain thought is derailed by the lyrics of the next song. Just one of those lines in music that has always pumped me up. The song is all about pressing on, regardless of how anyone else feels about you or what anyone else does to try to stop you. I switch the shower off, shivering due to the glacial setting I chose. The sooner I wrap myself in that towel, the better. I drape the smaller towel over my head, unable to quite master the tying the same way Mum does it. Not like it really matters, as I have a shower cap on anyway. It's just good to try to copy all of the habits and examples Mum has been showing me. That and it stops the shower cap or the wet spots on my head from dripping on to the hall or bedroom carpet, nor the bed itself.

I know that I'm walking into a surprise. As soon as I enter my room, I will see the outfit Mum has chosen for Molly's debut. It's wet, and probably cold outside, so I doubt a skirt or dress is waiting for me. I just hope it doesn't look silly once I have it on, whatever it is. I certainly wouldn't go out in this weather wearing yesterday's ensemble. 'Barbie' would freeze to death or catch pneumonia.

Armour

On my bed, as expected, is neither a skirt nor a dress. No, as I walk into the room, it is impossible to avoid the bright-blue jeans on the bed. It feels a little anti-climactic to be wearing jeans on my first official outing as Molly however the dreary weather make them a sensible choice. It also might turn out to be a better idea when starting out just so I'm not being too loud or obvious in the very beginning of my days of girlhood.

The jeans can't go on first. Stepping closer to the bed and lifting the jeans, I see the full ensemble. It's not every day a girl invited you to experience them changing. Let's get dressed!

Dropping my towel to the floor, I feel flashbacks from all those years ago. What if those Russian spies are watching me right now? And are they happy to be watching me? I suppose that latter thought didn't exist before, but times change.

Although no one is in the room, and my door is closed, I rush to cover up in some way. That being the powder blue panties waiting for me. No childish brands or embarrassing logos, and their actual length is pretty much the same as the Barbie ones from yesterday. They are never tricky to put on, but I'm equally still not used to wearing such a weird material. It's almost like boxers, except softer and cooler. The bra is like the vests I used to wear under my shirt in primary school, only shorter, tighter and it feels much more revealing, even though it will be covered by the next item. It's also just another sports bra, no hook to fasten or anything like that. I'm glad it's not a tie-up affair either. I struggle enough with a school tie, tying a bra would be difficult to say the least.

Underwear on, there's no way I'd ever go out in just this, unlike some of the other girls I see on Facebook with their bodies almost completely revealed. No, I need something warmer and that's what waits on the bed.

Jeans first — I expect them to be skinny, but they are in fact just simply straight-leg jeans. That's a relief, Mum clearly put some thought into me feeling as comfortable as I possibly can on my first girly adventure. I'm so used to the button being on the other side that it feels surreal to be fastening girly jeans without having to be quiet or sneaky about it.

The colour of the jumper Mum has chosen for me would be awful for being discreet anyway as it is the famed Barbie pink from yesterday. As I unfold it, I read the slogan which says, '*It's a Girl Thing*' and notice a small lipstick-kiss emoji at the end. The whole text and emote pattern is in subtle black glitter which stands out on the pink wool like red wine stains on a white linen tablecloth. I assume the slogan choice is not an accident — it's a very cute jumper!

Thick, winter socks complete the outfit so far with the shoes still a mystery. Hot pink with black barbie logos all over, straight out of Primark! Cute! Primark has always been one of the best places for clothes, male or female. I'm excited for when Molly can visit one for the first time!

Can't get ahead of myself though. Just as I go to leave the room, I realise a fatal error: I haven't done my make-up!

I talk myself through each individual step of the make-up, so some of what you are about to read will be pretty much direct quoting.

What did Mum say yesterday? And all those tutorials? Hmmm… ah yes! Start with moisturiser and primer. It's chilly against my cheeks and numbing to my nose but it's also almost luxuriously smooth — like rubbing your face in Greek yoghurt. Foundation follows, a much warmer and thinner paste and one which adds colour. It's tough to tell which colour exactly since there is no mirror in my room and I am working with a phone camera. I remember one influencer yesterday saying that phones can sometimes misrepresent the pigmentation on the skin and what am I saying? I dab it on anyway, hoping for the best and use the blush and bronzer to round out the base. Satisfied enough that I neither look too dark nor too artificially tinted, I start on the eyes — where the real magic happens. I stick well within the comfort zone with a shade of pink. I may have a whole palette to explore, and I will. Day one doesn't seem like the right time to be any bolder or more daring than this whole situation already is.

Mascara gently applied, that famed 'Strawberry Dream' is the obvious choice for eyeshadow. I just brushed it on the exact same way Mum did yesterday. I'm not quite as complete in my application of the powder but I manage to reach the important bits. Just as I am about to do my lipstick and complete my face for the day, it occurs to me that I should probably clean my teeth first. It's just common sense that the toothpaste would ruin the make-up on my lips.

Two minutes and thirty-six seconds later, the lipstick is in my right hand and touching my lips. All over, painting an outline and then brushing away any bits that look a little too preposterous. I don't trust lip liner just yet, I'm just not quite experienced enough. I'll learn though, I'm sure of it!

Just as I go to start brushing my hair out, Mum summons me to her room.

"Molly!"

"Yeah?"

"Come and show me your outfit! I want a photo of my special girl."

"Coming!"

She's surely not going to share these photos, not with my hair still such a mess. Not like I can do much with it in its current state. Some girls can pull off the short hair, I'm not one of those girls based on early evidence.

Still, I take a few deep breaths and brace for the worst as I step out into the hall and knock on Mum's bedroom door before going inside.

Final Touches

Confidence or timidness, it doesn't matter at this point. I just hope I haven't let Mum down with my effort. I'm sure if it's a disaster, she'll step in and sort it. Walking should be easy since there are only socks on my feet, yet it isn't. My thighs are close to turning to jelly with a mix of anticipation and nerves.

"So how do I look today? Have I done it all OK?" The questions are a sure sign of my fear of disappointing her.

"That's actually a really good first attempt at doing it all yourself, doll! The make-up is almost there; I think there may just be a little miss on the eyeshadow. It just isn't popping the eyes enough; eyeliner would also help there of course."

"I just didn't feel confident enough for eyeliner yet, I guess."

"Well, come here and I'll quickly put a little on you."

I knew she'd help me, even when she said she wouldn't. She's a kind woman.

Anyway, two minutes and a lot of 'open your eye… now close it' later, Mum is happy with the 'pop' of my eyes now and I am too! She sets the eyeliner with spray then gives a me a warm hug and a little peck on the top of my head. Mum was never this close to Ollie; I suppose it was just weird for that sort of interaction between a mother and her teenage son. I mean, I also didn't want her to hug me before in case it bruised my fractured, battered and unwanted male ego. With that ego gone, the quick embrace is like a comforting blanket over me. Like when a baby is brought home for the first time, Molly is only two days old, and she feels every little thing like it's brand new.

Still, the show must go on and the curtain is about to be raised for Molly's debut. I'm still nervous as Mum leads me downstairs to the living room and fetches me a glass of fruit juice just to calm the nerves a little bit. It also gives her time to show me my shoes for the day. Not expecting heels or anything fancy, it's intriguing to see a fancy shoebox in her hands.

It is all a ruse however, as in the box is just a pair of low-heeled, black boots. They have zips on the inside and are undoubtedly for women.

"I thought it was a good idea to keep your footwear practical and comfortable for wearing all day. Plus, it's a cold day and I couldn't have my daughter's feet freeze! These will also be a good choice for loads of outfits, making them a good everyday choice. They should also make a little click, just enough to remind you that you are Molly now."

They are very easy to put on, just slip the foot in and zip them up. As for the heel, she isn't lying either. As I stand up to test them out, it's impossible to ignore the unexpectedly loud click from the short heels. They only rise to the ankle so stop at just the perfect height for the jeans I'm rocking.

"Last steps now! Just a bag and a coat and we'll be set to go."

"Where are we going, again?"

"There are a few places to visit today, but I want them to be a surprise to you."

"OK, I don't deal with surprises all that well…"

"Ollie didn't. Molly might, you never know!"

I strongly doubt it. Even if I am a girl now, it can't change *that* much about me, can it?

The coat is simple, waterproof and black. Like many jackets, it has a faux-fur trim on the hood and buttons to accompany the zip and allow a little extra protection from the bitter Scottish autumn chill. This is also helped by the brown faux-fur lining on the inside of the coat. It's not a new coat — Ollie had it before me.

Mum checks that she has packed my bag with all of the essentials (my lipstick, my new purse, my phone and some perfume) before putting it over my shoulder almost as if she is knighting me and welcoming me to womanhood. The irony in that sentence isn't lost on me either, but I can't think of a female equivalent since I've never watched anything I can make a more accurate reference to!

"Are you warm enough, petal?"

Still not used to nicknames like petal or flower or doll yet, clearly.

"Oh uh, yeah. The coat is really nice!"

"I'm glad to hear it. I think everything other than your hair is pretty much perfect!"

Not much I can do about that. Of course, Mum has thought ahead and dresses my head with a soft, black beanie. It has a little shiny patch in the centre, but I have not time to read what it says as Mum straightens it up and ensures it is slightly over my ears. It's easy to hide my short hair under the hat, and I'm happy that it is now hidden. I long for having long, flowing hair but it's not going to come easily.

"Much better. Let's go! I have gloves and a scarf in your bag in case you feel really cold, but I'm hoping you'll be warm enough to keep showing those lovely nails off!"

Door open — it's time to head out. It's one of those noises that is usually lost to the atmosphere or forgotten in its everyday nature. The curtain truly raised on Molly's first time outside and the sound of Mum locking the door behind me confirms it. Time to be myself.

'Car Convo'

The same breeze hits my face as has done almost every day for sixteen-plus years and yet today, it feels entirely different. Probably due to the heavy chemicals on my skin which haven't been there before, the wind reacting especially with my lips which feel much cooler than usual. It's not a particularly cold day — definitely coat weather but it isn't anything special.

But the chill today isn't just on the outside. It feels as though everything from my heart down has been converted into a state-of-the-art cryogenics lab. It's all a result of nerves — the last time I had jitters like this was before the big school play four years ago. Even then, I was only ever a backing singer. Today, I'm the star of this movie. And whether it's a horror, a thriller or a drama — it's almost entirely in my hands.

The walking helps as much as it hinders. Walking is something I've used to combat all sorts of feelings in the past and each little step always makes up a return to my senses. Whatever I have been worrying about or stressing over, walking was always a good way of blasting those negative feelings away. I remember all those days spent on the playground, just talking to myself and walking around.

The walking doesn't help as much on this day since I'm thinking about my posture, my movements and my appearance with every step. One foot goes in front of the other and is announced by a click of my heel. I do my best to keep my legs as straight as possible while putting one in front of the other. It's also important not to go too far across when trying this because then you're walking squint and risking tripping yourself up. To be honest, I don't know what all the fuss is about walking like a woman. Mum doesn't appear to walk this way, yet she encourages me to keep going as I am until I reach the passenger-side door.

Every movement brings about a new level of strange reality. Reaching my arm out to grab the door handle with my left hand, I'm seeing my hot, 'Barbie' pink nails. Sitting down in the passenger's seat, I feel my underwear riding slightly up and it is much softer than the boxers I have been used to wearing for years. Instinctively, I pull down the sun visor to have a look at everything I'm doing in the small mirror. The smile has to be on at all times, except a little pout or lip bite every now and again. I observe my make-up and critique myself, all while Mum makes her way to the car so we can actually go somewhere.

"You look great, Molly. Don't worry about that, just try to enjoy this. It's all going to kick off from here."

"It's so hard not to think about it! I just don't want to look silly!"

"No matter what you do, people will always find it a bit odd or stupid. Focus less on how other people see you and more on how you react to those other people."

"Yeah, you're right."

"Of course I am! Now, let's get this party started!"

The car roared into life, sealing my feminine fate. No backing out from here, no adjusting anything. I truly am destined to start my life as Molly from this moment. Everyone who sees me will see a girl, not the boy I once hid as.

"So… can you tell me where we are going now?"

"I suppose I can tell you the first stop. We are going to need petrol, so you can come out of the car with me and settle those nerves a little. Once you've had your first experience in public as Molly, it will all be so much easier."

"Oh, right. Um, I guess that's a good first step in coming out publicly."

"It'll be good to practise all that feminine movement you've been working on in front of an unsuspecting audience."

"About that… are you sure the movements aren't too… much? I mean, you don't move around like that."

"Well I'm not a sweet little sixteen-year-old princess! You can be as dainty as you like now, honey. You have waited more than long enough to keep anything bottled up inside."

"What do I do if I notice it's way too... much?"

Mum slows the car down as it reaches the spot at the petrol station, giving her the perfect opportunity to look me in the eyes.

"You be yourself! If it feels like too much to you, dial it back a little bit until you are comfortable. If you're happy with how you are presenting, that's all that matters. F*** what anyone else thinks."

Mum has always had the occasional swear word in her.

"Mother, that is no way for a lady to speak!" I announce in a pompous and clearly sarcastic tone. I never call her mother anyway.

"Do as I say, not as I do. You must do your best to be polite and curse-free. My innocent girl is too precious to be using words like that."

"OK, Mum," and I smile.

"OK, enough chat. Let's give Molly her first test run... right after I fuel up."

The last thing you want to do at a petrol station is leave the car while the petrol is being poured in. If you think the smell is bad inside the car, it is nothing compared to the intoxicating fumes outside.

Two minutes later, and a little tap on the passenger-side window informs me that now is the time to leave the car. No going back. It all starts here, at the local petrol station. What a glamourous location to have my first Molly outing!

The Petrol Station

$\mathcal{D}$eep breaths, calm those nerves. Nothing to stop this from happening now. I open the car door from the inside and immediately start looking around to see if anyone is watching. It's as quiet as you would expect on a Tuesday morning — a couple of people going about their day and filling the car up, and one other, older gentleman checking the tyre pressure on his Audi.

Despite the lack of care from the strangers around me, my legs are turning to jelly once more as I summon the courage to move and stand up outside of the car. I close the door behind me, still in a slight daze about any of this being real. Reality is about to smack me fully in the face, I just know it. I can't let the fear win forever, here goes nothing. Or quite a big something.

I can feel the smile fading from my mouth, so I do my best to correct it while I walk, head slightly lowered, into the shop behind Mum. It's tough to feel so confident when it's the very first time you do even the most routine of tasks, so this is quite the challenge.

The small, annoying buzz from the door confirms to the shop assistant that someone has entered. Rather than the constant little taps from my heels off the concrete outside, and now off the clean orange-y tiles of the inside of the petrol station, this buzzer tells everyone that I'm here. And while it goes off for everyone who enters, and it's nothing specifically 'outing' me, I can't help but liken it to those Russian alarms from my spy fantasies of yesteryear. This time, my disguise is off.

"Everything OK, petal?"

There is a slight delay as I do my best to silently fix my voice, despite my nervous disposition to do so.

"Yeah. I'm good," I squeak, unable to totally conceal the uncertainty I'm feeling in this moment. I close my eyes and focus on thinking about every little movement again. In my head, I can hear my own words. 'One foot in front of the other, wrists a little limp and move the hips to shift the weight. That's how you achieve feminine swagger when walking."

I start to build into my stride a little more as Mum picks up some semi-skimmed milk.

"May as well grab it while we are here, eh?"

"Yeah, don't want to run out," I say, purposely distracting myself by looking at my now very feminine hands. Girls check their nails all the time just out of sheer admiration, I'm just doing the same.

To be honest, as someone who is different, I often struggle to make eye contact anyway. Having something prettier to look at than the ceiling or the floor is a brilliant upgrade!

I have always been mocked for being unable to hold eye contact and for looking up or down when I talk to people, but I can't help that. I've just never been able to look someone straight in their eyes without feeling either impolite or intensely intimidated.

As we approach the assistant, I have a worrying burst of confidence. As Mum pays, the woman is looking at her, and then at me.

I look right at the woman who is looking at us and it feels super weird. Am I being rude by looking at her? Mum always says it is rude to stare but is it also rude to not look at someone when they are talking to you or who you are with? How am I even meant to know?

"So, no school today?"

"No, Molly's actually out of school due to her condition."

"Ah, I see. It's good to see that you're well enough to be outside though." She is making eye contact peering into my soul, and I can feel a million little judgmental voices filling my head with sadness.

She knows what you are, she knows you are a freak. She knows you are a sissy; she is disgusted by you. She's laughing at you on the inside.

What did all those guides say? Try to fidget femininely if you feel like you can't look at someone. I choose the reliable choice of looking at my nails as I respond.

"Yeah, it's not an illness in that way. Just some things needing sorted out."

And once again, I sneak a little look up once more to see the assistant's face as I finish my admittedly very confusing reply. Her brown eyes are still looking right through me, as they were upon my first peek.

"Well, it's nice to be out of the house at least! That's pump four, yes?"

That latter question is obviously not for me to answer so I hold my tongue and instead start femininely swaying once more.

"OK, we best be going, petal! Lots to do today, remember?"

Mum's words are another snap back into reality.

"Oh yeah, let's go!" I respond, doing my best to finish it with a high inflexion and even, a little giggle. I am so in character at the moment that this stuff is just instinctive.

I suppose 'in character' is the wrong way to word it. It's more accurate to say that I just feel so natural acting this way, looking like this and being seen as who I truly am, after so many years of waiting for this feeling. I've never taken any drugs, but this feels like I've had a heavy hit of something.

We turn to leave the station, my head, heart and heels all giddy with this one brief interaction. Mum's words once again do their best to steady me.

"Well now we've got fuel, we can start today's plans."

And just like that, the small buzzer sounds, and we cross the threshold of the petrol station. We head back to the car, and I reflect on what has been a remarkable high. Even if the shop assistant knew, she didn't say anything. As Mum sits back down in the driver's seat — and while I fasten my seatbelt — I can't help but ask Mum an important question. Much like a kid turning in a piece of homework, I need to know how I did.

"So, did I pass as a girl there? Did I look like your daughter?"

"You were great! But more importantly, I can tell you enjoyed it! You never want to talk to anyone, even talking to me is sometimes beyond you!"

"Well… maybe that was an Ollie thing."

My reply is either optimistic, incredibly unrealistic or total lunacy — you decide!

"If that's the case, I'm glad Molly will be around from now on. No going back, this is clearly who you are meant to be!"

"Aw Mum, that's so sweet."

"We now need to get *where* we need to be, but I'm leaving this one a total surprise. A phone call I made while you were practising yesterday may be the cause of it."

"Oh, I still don't like surprises."

"You'll love this one."

The car started and we left the petrol station. And much like when an army leaves a battlefield after an important victory, I leave the petrol station (the grounds of my first successful outing as Molly) with the same satisfaction — and hunger for more of that adrenaline.

The Cards Will Fall

I would know this journey anywhere. I could call it turn-for-turn even if I was wearing a blindfold. Just the unique mapping of the turns is enough to confirm to me that we are visiting the doctor's surgery. My local GP is based close to the centre of town but in what used to be an office building. As such, the car park is quite large for just a neighbourhood medical practice. One thing I don't know is... why here? I don't have a check-up scheduled today. I certainly haven't felt unwell recently. The last ten minutes were the best I've felt in years! Why are we here of all places on today of all days?

"The call I made was to have you seen to by the nurse. It's also so we can register you under a new preferred name. We can't legally change it yet; we don't have the documents. Luckily for us, doctors and hospitals have found a way to update medical records without needing proof of ID, just by changing your preferred name on the system. No other details have to change, and they can't yet."

"Oh... so why am I seeing the nurse?"

"We're going to... tell them about yourself. Just a little bit. More accurately, you're going to lead it. It's perfect practice for the meeting at the school on Friday, and you can just behave exactly as you did in the petrol station. Be yourself!"

I suppose nerves will always be a thing whenever I need to go anywhere new, now as my real identity. However, I am still feeling confident after my last victory and the internal shivering has weakened, though it is still there and noticeable.

The doctor's surgery is a simple, one floor building — it's no wonder the company who previously owned it needed a larger workspace. The sand-coloured exterior is not repeated on the side, instead opting for a shade of pink which looks sort of like that medicine people take for indigestion. It has the same bubbly consistency as well, clearly a quick and messy paint job. The small front room acts as an entrance and nothing more. Through the second "automatic" door (often you need to push a button to actually open the door, defeating the purpose of making it automatic in the first place), there is the reception desk. It's only ever had two people working behind it at most, no need for any more than that due to the consistently small demand. Even through flu season, this place is never really dealing with chaos. I've always associated it with comfort and calmness. It's always told me that while I don't feel right in that moment, I soon will feel much better. And I think that sentence sums up this entire situation. I don't feel right at the minute, but I soon will.

Mum does the talking this time, mainly to confirm the appointment of 'Ollie Clarke.' They don't need to look very far to work out exactly what is going on. They don't out me in any horrible way, but legally they have to confirm that they are seeing the right person. The young lady behind the desk smiles as she confirms the appointment, her blonde hair barely touching her shoulders and her make-up very casual. She is definitely wearing some, but it is very natural. There may be some regulations on how the workers can look, or maybe that's just how she does her make-up. It's not my place to know!

"That's you booked in to see Dr Grayson. Please take a seat in the waiting room just through there."

They know that most people who come here are repeat visitors, must be part of their training to always advise people where to go in case they have never been before. The waiting rooms never change — same unappealing walls, wooden furniture — the only exception being the blue, plastic chairs lining the walls.

The typical waiting time is about fifteen minutes. Perfect time to take my phone from my bag and check if anyone has been trying to contact me. I'm not all that popular, but I do have a few loose friendships. I reach to my right side to open my handbag. *Zzzzzip*, just like that. No need to take the bag off first, it's all right by my side. Much more convenient than a backpack! I reach for the small, black device which often has a stranglehold on my attention. Let's see what's new.

Facebook notifications, Pinterest ideas, random background app updates (half of them for apps I have never used) and then… an actual message! Wow, sound the alarm!

It's Chris…

'Hey dude where r u? U skippin school or sumthin?'

Ah… fudge! What do I tell him? I can hardly just lay it bare for him. The honest message would look like this;

'Hey, I'm just at the docs. Got to tell them I'm trans and I wanna be a girl.'

That obviously isn't going to fly. A boulder falls into my stomach, rippling throughout my entire nervous system. Sooner or later, the house of cards has to fall — I will have to come clean and come out. Not right now though.

As I'm considering the best way to answer the very simple message, I hear the call.

"Ollie Clarke?"

In case I didn't remember my own name, Mum subtly squeezes my left arm to say, 'phone away, let's go.' I stand up, trying to shake the nerves caused by Chris' casual message. It will just have to wait. For now, it's time to talk to the nurse, maybe even the GP. This could be seen as a formal coming out, in a way.

The Easy Questionnaire

"You're right through here, with Dr Grayson."

Ah yes, good ol' Doctor Grayson! He's been bald and clean shaven for as long as I can remember. I often joked in the past about his head resembling the cue ball on a pool table, but it was all in good heart. He always wears his long white coat with pride and does his best to serve everyone with a smile.

Alongside the doc is a woman I have never seen before. Jet black hair tied up in a messy bun and a pale face. She stands in a suit, a purple shirt beneath it. She doesn't look old, and she doesn't look like Dr Grayson's assistant.

"Don't mind my colleague there, she's going to talk to you in a bit. Firstly though, I just need to run through a few of the questions."

My voice is already dropping in pitch, I can feel it. I still have to just go ahead as if nothing is bothering me, but the deeper voice is irritating.

"No worries."

"Oh, and is it OK if we ask your mum to leave the room? Just so there are no distractions, no offence Ms Clarke."

"None taken!" Mum replies gleefully as she leaves the room and returns to those blue chairs outside. Just like that, I am alone with the doctor, this new woman and my own dysphoria out on the table.

"How are you feeling today, Ollie?"

"Healthwise, pretty good actually."

"Great! Now of course, we know that today isn't about physical health but your own mental health. Is that right?"

"Y-yeah, it is." It's always a question that causes shivers.

"Well, rather than ask the questions verbally, we have an online survey for you to fill out. It's a mood questionnaire where you can discreetly tell us the exact problem. My colleague will then take these results and talk to you about them confidentially. Sound good?"

"Y-yeah, just on your computer?"

"Mmhmm, I've already hid anything you aren't allowed to see so just go ahead and take this seat."

It always feels weird to be taking the doctor's seat, even when he asks you to sit there to use his computer. That feeling of being somewhere you shouldn't has defined me so far, and it still does.

"OK, thanks."

"The questionnaire is very simple. Read the statements one-at-a-time and click a number 1–5 based on how strongly you agree with each statement. And please, be honest with yourself when answering. Don't hide anything, we are here to help. There are many people your age who struggle with their mental health for all sorts of reasons. We are not here to judge you."

'We are not here to judge you' is probably the best line I could hear right now. Everything this week just feels like I have signed up to a talent show and have all my routines to learn for performing in front of the whole world! It's good to hear a reminder of the scale I'm working at. It's just me, no one really knows me and very few people have to.

I adjust the chair to be at the correct height (Dr Grayson's a giant, at least six-foot four inches) and sit down, crossing my legs over as usual. I take the mouse in my right hand and move it around in a circle just to check it is all working. On to the questions.

1. You are unhappy.

Clicking the '1' means I am not unhappy. Clicking the '5' means I am. Weighing everything up, I click a '3'.

2. You have had trouble sleeping recently

No, not really. Nothing out of the ordinary. '1'.

3. You feel out of place

There we go! '5'!

4. You have been bullied/mocked by your peers

I'm always the butt of a joke or two, but I wouldn't say bullied. I am worried about future bullying, but does it take that into account? I'll click '2'.

5. Your appetite has dropped

I don't eat all that much, haven't since I lost all that weight through

78

natural puberty. '1'.

6. You have thought about hurting others, or yourself.

What sort of barbaric statement is that? '1'!

7. You are scared, anxious or nervous about something

I click '5'! Pretty much everything is making me nervous. And these questions are making me more so.

8. You have low self-esteem

Well this is another '5' if we forget about the brief euphoria this morning. I'll say '5' for accuracy's sake.

9. You want to change something about your life

Another '5'; this is becoming a little easier. Let's see what the next question is.

Thank you for answering these questions, we are here to help you.

Well that barely scratches the surface! How vague do they want a questionnaire to be?! Trying not to let my frustration out, I simply inform the doctor that the questions are all done.

"Perfect, I hope it wasn't too tricky for you. Some people find admitting certain things quite tough, it's OK if that is the case with you, Ollie."

I mean, I know my patient record isn't updated and legally can't be. I also know that my preferred name change hasn't gone through yet. Every time I hear that name, it hurts because I know that's who everyone thinks I am. That's how I appear to everyone, that's how they know me. Teachers, peers, friends, family — they all know Ollie. And Ollie is dead, they just don't know yet.

"It was all right, not great."

"Well, hopefully we can lift that mood a little now. A lot of times, your mood is affected by emotions, thoughts, fears and dreams that we keep bottled up inside for too long. Having no outlet for it can lead to big problems — that's what we are trying to avoid."

"Yeah, that's good. I think it will help to just say what's wrong."

"And that's where I come in!" At last, the younger woman chimes in and gives me some idea of why she's here. "I'm Mrs Styles, and I'm a psychologist. Specifically, a child and teen's psychologist. I look at the problems facing all you lovely young people and we work together to work through them. Shall we go elsewhere?"

"You'd best, I've got another patient coming in!" Ah, good ol' Dr Grayson, he has a reputation for chasing his tail like that. Mrs Styles leaves the office, and I follow her to a room just down a bit and across the corridor.

"My office is not the tidiest, do watch the mess! My younger patients like to play with toys while I speak to the parents. Now, take a seat and let's find out more about you."

State of Mind

"Go on and take a seat on the couch. There is a recliner, but I will ask you to take your boots off before you put your feet up. I don't want dirt on the sofa, it's the one part of the room that's clean!"

I like this Mrs Styles. Her chaotic sense of organisation, her simple sense of humour and her general laid-back attitude are all blending nicely with my personality. I'm feeling almost at home, despite being at the doctor's — in the psychiatrist's office.

"Before we begin, would you like a cuppa? I've got tea, coffee, hot chocolate or plain old water."

I am not about to say no to an offer of hot chocolate — nature's most delicious drink.

"Ooh, yes please, a hot chocolate sounds lovely."

"I thought you would say that; it's a very popular ask. I'll be back in a few, just try to clear your head of any clutter while I get our drinks."

I unzip my boots and remove them, revealing the Barbie socks once more. I feel kind of proud showing them off and being so outright girlish in this moment. I place my boots on the floor to the side of me, as not to block the recliner from extending out. Then I pull the lever on the side of the sofa and just like that, I've got a footrest.

I close my eyes and lean my head back against the luxurious couch cushion. Clearing your head is a lot harder than it sounds, there's so much going on in there. The most worrying thing of all is still Chris' message. I can't just ignore him. I can't tell him the truth. And I don't want to lie to him; he's a good friend of mine. This would count as a white lie, right? Hiding my true identity so it would all be revealed naturally? Lying to postpone the disgust, embarrassment and humiliation? Jeez, I really need to distance myself from it.

I keep my eyes closed and start running through my outfit. I'm undeniably girly and my clothes show it. If I can just accept that one truth, I'm positive that this chat will be much easier. I can hear my thoughts loud and clear. 'Bra, panties, make-up, flowery jeans, femme sweatshirt, Barbie socks and heeled boots. You're such a girl. You're suuuuch a girl.'

Ever tried to change the voice of your inner monologue? I tend to extend vowel sounds to make it sound as childish and feminine as possible, but I wouldn't dare speak like that. Maybe I just need to lean into the change more and lose all of that machismo and bravado that I don't even want or need. That deep man's voice just isn't my speed.

Eyes still closed, I attempt to adjust my voice without making any sound. This sometimes works — you basically just try to raise the pitch of your voice by lifting your voice box (or larynx) up inside your throat. It's vital to only raise it as far as you are comfortable and where there is no strain put on the voice. However, without being able to hear it, you're pretty much guessing on where it is or isn't. All I can tell when I do it silently is when it starts to hurt and that's when I know I need to tone it down a bit.

The best I manage to stabilise it out to is an androgynous droning base pitch and with a smile, it doesn't sound terrible. Smiling makes everything sound naturally higher, so the smile is crucial!

After what seems like far too long to be making just two drinks, Mrs Styles re-enters the room. My eyes are still closed but I can tell as I hear the mug being placed on the small mahogany coffee table sat just to the side of the sofa (where the lever for the recliner is also situated.) She then sits in her special 'doctor's chair' (you know the kind. It's a dark green with a heavy-duty back pillow on it). I suppose if your job involves this much sitting down, you ought to do it in as much comfort as possible.

"I hate to interrupt such a peaceful moment, but it is time for you to open your eyes. Your hot chocolate is just to the side of you, give that a taste and then we'll get started for real."

I lift the mug to my lips and take a decent-sized sip. I can feel the ceramic of the black mug against the sticky chemicals of my lipstick but thankfully can't taste them much. The drink is very rich — it must be a strong, dark hot chocolate powder. It's not overpowering, but you wouldn't be able to drink two in a row. I couldn't anyway. I put the mug back on the coaster on the table and turn to face Mrs Styles, mind now more cleared than it was before, but not totally void of worries.

"So, Ollie, your mother has told us about your situation over the phone. But this is a quiet and protected space for just you and me. What's on your mind?"

"I… where do I begin? I guess with the clothes, you must find it quite weird…"

Mrs Styles reassured me, never once raising her voice. "I have seen just about everything, including exactly what is going on inside your head. I just want to hear more of your side of the story before I go any further. Tell me about yourself. What is your name?"

"I'm uh… Ollie." I panic, does she want my real name or my preferred one?

"Hmmm, and are you happy about that? About being Ollie?"

"Well, to tell you the truth, no. For years now, I have felt like I am someone else. Like this person I am at the moment just isn't me."

"So Ollie is not your name but the name you were assigned at birth. What do you call yourself?"

"Molly… my name is Molly… I want to uh… be Molly… and… be a girl. A woman even."

"Well it's lovely to meet you, Molly. And hey, what you just said there is probably the hardest sentence you'll have to say to me today. Without maybe even realising it, you just defined your own identity. You say you want to be a girl, yes?"

"Yeah, that's… yeah." My confidence isn't rocked so much as it is in little shards scattered across the room, along with all the dolls and toy cars. I can feel a tear or two forming in my eyes and fighting the urge to release them is agonising.

"The tissues on the table, take one if you need it. This isn't going to be easy, but this conversation is a must have. I need to know as much about you as possible so that I can help you, and so we can discuss next steps and future plans."

"Thank you." I take one tissue, dab my left eye and then do my best to regain my composure.

"If you say you want to be a girl," Mrs Styles carries on, "then you are a girl. That's regardless of anyone's expectations, or beliefs, or standards. If you see yourself as a girl, if you treat yourself as a girl and if you want to become a girl physically, that's already enough to say that you are a girl. It's not an overnight process. Sadly, we can't just wave a magic wand on this no matter how great that would be. But the first step is accepting yourself — do you accept yourself, Molly? Do you like yourself? I noticed your self-esteem is low from the questions at the start."

"I love everything that I am becoming and all that I aim to be. It just feels like I'll never get there. I see all th-these gorgeous women and pretty g-g-girls everywhere and want to be just like them, but I just don't think I'll ever be like them at all…"

"The key there is to remember that even other women and girls — probably including some of those whom you admire or look up to, envy even — they all have those same emotions that you just shared. Everyone feels like appearance needs to be a race to find the next trend, with everyone else playing catch-up behind them. Even I struggle not to fall into the odd expectation trap. Then I remember that I'm a psych for young people whose office is always an absolute mess and all of a sudden, I stop taking myself so seriously."

"Right… but how do you do that? How can I do that?"

"People are complex, they are also individual. We all have unique thoughts, feelings, aspirations, fears, doubts and desires which shape our personalities. Rather than accepting Molly as a girl from the off, you first need to accept Molly as yourself, and yourself as Molly. It's easy for it to feel as though you are playing a role as a character, yes?"

"Yeah, it can feel a bit like dress-up at times. I suppose that's just because of how often I've snuck into Mum's room and dressed up in the past."

"When the dressing up is associated with shame, it can be a lot harder to accept yourself as that woman. You associate dressing as a girl with getting caught being a girl, instead of as expressing your own usually hidden femininity. Now that you don't want to hide it any more, that acceptance isn't easy. It's like you are reborn almost. Your past can become fuzzy. Don't erase your past, don't lose those memories — be determined to make more as this true version of you. You have always been a girl, the only thing that is changing is how proud you are about it!"

Another long sip of the luscious hot chocolate and that 'tearing up feeling' is still present. It must just be because Mrs Styles is absolutely right.

"You briefly mentioned it, so I'll ask: when did you first find out that you are Molly? When did you first discover that you are a girl?"

Third sip, it gets better with each one.

How I Knew

"It all began a little after my ninth birthday. I don't know exactly why, but I started feeling urges to try on my mum's stuff. Whenever she went out, I would sneak into her room and model her dresses and skirts. I was always super cautious about it and was usually back in boy mode well before Mum came back home. That was until this week."

Mrs Styles eyebrows raise as she nods just once. "So, your mum saw Molly for the first time ever this week?"

"Y-yeah. My friend had just gone home, and I thought I had a couple of hours to be mys-self." I stammer as I try to keep my head on my shoulders and partly due to just needing to breathe.

"Mmhmm, right, I see. OK, this is all perfectly expected with someone like yourself, Molly. How did your mum react when she saw you?"

"She was… I don't know. It's so tough to explain her initial reaction. She was distressed for sure, but she wasn't actually angry with me." As I sit there, recounting the events that changed everything, the flashbacks vividly plant themselves into my mind.

"She… was a little upset at first… but I think it was still because she was recovering from the shock. Once she saw how I reacted, she saw right through me.

'I-I...'

'You want to be a girl.'

"Just like that, my life changed forever."

"How did she know? Had you given any clues in the past?" Mrs Styles is clearly intrigued by the story.

"Not that I'm aware of. She said it was more than just 'boys being boys' and she was right. She said I was dressed far too girly for this all to just be a phase."

"It could be that she has known about it for years but is trying to protect your embarrassment. Her instinct here will be to keep you happy, and nurture you as she has done. Nothing of what you said has made it sound like your mum has been hard on you. You're lucky to have her on your side, and so outrightly proud of it as well. The way she stood by your side when you first came into Dr Grayson's office, the clothes she has kitted you out with — she wants this for you just as badly as you do, or near enough."

"Isn't that what all mothers are supposed to do? Support their children?"

Mrs Styles throws me a serious look. "Yes, you would think so. Unfortunately, not everyone is as lucky as you. There are entire countries, whole religions, huge communities who don't validate their children's biggest wish and purest human right — the right to be yourself. You may not realise it, but your mother is a special case. She one-hundred percent supports you and having that powerful ally in your corner will make a world of difference."

I can't help but smile. This feels like a reverse parents evening where I'm hearing how Mum is doing in her work. A fourth sip of the now slightly cooling cocoa, and the topic shifts forward a little.

"So…" I begin, "What do I actually do now?"

"Well, you've come out to one person. I'm guessing you won't be doing this by half. You won't be going to school as boy Molly and coming home to become girl Molly, will you? Is this a full-time change of appearance?"

"Yeah, we are going shopping for uniform on Thursday." An avalanche occurs in my stomach — just two days away from buying my new school clothes and trying them on in the shop!

"That's quick for sure, but it's admirable sometimes to just rip it off like a plaster. Some people bottle it up inside them for decades and spend half their lives living a lie. Others were just not fortunate enough to truly express themselves. This doesn't mean they aren't transgender, but it may mean that they don't feel the true extent of the happiness they can gain from life. So long as you are ready for it all and you don't rush it too drastically, you will likely be all right and be much happier presenting as a girl full-time. Are you ready for that?"

"Ready as I'll ever be; it's time to be myself."

"Well said!"

"So you said... present as a girl? Is that all I can do? Present?" I say while taking my fifth sip of the drink. It's over half-way done now.

"As you are in the very early stages, there is no way a gender specialist would see you — not a public one anyway. They usually ask you to spend a year presenting as your desired gender before they allow for any medical adjustments. As such, I'm not going to disclose much more than that, but I can email you some websites just so you can read up on the methods of treatment you may be offered down the line."

"Oh, OK. That makes sense, just feels like a long time."

"Everything will feel like a long time at this moment because you have just started. When you have a final goal in mind, it's easy to get ahead of yourself and try to skip to the finished product. You just have to take it a step at a time, and not let your imagination race too far past the realistic expectations and boundaries. Sadly, you can't just wake up tomorrow as a physical female."

"Yeah, it sucks but at least I am getting somewhere. First steps and all that, eh?" My voice's pitch has dropped down again. It's not totally gone but it is deeper.

"Yep. Now, as far as the end goal goes, that is totally up to you. Some transgender people present as their true gender identity but never go for any of the medical adaptations. Others go all the way and aim to be as close to the natural physical woman as possible. For others, they simply accept that they are who they are. Almost nothing physically changes. From where I am, it seems you will be the first type for now and aiming to become the 'ultimate lifeform' as you likely see it."

She's good. I didn't realise she is a mind reader in the literal sense. Yet here she is, turning the pages of the book of my life as if it is just sat on her coffee table.

"Y-yeah, i-it would be nice to... lose... my... yeah." I can't bring myself to say the word aloud just in case it offends Mrs Styles.

"If that's the way you want to go, nothing can or will stop you! But always keep an open mind, and always try to understand that there are more transgender people like you out there than you would suspect. The clinics are often host to long waiting lists."

"I get that, I'll just have to be patient!"

"Yep, I'm sure you can do it though. You seem like you have resilience and steel about you. Stay true to yourself and you'll be OK."

I would be lying if I didn't think that Mrs Styles has been repeating herself a lot in this chat. I imagine that's how they are taught to approach tricky conversations like this. Just try to reassure the patient.

"So, do you have any questions?"

"I suppose I have one, but a tricky one. Why… am *I* trans? I've heard it on YouTube videos and read it online, but I am hoping you can give me a bit more context of it. Is it chemical? Is it just chance? Is it genetic?"

"Yes, yes and sometimes, yes, though indirectly. Sorry to say this, but it is unclear. Now, I do know from your file which I read before you arrived today that you have autism, correct?"

"Yeah, it was assessed *years* ago! Does that relate to this?"

"Scientifically and statistically speaking, you do have an increased chance of having gender dysphoria if you also have ASD, like you do. It's not totally to blame. Not every trans person is autistic, not everyone with Asperger's Syndrome is transgender. But there is that higher chance. I'm sorry, that's the best I can do for why you have dysphoria."

"No, it's OK. I understand. It can't be easy to nail down just one specific cause."

"The cause of being transgender is gender dysphoria. It's that dysphoria that we can't explain entirely. We know what dysphoria is, we just don't know *why* it is. Does that make sense?"

"Yeah." I finish the drink at last with a smooth sixth sip. "So dysphoria is just that feeling of not feeling right in your own body?"

"Yes, dysphoria takes a multitude of forms. In this case, you have gender dysphoria. Your gender in your head is at odds with what is physically between your legs and all of the physical evidence every time you look in a mirror."

"Yeah, I don't like looking at myself usually. But today…" I pause to run my hands down my jumper, "I love the way I look!"

"So keep doing whatever you must do to be happy. That's the number one thing. I could go a lot deeper into the psychology of gender and such with you, but I do have other patients. Not to mention, you need to go with your mum to your next stop, wherever that is."

"She's keeping as much of it a surprise!"

I put my boots back on and push the recliner back down with my legs, keeping my feet on the floor so I don't mess up the couch. I then stand up, feeling quite stiff and weak just through lack of movement. That couch is so comfy, I would honestly stay all day if I could.

"So will I see you again for a chat?" I ask optimistically.

"Yes, I will actually be a contact for the school. If you need support while at school, I can come in and we can have a talk. Besides that, I do usually perform little check-up talks for my patients. Sometimes via call, other times you'll be right here."

"Cool, sounds good!"

"OK, we best get you back to your mum."

We leave the office and I return to the waiting room. Mum thanks Dr Grayson and Mrs Styles then we both leave.

"So how did that go?" Mum cheerily asks

"It was… a lot."

En Route to the Salon

We are not even quite back at the car before Mum tries to find out exactly how the meeting with the psychiatrist went. I prolong her excitement and anticipation by waiting until we are back in the warming shelter of the car before opening up about it.

"It was a tough chat, but the doc is really nice. She was very gentle about it but didn't give me unrealistic expectations."

"That's good! What was it she was asking anyways?"

"Oh it was basically all about how I first knew I was trans and everything that's happened since you found out."

Mum jokes. "I hope you didn't make me sound too much like a villain!"

"Actually, Mrs Styles says that you're doing a great job of supporting me and that I'm lucky to have you in my corner with all of this." It feels good giving Mum her 'parents evening' report. She's clearly touched by it too, as a genuine smile appears on her face.

"I just want what's best for you, princess. If that's raising you from this point as my daughter, I'm all right with that."

"She was saying that a lot of people end up totally alienated. No one accepts their true desire to express themselves! How awful is that?"

"That's terrible! I mean, I don't know what the rest of the family will say to it, but I don't care. I certainly don't care what my friends think of it. I'm proud of you, unconditionally."

Ah… yeah. The rest of the family, I forgot about them. It's not a huge immediate family. My older brothers are off at university down South, and we don't talk about where Dad went (fairly classic, ugly split up. To this day, I still don't know why.) I don't have a sister, making me the only girl of the next generation — and only Mum and I know it so far. Cousins, uncles, aunts — all out of the picture. We only ever see each other at big family events.

"When do Matthew and Kyle find out then?"

Mum shrugs, for once not having an answer. "They'll find out when they find out. They'll be home around Christmas, they always are. I'm sure they'll be fine with it. Hell, I bet they'll want to protect their little sis even more!"

"Yeah! I'll need it!" I humorously add.

"So, was that all Mrs Styles wanted to chat about? The start?"

"Nah, we went through some scientific stuff about why dysphoria exists and why trans people are a thing. Then we discussed the goals I have with my transition."

As the car takes the second right to head back towards Pitton's Suburbia via a quieter road, Mum starts to chip away and unlock the finer details from within my mind.

"So whether you'll go on hormones and all that? What did you say?"

"I said I want to look into every option. She did say the waiting list takes a long time and that I can't even join it yet. I have to have lived and presented as a girl for at least a year."

"Well, it will all happen at the right time, hon. Good things come to those who wait!"

"That was pretty much what Mrs Styles said too. No other way of looking at it, going private apparently costs a fortune!"

"Well, you can become really successful and do it that way if you like!"

"Hmmph fat chance! Anyways, you haven't told me where we are going now."

"We are going to see about the options for your hair. I don't know whether it will be a wig or extensions, but we need a quick fix as well! Can't have you going into school without gorgeous hair!"

"Ohh! Yeah, I suppose they don't happen to have any rapid hair-growth formula."

"Even if you ever find a bottle of that, do **not** use it! Imagine all the gunk they put in a bottle of that! You are better doing it as naturally as possible. At least it has been a month since your last haircut. I reckon in less than a year, you'll have something we can work with. But we'll ask the expert before we do anything!"

Like I already said, Sharon owns her own salon, but I have never actually had my hair done by her. I've obviously never had my make-up or nails done by her either and that's not the aim here.

"I would ask if you are excited, but we probably won't be getting much done today on your actual hair. More just advice on what to get you while it grows. We'll then add that to Thursday's shopping list!"

"Fab, let's see what Sharon has to say!"

"Maybe just try to pick your voice up a little before we go in?" Mum has a point, it has dropped a lot since this morning's petrol station visit.

"Yes, Mum."

This time, I don't have to adjust it in complete silence, although I know Mum isn't best pleased with the rather obnoxious noises I'm making as I try to steady my femme tone. One minute, maybe two minutes tops later, I'm ready.

"Ahem, how's that now?"

"Much better, doubt Sharon will have any tips for that so just keep doing your best with it. I'm sorry if this feels like too much pressure, I just want to help you feel comfortable with yourself after years of being unable to."

Years? How does Mum know it has been years in the making? I haven't told her that part. Maybe she's just assuming, but she would assume right and that's a little creepy.

"Come on, daughter of mine! Time for you to actually talk to Sharon about your hair."

We leave the car for what feels like the hundredth time today, though by my count it is only the third. More of that clicking off of the car park surface and then the pavement. It may be the noise that will haunt me with its repetitive and steady rhythm, but it also feels so good at the same time. With every step, my femininity is proudly booming from my feet. They also make my steps a little more feminine, all the better when I'm just about to let more people see Molly for the first time. It feels like a confident strut akin to that on a catwalk as we reach the heavy glass door. One dedicated pull on the cold, metal handle and we are in.

"Hiii there, ladies!"

That'll be her.

Different Hairdos (and Hair-Don'ts!)

Flashback to the 1980s in your own head or, if you are too young for that like me, picture any salon in any eighties movie. That's what you are greeted with in Sharon's Salon, which is imaginatively named… *Sharon's*. I wonder how many seconds went into naming that.

Loads more time went into the décor of the place, however. The walls were all done in black-and-white check pattern with bright red chairs which really stand out in the otherwise checkerboard room. The mirrors are all wall-mounted and a lot bigger than they ever have to be. Usually, I would be heading upstairs to the green walls of the gents cuts floor. Not today; I want to be pretty!

On the walls, besides mirrors, are pictures, posters and memorabilia — all of which from her favourite music stars. From Michael Jackson to Queen to Whitney Houston. Her 'Best of the 80s' playlist playing down the speakers of the salon floor almost matches the decorations entirely. I hear something by Queen and Freddie Mercury's iconic yellow jacket and legendary moustache greet me with one look at the wall beside me. It's weird, almost feels as if he is going to pop out of the picture in some kind of grand return.

Now what about the woman who runs *this* show? Sharon is a very proud woman. She's unapologetic, she's honest and she's lovely. Her hair seems to change colour almost monthly — this time it is a bold, darkish red. She styles it with spray and keeps it quite short, preferring to spike it up. She isn't the most feminine in her appearance; her dark red lipstick the only make-up she tends to wear, and it always seems to be that same shade whenever I've briefly seen her. Mum says that she's a lesbian, which isn't the most common thing here, but it also isn't as unique as myself. She says that some lesbians dress in quite a manly way, but also advised me never to tell her that I heard that.

This is what I mean with Mum. She's fantastic and the best mum I could ever ask for, but she does have a few… let's say, views in poor taste. I've never once found myself judging someone's outfit and basing it on who they love. Then again, I can imagine that's what will happen with me once more people find out who Molly is.

Anyway, enough of the context and explanation. It's time to actually talk to the woman herself.

"Hi there, ladies!"

"Hi, Sharon. How have you been?"

Ah yes, the few minutes of expected chatter between the two women. I should probably be paying attention to them chatting as it's good practice for hearing how women should chat to each other. Nevertheless, I stand admiring the décor for a few minutes while hearing the odd word in between my fascination of the plethora of artists on the walls — a few I've never even heard of! They're talking about a wedding of some kind, it's not Sharon's. I don't even know if it's someone in her family or just that of another client in the salon. There's not much privacy in the inner circle of the salon gossip girls.

"Well, as you can see, I've brought along a special visitor! Say hi, Molly!"

"Hiya!" I confidently follow the request.

"Hi, Molly. Pleased to finally meet you!"

Finally? That's an odd word to use. She has surely only known for a day or two at most!

"Happy that you can finally meet me, too!"

"So your mum has told me that you're going to start appearing like this all the time? That's wicked, you're going to be so cute! And you know that my salon welcomes anyone, so I'll expect to see you when you finally have hair long enough to do something with."

I crack a smile at the thought of that dream eventually becoming a reality, one day in the not-too-distant future with any luck.

Sharon continues, "But until then, you'll need some alternatives, right?"

Mum re-joins the conversation. "Yeah, we obviously can't do much at the moment with yourself, but we are hoping you'll know the best thing to do."

"Well, Lola's always wearing different sorts of wigs when we go out to things together. She has long enough hair, she just likes to experiment with colours, styles and all that without all the hassle of having to undo it."

From this, I'm guessing that Lola is Sharon's partner. Again, just going to bite my tongue on that one until I know for sure. And I'll only know for sure if Sharon ever mentions that fact.

"So I think if you picked up a decent wig, it would be the best way to go about it. Extensions are useful, but not when there is no length to the hair at all. Not to mention, they're an absolute faff to take out and put back in. With a wig, it's a case of putting a cap on to hide your own hair then styling the wig on top. You'll need a comb and a couple of brushes, but I think the wig is best."

"Thanks, Shaz. I was thinking the same thing for her hair but wanted to run it by an expert. We're going shopping for new uniform and other new clothes on Thursday, do you know any good wig shops at all?"

"There's one in Dundee, I know that much for sure. That's where Lola gets all her wigs, bless her. Maybe you can speak to her about it all tomorrow? I'll see if she's got time for a quick phone call so you can pick her brain about it."

"What do you think, Mols? Sound good?"

"Yeah, I'd love to speak to Lola about it. As you say, she knows more about this than all of us."

"Braw, I'll ask her tonight and let you know."

Just then, the door opens and a bubbly, skinny, petite woman walks in.

"Speak of the devil! Hi, hon! I thought you were working."

"Ah it's a right bast***, the heating at work broke while we were on lunch, so they sent all the staff home for the day. It's annoying because I was doing really well on the calls, but it's a bonus day off and a chance to surprise you!"

This… is probably Lola. And she is… probably Sharon's girlfriend.

That much is then pretty much confirmed as Lola quickly gives Sharon a peck on the cheek and receives one in turn. Lola then turns, suddenly noticing our presence. It's just the four of us in the women's section of the salon at the moment, yet Lola didn't see anyone else right away. It's cute in the sort of 'be sick in your own mouth' kind of way.

"Oh, hi ladies!" She sounds very chipper, a real perky one.

"Hi! I'm Molly!"

"Ah Molly, I've heard a lot about you over the past few days! You look gorgeous!"

"Thanks, you look lovely too!"

I am not lying there either. Lola has golden hair which she is wearing in a tidy bun. She's wearing glasses and a substantial application of make-up. She has come from work so stands in a yellow plaid skirt-suit and low, black heels, which don't do much to shield the fact that she must only be 5ft tall without the shoes. And most importantly, the smile still hasn't left her face from the moment she appeared. Even when she was complaining about her work closing, she did so with a smile.

Sharon steps in to try to move the conversation along, she may have more clients coming soon.

"Honey, Molly is wondering about wigs. She is going into school on Friday for a meeting and hoping to be full-time girly-girl from that point on. I mentioned how you wear quite a few of them."

"A whole cupboard in my room is just for my wigs, I must have like a dozen! All different colours and shapes and lengths! What would you like to know?"

My mum thankfully tells Lola to spare me the embarrassment of not knowing what I'm talking about.

"We want to know which colour and length you would recommend for Molly. We likely want to only pick up one really good wig instead of having multiple."

"I would advise that you pick up a wig of a fairly standard hair colour. For Molly's skin tone... hmmm... Either a nice, bright blonde to really stand out, or a gingery one for the same reason would be best. I don't think brown is special enough, it doesn't stand out in the right ways. Length-wise, definitely go for a longer one. I'm thinking more than shoulder-length, but not outrageously long for every day!" She's unbelievably cheery as she continues with her inspired advice.

"Ultimately, see what feels right when you go shopping for one, but that would be what I would go for if I was you! I'm excited to see what you pick though so please show us pictures often!"

"Ha, I'll be sure to let you know!" Lola's a breath of fresh air on this dim town.

"And I would also seriously recommend picking up a couple cheap ones on Amazon or whatever. It's good to try new styles and you can always show up to an event with an instant talking point. People always ask me about my hair, some don't even know I'm using a wig sometimes! But before you ask, these are my natural locks!" She points to her beautiful bunch of golden hair, sitting proudly like a halo atop her head, in a black band.

"Right place, right time as ever honey," Sharon lovingly shares.

"Thanks so much for your help ladies, we'll be going now but I'm sure Molly will have more to ask you both as she gets started!"

"Message us anytime!" Lola once again showing unrivalled enthusiasm. "And good luck!"

And just like that, the day of chaotic and crucial meetings has come to an end. I know a lot more now than I did yesterday, but I take an hour or so once we get back home just letting all that info soak in. I take time to note down any key advice and events of the day in my little 'Transition Planner.' It was an idea I got from a YouTube video, and so far, it has a lot of handy information from all my studies.

White Lie

If I ran through the events of every night, over and over, this book would start just being a repetitive mess. If something happens, I will tell you. However, last night — that Tuesday night, nothing did. I cleansed the make-up from my face, changed into a cute yet simple black nightie, and fell into a blissful slumber.

And as I awake on this Wednesday morning, I'm confused as to what today's plans are. This is when Mum hits me with some surprising news.

"There's nothing actually planned for today, nowhere we need to be, and *I* need to go back to work."

Mum has been given a few days of leave just to help fix me up and for 'getting over the shock.' Mum successfully got over the shock on Sunday night with a laugh over dinner and quite possibly, a cheeky glass of red wine once I retreated upstairs to play my game. She has been viewing them as bonus days off, and that's fair enough to her. Even though she has been my chauffeur and my helper throughout the week so far, she tells me something surprising.

"You know, it felt really nice to spend a couple of days getting to know my daughter. Hopefully, this won't be the last time you'll want to spend time with your mother." She smiles but it seems to be battling genuine worries about losing the bond that has been so quickly strengthened thanks to my awakening.

"Mum, we've got many mother/daughter dates ahead of us, don't worry. Now while you're at work, what would you like me to do?"

"Hmm, I honestly don't know. Shower and get dressed of course, I've put some comfy 'loungewear' through on my bed for you... hmm." Mum continues to wonder what my goals for the day should be.

"Well, I'll practise my make-up and I'll look at different wig options as well as clothing. You know, make a list so we know what we are looking for tomorrow."

"That's a fab idea! Oh, and if you could also do those dishes from last night, I'd really appreciate it. You aren't ready to take on cooking yet, you can barely work a microwave! But we'll work on all of it and before long, two young ladies will running this household like a tight ship, no a shi—"

"Mother, if I'm not allowed to curse, you shouldn't be either!" I confidently interrupt her, even though my voice hasn't been sorted at all yet. It still isn't instinctive once I've been awake for 5 minutes.

"Fair enough, guess we'll both need swear jars!"

"Yeah right! Anyways, you best be going but don't worry, I'll be all right here!"

"I know you will be. Just… I'm so proud of you, honey. You're looking more like a woman by the minute, even if you don't feel it. I'm really happy you don't have to hide it any more, soon not even to the outside world."

Mum follows up an emotional speech with a little kiss on my forehead while I am sat up in bed, which is as glamorous as it sounds.

"Have fun at work. I'll see you tonight when you come in."

And just like that, Mum leaves my room, closing the door behind her. I can hear her putting her boots on downstairs, fastening her coat and then grabbing her keys and heading out the door.

A day off where nothing is actually happening? It feels like I should be guilty for what is technically skipping school, but I invite you to consider the alternative. Molly, still not entirely feminine enough for consistent (daily) public appearances, in the dog-eat-dog world that is high school. I'm not even at a particularly vicious high school, just the court of public opinion would not be the most welcoming. They won't be anyway.

I make the mistake of looking at my phone. Aw crap, did I really forget to reply to Chris? That just makes me look like an awful friend.

My right thumb is nervously shaking as I tap the screen to unlock my mobile phone. An ungodly thirst builds in the back of my throat and spreads to the front with speed and precision. I drink the remainder of last night's glass of water, which helps a little.

I click the little blue icon for Messenger, and just as expected, top of my messages is the one Chris sent yesterday — the one I read while waiting for my appointment with the doc and the psychiatrist.

'Hey dude where r u? U skippin school or sumthin?'

Now or never, I need to reply to this message. Do I dare to tell the truth? Before the big debut and reveal? Absolutely not! This high school, truths and lies all spread like wildfire there. I'd be done for before I even begin my new school life.

I run through about six different drafts of the message but settle on this one.

'Ah, Mum took me away with her to see my aunt for a few days — family shit, y'know?'

Not a bad lie, not a terribly unbelievable truth. In my logic and overthinking, I decide this is the best I can do and hit send. One monkey off my back, now to actually get up off my back.

I take my glass from my bedside unit and go downstairs to the kitchen to refill it, after rinsing it first of course. Along with this, I pop some toast in for a change, and because I have time today. Two minutes later, I spread the butter and spoon the strawberry jam on to the slightly toasted bread. Then, I do something I have never done before — I grab one of the trays!

We have these trays which are for eating in places other than the table. I never tend to take one but today, on a day off, it just feels right. I start saying my next steps for the day aloud.

"I need to eat this, shower, shave and get dressed. Dishes need done at some point, then it's just more studying and deciding who Molly truly is and what she looks like"

Intervening in my own psychotic meltdown of talking to myself — something I have always done and will always do — I return to bed with my tray of toast and water. And as I choose the first video of the day, another in the 'Girl for A Day' series, I can't help but feel a sense of intense satisfaction. This truly **is** the life! Breakfast in bed, cute nightwear and freedom to watch anything I like. Hopefully, the expert artistic efforts from this make-up team will take my mind off the impending confusion and disaster to come when I finally remove the mask at school. I can only wish to one day be this good at getting ready — maybe it's easier on someone else. Sometimes, it's really hard to tell that the 'boys' were ever boys at all! And it's all for proms, or fancy parties or weddings — I would give almost anything to experience it just once! Anyway, best eat my toast before it goes cold!

The Window

Well, this is lovely, but I really need to get on with my day. The third or fourth video from the makeover team is impressive, but I can't just vegetate all day. I take the second trip downstairs today to put my dishes in the water — I must do those later! For now though, something else needs washed — me!

It's a toss-up between shower or bath, but I actually choose bath since I have plenty of time. Not only that, but I can also do other revision, training and practising of all the feminine habits I want to master. Sitting with a razor in one hand and the soap in the other in a nice warm bath, this is once again the best life! I'm practising all sorts of different phrases with my improved voice.

"Hi everyone, I'm Molly!"

"Um… I don't know; what do you think?"

"What are we going to today?"

Again, the focus is to try to nail that inflection at the end. The pitch needs to raise on the last vowel sound of the sentence to sound naturally feminine. Men naturally drop their voices at the end of a point while women tend to up the pitch a little and make it sweeter. We really do just about do everything better!

The other challenge is keeping a constant smile going, and all of this while my music plays. I decide to test Mum's theory about my music taste having to change and switch from the regular playlist to one titled *'Girls Modern Music Classics'*

Some of it is alien to me, others are those currently playing on the radio or those so famous that you couldn't possibly fail to recognise them. ABBA have always been a little guilty pleasure for my music taste, so to hear one or two of their biggest hits as I lather up and scrub down is fabulous!

This bath also doesn't last as long as the one I took on Monday, all just because I know some of the steps now instead of reading a step-by-step guide.

Smaller towel in my short, brown hair and a large towel waiting to be wrapped around my body, I'm happy enough with my efforts that I drain the bathwater down the plughole and move on to moisturising. The humidity in the room makes it feel quite itchy, all the more reason to rehydrate that skin. Almost head-to-toe, I rub moisturisers into my body to try to soothe the burning and discomfort.

Slightly less sore, I dress myself with the towel and head quickly through to Mum's room, the heat of before replaced with a truly unpleasant chill. The sooner I put these clothes on, the better — in every sense. But what do we have today?

Loungewear is the exact word I would use for this outfit — it looks almost like thicker pyjamas. The underwear set is basic and black but does include a bra, so it's not entirely effortless to get changed. Through some videos I've watched, I know that many girls hook their bras from the front first and then turn them once that's done. No one is around to judge me taking this cheeky shortcut, so I do just that. They didn't lie — it is a lot easier! I can't help but feel slightly put off by the lack of… anything inside the cups of my bra, so I grab a pair of socks from my room quickly and put one in each. It's hardly any size at all, but it feels nice to have something there!

Next, on to the pyjamas… I mean, loungewear. It's jet black with a white slogan up the side of the leggings and the same slogan across the front of the jumper. I say slogan, it is just one word — 'Pink'. That's A) a lie, and B) an actual brand! This must be Mum's; she's just letting me wear it today! The white writing isn't entirely white. It's an animal-print design but just on the lettering and only in black and white. You would think this makes it tricky to read but the writing is more than large enough to see at a moment's glance.

Black 'boot' slippers complete the set, and they look **so** warm! They have little buttons on one side to make them look more complex than they are. I put them on and I'm not disappointed by the warmth of them. I then quickly remove them to put socks on first, then put them back on over the top.

Next up, it's teeth cleaned and then make-up! I keep it fairly simple for the most part, but suddenly feel bolder when it comes to eyeshadow. Instead of opting for the safe pink, I go for an almost seductive red. I also try to apply it higher than usual, to make my eyes and eyelids appear properly shiny. I bolden this look with the mascara and think about eyeliner.

"Ah, no one will see it. Let's just try it out."

And so begins ten excruciating minutes of trying to perfect a flick. I opt for the quick fix and smudge a little with my fingers to create a faded flick at the side of either eye. Not terrible, hardly great!

Pink lipstick won't do today, where's my red? Oh yeah, I don't have one. Mum does though, I'm sure she won't mind her daughter just borrowing it. Two minutes later, I have dark red lips, working nicely with the Hell-like eyeshadow. It's taken me two days, and I've gone a little goth!

I can't quite shake how ridiculous the hair looks, so I grab yesterday's hat. Now that I'm ready for nothing, I face the next challenge of the day — dishes!

I return to the kitchen for now the third time today and empty the dirty dishes out of the basin, one-by-one. My music has been playing the whole time, so I notice my hips moving to the rhythms blaring from my phone as I stand over the sink.

Once emptied of crockery, I pour the disgusting water down the sink and start to refill it with fresh, clean H_2O. There aren't many dishes, just those from last night's dinner and the ones from breakfast today. It's better to wash them one at a time in the basin, and not leave them to stagnate again in the water. A generous drizzle of washing-up liquid and I can finally begin.

It's easy enough, made even easier with the sponge-on-a-stick that Mum bought a few weeks back. It is already loaded with dish soap but it's good to have bubbles forming in the basin too.

As I reach the second last dish, jamming out to the girly tunes, that's when it happens. See, the big kitchen window behind the sink has a blind but it is almost impossible to reach. I don't think this through and just leave the window a clear viewpoint for anyone looking to see a crossdressing freak. And that is what happens. Or at least, I think it is.

An old man from the same row of houses is walking his dog. The pooch is adorable, a wee Jack Russell with brown and black patches of fur and the cutest little face! If only the owner was so agreeable.

Unfortunately, Hank is anything but. A proper old man, what the kids would call a boomer. He walks his dog every day in the woods which border our street. You can often hear him cutting the grass at any time from seven a.m. to ten p.m. Why do people cut the grass in the dark? You can't see the grass. How do you know it needs cut?

I only notice my mistake a little too late, and Hank stops at our back gate. The planks are spaced out widely enough that you can see what goes on in our kitchen from any opening in the fence.

He stops, he looks, he *keeps looking* and my eyes at last lock to his position. I need to face this. He turns to head along the path to his, but I can read his muttering lips enough to know that he is muttering. And that instantly means he is muttering about me.

I have a hat on; my make-up is heavy. Surely he couldn't tell. Maybe he didn't even see, maybe he saw a bird or something in the garden. Maybe he was just catching his breath. That could be why he was then muttering. Nah, he can't have spotted me, but *did* he?

Scouting for Girls' Clothing

There's only one way to get over the storm building inside me at the thought that one of my neighbours could out me before I'm ready, and that's to take some time to look at girly outfits on Pinterest. Normally, this would just be pure fantasizing. However, it is now within my reach. Tomorrow, I will be shopping for girly clothes, shoes, even a wig! It's all very surreal, like an out of body experience. It feels like any minute, I'm going to awake to find that Molly is the one that's dead.

But that's not the case — Molly is still here. **I** am still here, and **he** is gone. Looking at all of these outfits just reminds me of that even more. It brings a wicked smile to my face as I sit on the couch in the living room, just scrolling through ideas on my phone.

Some of the outfits are pretty close to what I see the other girls in my town wear, while others are the furthest thing from it. There's a groundswell of outfits inspired by Japanese pop-culture and especially anime. I've only ever heard of one anime but to see outfits from it being modelled in real life is so fascinating. Maybe one day but for now, I need to look at the practical outfits. Dresses and skirts are the backbone of my dream wardrobe, but they'll have to be more conventional to begin with.

My real weakness is that stereotypical 'school-girl' look. While the guys my age would be foaming at the mouth to see the girls wearing it, I've always wanted to dress that way for my own satisfaction. The way the boldly coloured skirts contrast the usually plain jumpers is just perfect. They are also usually complemented by some high heels. And I imagine it's all the cuter when finished off with tying the hair into pigtails and a heavy make-up job.

One day, I'll be wearing that stuff regularly. And if we are talking about crazy and unrealistic fantasies, maybe one day, someone will be foaming at the mouth over me. It would be nice to feel wanted, but I first need to feel accepted.

After saving what must be the 1000th plaid skirt cute jumper combo to my wish list, I receive another message. This time however, it's not Chris. It's from Sharon's partner, Lola.

'Hi Molly, you precious little flower! Sharon helped me find you on Facebook so I could send you this. Enjoy shopping tomorrow! :D'

Much like her own appearance, Lola's messages are not at all bashful. The 'this' that she sends me is a YouTube video titled 'Wigs and Wig Care For Beginners'. It gives me the perfect opportunity to escape the clothing rabbit hole I've been down for admittedly a little too long and turn to thinking about my hair again. Firstly though, I need to reply to her. This isn't as bad as messaging Chris, nothing to hide.

'Hii Lola, thx so much. I'll be sure to watch this rn. So excited for tomoz! :)'

The video isn't the most interesting thing ever, but it does have some really good advice in it. I click around the channel page as well to see if they have more tip videos and save them to my 'Watch Later' for when I need to know something new about wigs. I hop back on to Pinterest after the video and type two different searches to compare some things.

Search number one is 'long blonde wig' and there are many different results. Some take 'long' to the extreme, presenting me with hair that goes down to the thighs in some cases. That would be a really impractical choice, but the shoulder/mid-chest length blonde hair looks amazing! It looks especially elegant when accessorised with bows, hairbands or tied up with ribbons!

The next search, as per Lola's advice, is 'long red wig' though I quickly realise this is wrong. By 'red', I don't mean **blood** red. That's exactly what I am greeted with as many bright red wings appear, trying to entice me with their bold shades and unapologetic confidence.

Not wanting something quite that brash, I alter the search slightly to say, 'long ginger wig' and this is much better. It's proper, classic Scots' hair colour and it too looks fantastic at my ideal length. All I really gain from this is that I know exactly what length to aim for. As for colour, I can't seem to definitively decide between being a blonde babe or a redhead! Women have all of the hardest decisions to make, no doubt about it.

I also spot some more exotic colours in my suggestions. Baby pink hair, royal blue hair, white hair (not grey but very white), half and half wigs, rainbow wigs — why does everyone make so many wigs?! Maybe this is the problem Lola has, and why she says herself that she has a dozen of them at very least.

As for the wig I will choose, I guess I'll just see what looks better in real life. It's one thing to like the look of something on the internet, it's entirely different to feel enamoured by the look of something in person. I suppose you can apply that to people too. Then again, I am perpetually single, so how the heck would I know?

Surprise Donation

It's amazing how quickly a day can disappear when you immerse yourself in practising and training. That's exactly what I do with the final few hours before Mum comes home from work. I do my voice exercises; I strut around and I keep smiling throughout.

I even decide to really test my limits by removing the comfy 'slipper boots' and socks and instead, putting on the first pair of heels which I was caught in on Sunday night. Strutting in heels gives me more of a wobble but also more of a confident strut once I'm finally able to take a few steps and not feel like I'm totally losing my balance. I doubt I will ever be able to (or want to) wear high heels to school but they'll be great for special occasions!

Anyway, just as I'm in the middle of a voice-training video, the front door is unlocked and opened. I sit back down and kick off my heels as fast as possible before putting the cosier shoes back on and going downstairs to welcome her home.

"Hi, Mum!" I exclaim happily while making my way down the stairs.

"Hi, honey; how was your day?"

"It was good, yeah! I did what you asked me to."

"You're a good girl! Makes my life just that little bit easier. I'm glad you're around actually, I believe we'll be getting a knock at the door for you soon. "

"For me? What could anyone be wanting me for? Do I have to go anywhere?"

"Relax, doll. No, it's just some stuff being delivered for you."

"Oh! That's fun!" I'm very excited to see what this mystery package is.

Until then, it's back to a little more training. I return to see my phone lying screen-up on my bed with a new message notification on it. 'No, please don't be Chris again!'

It isn't — it's almost worse. It's the gaming group chat. All of the guys are in it, all 7 of us! Rami is the one who has put the call out for the squad.

'Anyone coming on tonight?'

He also isn't the only one as a few active responses start rolling in. I would like to play, but I can see that Chris has said he is on. In order to not contradict myself, I decide to just ignore it. Stephen goes as far as to @ me but Chris answers, telling him where I am. Or rather, where I *told* him I am.

'Ollie's away'

Close enough to the truth. We all know Ollie is actually away for good. Dead in other words.

I may still decide to play a game tonight, but I'll just appear offline. I usually do anyway, I don't want to be bothered by random players when I'm just trying to relax. At the same time, there are a few better things to do. Tomorrow is a big day for me, I need to make sure I am pretty much picture perfect and sound perfect. I need to be entirely indistinguishable from a cis-girl.

Just as I find myself worrying about how much there is to do, there is a knock at the door. I don't dare go down to answer it in case it's someone who knows Ollie. I wouldn't want to break the shock news early. I mean, it could even be Hank, coming to break the news of what and *who* he saw earlier.

Thankfully for my poor, tormented mental state, it is not Hank. It is however someone who knows my mum — I can hear her pleasantly chatting away with the woman at the door. I can tell it's a woman as the voice is too lovely for a man's voice! I didn't hear her say at any point that we were expecting one of her friends to visit but that's what it sounds like.

I do my best to subtly listen in on the conversation, but the details are quite shocking.

"You know, I asked Courtney to put a bag of clothes together for the charity shop. When you asked if she was throwing anything out, you couldn't have asked at a better time!"

Sh**! Courtney? Only one of my mum's friends has a daughter named Courtney and that girl is *in my year at my school!* No, no, no, I can't believe this! She's going to know; she's going to tell everyone! The visitor continues talking.

"Even better, her shoe size just grew so she just got a bunch of new shoes. Her old ones are all in pretty good nick, should work well for whatever you're doing."

"Thanks so much, Evelyn. Are you sure you don't want anything for all this?"

"You can buy me a drink on our next bingo night!" Evelyn (as I now know her) jokes

"Works for me! I best go, my child will be wanting her dinner."

Lose the Evidence

Mum's little slip of the tongue puts my own heart in my mouth. Luckily, it isn't even so much as followed up on. The door closes after some friendly goodbyes (too many, really) and I make my way back down the stairs once I am sure the coast is clear.

"So... what was all that about?" I ask, pretending that I didn't just eavesdrop on her chatting.

"I may have asked around for a favour or two. Buying you an entire wardrobe is simply impossible, even with my good wage. I asked a few of the mums that I know who have daughters around your age and around your size — 12 or 14. That was just Evelyn Jennings from the other side of the street, you know her daughter apparently?"

"Yeah, it's not like I know her well at all. We're in P.E. together. That's about it. We don't talk outside or that."

"Well maybe Molly will find it much easier to get on with her. Could be a really good friend to have, someone so close who knows exactly who you are. She can support you, give you tips, you two could hang out together and forget those filthy boys!"

"I think you may be getting ahead of yourself. Anyway, do I open the bag now?" I ask, gesturing towards the tied-up black bag, courtesy of Mrs Jennings.

"I'll just reveal it one outfit at a time as the days go by. I didn't ask for school stuff because that's the one thing I really want to buy you brand new! Well, also underwear! She was never going to donate that!"

"Eww, I don't blame her either! Why would I want Courtney's used underwear?"

Mum just chuckled. "Yep, way too innocent to be a man. How did I not spot Molly sooner?"

"I honestly don't know! Do I really have to wait to see what's in the bag?"

"I'll give you a deal. You go and empty all of the male clothes from your room, put them all in a black bag — uniform included. I'll take them to the charity shop tomorrow before we go shopping. Once you've emptied your room, you can come downstairs and watch TV and I'll busy myself ironing all of your new clothes and putting them into your wardrobe! You come back up, it will all be ready for you, princess!"

"That seems fair. Can we eat first though? In all my excitement, I didn't have lunch!"

"Go make a start on your clothes, and I'll put dinner on."

"Deal. Thanks, Mum." I give her a quick embrace and head upstairs to start throwing my clothes out.

My wardrobe and my drawers have never been even slightly organised. I hate leaving clothes out, so they have all been put away but seemingly with absolutely no system. The one exception is school uniform which is always hung up or Mum would be very annoyed.

The way the system is meant to work is that my underwear goes in the top drawer (I can usually stick to that one) with T-shirts and shorts in the second drawer and the bottom drawer being the home to any pyjamas that I often used to wear to bed. Then in the wardrobe, I hang my jeans, my shirts, my jumpers, and any occasion wear (a few suits and a kilt).

I lay the open black bag on the floor in the middle of my room and start the wholesale clearance. Nothing is safe, not even the shoes on the bottom level. There is nothing pretty about them, they should all go. A small part of my mind goes back to each respective event as I put the suits into the bag. The weddings of my oldest brother, my cousin Zara and a close friend of my mum's. Why all three had to come in the last couple of years, with the suits still fitting me to this day? I'll never know, and I no longer need to worry about them. Into the sack they go!

Half way through this total manic panic, I rush downstairs to grab a second, and even a third, black bag then race back upstairs to continue the clearing out carnage.

I pause to take a breath (and a drink) as I admire my work. In what feels like no time at all, I successfully rid my room of any manly clothing. It's so strange to see my storage spaces looking so empty. I can't help but speak into the wardrobe just to hear the subdued echo from its walls.

This must be what it's like when someone dies — all of their stuff thrown away or sent elsewhere — the room a husk of its former self. The personality in my room has all but drained entirely. All that remains is empty spaces, my chair, my bed and my TV/gaming setup. Every relic of the boy who once was, is now firmly out of sight and out of mind. I go to settle back into more practising but the summons comes.

"That's tea, Molly!"

I will never not love that call. Ever since I started eating less at lunch to try to be less fat (and therefore more popular in my head), dinner has become more of an event.

Take His Place

*O*nce I have eaten dinner, I sit downstairs as requested. One of Mum's favourite hobbies is surprisingly ironing, so this surprise donation from Courtney is a present to her as well. A whole bag full of clothes which likely don't even really need ironed, but Mum isn't going to pass up on the chance to do more of what she loves. And I can't say I have a problem with it. All that changes is my place of study.

Mum gently throws the heels I had on before dinner to the bottom of the stairs as a subtle clue to keep practising. Once I sit for a little bit to let my body digest the meal I just finished, I put the heels back on and resume challenging myself. Voice, movement, mannerisms, keep the balance! Trying to do it all at once is a challenge, made even more challenging by it being very new still. You can put as many hours as you like into learning when you first come out, I still feel like I'm totally new to it all!

The clicking is intense no matter where I go but the carpet upstairs usually means my walking practice is quieter than it is right now. Each step sounds like it is taking place from a cave at the seaside or a cliff overlooking a vast chasm in the rocks. In reality, it's just the laminate flooring of our living room. There is a rug, but it is really small and there's not much room to practise movement on just the small rectangle of luxurious fabric.

When I can hear it over the clicking of my lovely shoes (the basic black pumps I was caught in on Sunday, to remind you) the videos are training me to say commonly needed sentences as femininely as possible. Being a student who loves to learn modern languages and is currently studying two of them at school, it's remarkably similar to learning the language of the fairer sex. Not just the language either. I also need to know the tone, the actions, the facial expression — everything which makes what I'm saying sound as sweet and girly as possible. Some examples of the common phrases I'm looking to put into practice when out shopping are:

'Oooh! This looks really cute!'

This phrase is tough when you aren't used to being socially allowed to make such noises at the start of a sentence (or at any point.) The only time a boy at my school ever says 'oooh' is when they are doing so in a mocking way. They do that to poke fun when someone says something that sounds way too fancy, over-the-top or just kind of camp. I'm guilty of doing this in that sense too. Or at least, Ollie was. He's gone; I'm taking his place!

'What do you think, Mum?'

This phrase will be needed a lot tomorrow. Mum knows better than me what will look good and more importantly, what won't look good on me! This whole saga must be quite strange for Mum as I finally listen to just about her every word.

'Excuse me, sorry.'

When walking past people or when I need to ask for help, this is going to prove to very useful. In that same sense, I've been practising 'please' and 'thank you.' It's generally about sounding brighter when saying these things, I obviously know the words!

'My name is Molly/Hi, I'm Molly!'

Never know when this will be needed, useful to work on it anyway. At least my name has a natural smiling point in it at the end, easy to sound cheery when pronouncing it. As I should — I sure am delighted to finally be able to call myself something so pretty.

A few hours pass and my eyes are starting to close. I sit down and take the heels off, exhausted and quite sore. This is the sacrifice we make to wear beautiful shoes — we hurt our feet! A small price, I'm sure we can all agree. And as I go to take a break from feminine studies for the night, I switch from the girly onslaught of digital content to a basic gaming compilation. Between five and ten minutes later, Mum shouts for me to come and see her work. I take a minute to regain my senses, all too aware that I'm close to crashing out. However, the cold bucket of water about to be thrown in my face is more than enough to wake me up again.

Mum stands outside of my room with the door closed behind her.

"Are you ready to see it?"

"Hell yeah!"

"More ladylike, please?"

"Oh yeah, sorry! Force of habit. I'd love to, Mum."

"That's better, angel. Let's go then."

Mum opens the door and steps in before I do. I follow her in to see nothing has changed on three of the walls, but the fourth is quite different! I don't know where she found it, but there's now an A3 poster of princesses on the least-hidden wall of my room. Besides that, little flower stickers have been placed either side, their pink shade standing out on the forever cream-coloured walls of my room. In Mum's eyes, keeping the room cream made decorating easy, no matter what I wanted to do. I bet she never imagined this would be my dream, yet she absolutely nailed it without me saying a word.

More flower stickers have been placed on the chest of drawers, and a different sign is up on the built-in wardrobe. It's one of those 'Keep Calm' parody posters but it's hot pink and bears the slogan 'Keep Calm and Be A Princess'. Most girls my age would find this décor incredibly childish, but I love it! Maybe, I'm just a big little girl.

"Now that you've admired what's happened to the outside of your wardrobe and drawers, you might want to look inside them. Not for too long though, I can see that you're knackered! You must be working really hard on all this stuff."

"I want it to be perfect. I want her to be perfect." I say with confidence and passion as I go to open the wardrobe. One gentle pull of the right-hand door, and all my dreams come true before my eyes.

Hanging up in *my* wardrobe is *just* dresses, blouses and skirts. How many did Courtney have just lying around?! The rail has some space still but there is easily enough clothing here for many different outfits. The jumpers aren't hanging up though, wonder if there are any.

At the bottom of *my* wardrobe, where the boring shoes and weird boxes used to be, is now just shoeboxes. I don't have time to look through them, nor the energy to really take it in at the moment. I can assume that each one contains a pair of shoes which Courtney has outgrown. My eyes begin to tear up as I try to hold back the emotional build-up. So many years of self-neglect, of mistrusting, doubting and denying who and what

I am just dissolving in front of me as I stare right into the future. I leave the wardrobe for now and have a quick check of the drawers.

The top one is empty.

"We need to grab underwear tomorrow, that's what will go in there."

"Makes sense," I say while a happy tear or two rolls drips from my eyes.

The second drawer is home to the jumpers and a couple of T-shirts while the bottom one is also yet to be filled.

"Understandably, nightwear wasn't something she wanted to donate."

"Yeah, fair. Wait, did she know it was for me? Did she know that her stuff was going to me? Does she know I have it?"

"She shouldn't, honey. You'll be fine, you're just in a bit of shock! It's kind of cute to see!"

"I… thanks so much, Mum. I love you."

"I love you too, Molly. Now, we have a big day tomorrow. You'd best get yourself cleaned up and ready for bed, I'll fetch you a nightshirt. Come to think of it, tomorrow, you'll be wearing your own nightwear to bed! You've come so far already, in just four days!"

"Crazy! I'll go get those heels from downstairs and make sure everything is off in there. Also, I'll get a drink of course."

"Good girl. Goodnight!"

"Night Mum."

A final peck on the forehead and a warm embrace, and I'm free to begin clean-up efforts. Make-up off, moisturise, bedtime.

Suspense

As I awake the next day, I pull the covers off for the daily reality check. No, I am not dreaming. This time, it's a nude-ish nightshirt which confirms it all. I can see my painted toenails wiggling at the bottom of my bed. And as I come to my senses about this whole thing, I come to terms with what today actually means. Today, on this Thursday (more accurately later, once Mum is back from her slightly shorter shift), Molly makes her full public debut. Not like Tuesday when I was bouncing between different errands then back to the car. No, today is almost entirely different. A firm extended block of time where there will be no hiding place.

I check my phone to see a text from Mum.

'Today's the day hon! Your outfit for the day is on my bed for you once you've showered. I kept it a surprise for you! See you later on, about 3-ish. Love you xx'

This could be the last day that I'll read that. 'Your outfit for the day is on my bed.' To be honest, I'm surprised that is even the case today. Must mean Mum has something quite special planned for our shopping adventure in Dundee today. It takes around an hour to get there, meaning it is a proper outing for Molly today. My true self has a chance to experience a different city with no place to hide.

The usual toss-up between shower and bath does not exist today — I need to be so precise about washing so it has to be a bath. I almost go to run one as soon as I'm out of bed, but I'd best eat first. Once I start getting ready, I'm not stopping until it's go time.

Back to the usual cereal today, mainly just because I fancy it. I consider going to have a peak at the outfit that is waiting for me, but I resist the temptation. It'll be so much more exciting if I wait until it's time to put it on. Instead, I whet my feminine appetite by watching a try-on haul as I have my breakfast. This one has an extra use to it — it's a UK school uniform try-on haul. I can't help but feel a little perverted as I choose this of all videos but it's not like there's anything lewd going on.

Just girls around my age trying on different styles of blouse and skirt, debating on whether a jumper is worth it and how best to style for being out in the playground. They discuss which hairstyles are best and how to fix your hair for P.E., the pros and cons of wearing heels to school and the ideal bags for all of your books. These videos almost feel like they were made for girls like me, learning the role at the age of sixteen instead of growing up in pinafores and pigtails. If I had my way before, that *is* how I would have grown up. Not that dwelling on it will do anything, just need to make up for lost time. And today is a momentous occasion as far as catching up goes.

Speaking of lost time, if I sit and just watch these school style tips all day, I'll be losing time I could be spending sorting my own look for shopping in Dundee. I'll just finish watching this 'Back To School Make-up Tutorial' and then I'm on my way to run a bath and get the day started for real! The main thing to take away from this video is that people are very judgmental about everything, so just wear what you like on your face. That's all I can really pick up, it's not like it gives me a colour guide or anything.

Running the water for the bath always brings on not only a bout of nerves, but an opportunity for self-reflection — a pep talk of sorts.

"This is it; this is the day. The day you've wanted for so long is finally here- "

I notice only after this much of the talk that my voice is not up to scratch. I pause the talk to correct that issue and then restart, in a much sweeter tone.

"This is the day, this is the one, Mols. You're free, and you're about to be unleashed on an unexpecting world. You'll have your new school uniform; you'll have your hair… you'll be ready to go for real!"

My almost manic outer inner monologue is interrupted by the bath being primed and ready for me to enter. I'm looking at every action in the routine in microscopic detail. Not a single hair out of place, lots of soaps used, even a bath bomb today for extra freshness! The bath is also mostly the best opportunity to tune the voice and make sure it can be maintained.

After an extended maintenance process on my body, my mind and my mannerisms, I gracefully leave the bath, freshly washed and shaved from face to toe. I could shave my head; it wouldn't add to the appearance but it wouldn't take away. The main reason I don't is because I have faith that eventually (and I mean a fair while away yet), my own hair will reach the length where I can do something with it that doesn't look awful. Until then, the mane I buy today will do enough to bridge the gap. Still not entirely sure what that will look like.

Anyway, time to head through to Mum's room with the usual double towel-wraps and see what this outfit is — and why she has been keeping it a secret.

My Dress

Strangely, all that is on Mum's bed now that I'm through in her room (a place I've found myself a lot more often recently than even in the years of crossdressing before Molly was found) is today's underwear. Today's set has a nifty blue-to-pink vertical gradient pattern on it, a bit like a sunset. The bra can't quite match it, so it's just a baby pink bra. But it's a *proper* bra. It's not one of these crop tops I've been using as makeshift bras since Mum discovered me, it's a proper bra that proper women wear. I guess I… am a proper woman now. No matter what anyone says, that needs to be my attitude.

Hooking a bra is much easier when you've practised it as a child, so I nail it first time! Trying to decide what to put in there, the least obnoxious idea I have is to go for the classic 'pair of socks in each cup'. It's an old trick, but it does the trick too. But that's all that's on the bed — just underwear. Surely this isn't what she means, cis-women don't walk down the streets in lingerie!

Before I go to message Mum, I start trying to think like her (a dangerous game, I know). She text me to say the outfit is on the bed. Maybe she laid it out before she went to work and forgot to put it back on top of the covers when she made her bed.

As I predict, when I lift the duvet, clothes are hiding beneath! And quite the strange ensemble as well, a whole new experience for Molly to face.

There's not too many other ways to say it — on the bed, there is a dress! An actual dress, in my size! It's mine, it's actually *my* first dress. I have of course worn dresses in the past but never anything that is designed for my age. To be completely honest, I'm not sure if this one is completely aimed at my age either — but this time for the opposite of the usual reason. See, Mum's dresses are obviously all aimed at women, not teenage girls (and certainly not teenage boys, like the one I killed a few days ago). Whereas *this* dress… it's…

OK, enough of the dramatics, I promise! On the bed is a blue-and-white check dress. It has a collar, and it appears to be about knee-length. It's in no way a fancy dress — try to imagine Dorothy in the Wizard of Oz. Better yet, try to think about what some girls wear to primary school. At least when I was at primary school, more often than not, girls would wear the expected trousers or skirt, with a polo shirt and a school jumper. However, there were also always a few who opted for gingham school dresses. This is basically what I have in front of me: a gingham school dress but sized and styled for a sixteen-year-old girl instead of a six-year-old girl.

This is not me being ungrateful either — I'm in love with this dress! It's love at first sight, and I can't wait to put it on. I will have to though. See, Scotland doesn't have the reputation for being the warmest place on Earth. If I wore just this today, with my bare legs out, I would freeze to death! Mum has obviously thought this through, and there are black tights waiting for me to put on first. The tights are fleece-lined on the inside, giving an extra layer of warmth. As I go to put them on, I stop to instead add one more layer of moisturiser to my mostly naked body. The softer and smoother, the better!

Allowing the indoor air to dry my rapidly cooling skin for ten minutes is a lot nicer than using a towel. When you use a towel on recently moisturised skin, it's likely that you will cover yourself in towel fluff — that's just common sense. I also can't go for my tights too soon in case the fluff does the same thing so what can a girl do while waiting for her legs to dry? I would say make-up, but that's going to take a lot longer, so I just sit and wait. I see a little bit more activity on the group chat and as I'm reading the results of last night's games, a new message pops up. It's Chris (the most active in the chat and most likely to send personal messages, if you couldn't tell yet).

'*Hey dude, when u back from ur aunt's?*'

Ah, yes, 'dude'. If only he could see me now, sat on my mum's bed in just lingerie, waiting for my legs to dry enough so I can put my tights and dress on. How much of a 'dude' do I sound to anyone right now? As much of a 'dude' as a lead actress or a Scandinavian princess or another totally feminine place in society.

I send the reply, knowing that I can't hide forever. I also know that I'm in school tomorrow for that meeting, and he may bump into me. I hope that doesn't happen, but life has a way of throwing curveballs, especially mine. I type out a draft message:

'*Heyy, yeah I'm home. I also might be a little different.*'

But I chicken out and replace the last bit, hurting my own heart in the process.

'*Heyy, yeah I'm home. Hope you all haven't missed me too much!*'

I hit send before I can rethink and add the honesty back in. In truth, I hope they didn't miss Ollie, because he isn't coming back. That Sunday night, as I sat in a skirt and heels playing video games with the guys, is the exact night where he died. And they have no idea that their friend is dead, and that I'm in his place now. Will they feel weird about playing with a girl? I suppose they won't know right away, but still.

My legs are certainly dry enough now for the tights to go on. I take a few breaths to calm myself from more message torment and continue getting dressed. At least I'm not rushed for time.

Tights feel great, fleece tights feel even better. My legs have been extremely cold for the last quarter of an hour, so this feels even better still as the warmth coats my legs. I learned from the videos that you should pull tights up from the bottom of the leg once they are around your waist. This way, you use all the material of the tights and stop it all from bunching at your feet. Tights look best when they are straightened out, much like hair and attitudes.

With the tights now fully covering the gorgeous panties, I can now finally put my dress on. Still feels weird — *my* dress. If this is a dream, this will be the exact moment where I wake up. The dress is in my hands, I check to make sure the label at the neck is on the side closest to me, so that when I put the dress on over my head, it will not be back-to-front. These style dresses sometimes have buttons, but not this one. This is a classic 'throw-it-on' style dress. Easy to put on, easy to take off.

The gingham cloth is surprisingly more elastic than it looks and it is no hassle at all to push my head through the designated opening. My arms find their places soon after and I'm able to pull the dress down to cover my body. It feels as though it will extend down forever but really, it's just because my whole body is a shaking mess at this point. Not at all by means of the cold air, but all down to the cocktail of emotions inside of me. As predicted earlier, it stops just below my knees. I'm dressed — *dressed*.

Next step to try to calm myself down is to clean my teeth. Out of fear of spilling anything on my dress, I have an amazing idea. I take the chair from my room and place it beside the sink in the bathroom, facing backwards towards the toilet. I then kneel over the back, using the chair back as an extra way of guaranteeing nothing spills on my dress. Two minutes and nineteen seconds later, I spit for the last time and run my tongue along my teeth to inspect them in the least conclusive way. I then correct my voice, since this is sometimes enough to allow my voice to revert to its much less glorious, former self.

As I go to leave the bathroom, I actually use the toilet really quickly, just trying to feel less nervous. I wash my hands with the water running too slowly to cause a splashback — I can't even have water spill on my dress. I need to protect this like it's my firstborn child. Make-up time, so I wrap a large, white towel around myself and get to work.

Still no mirror in my room, I opt to instead move my make-up bag through to Mum's room to make use of her setup. But what colours, what looks do I go for?

It's always a base of moisturiser, primer and foundation so let's start with a quick wrestling count — can girls like wrestling still? 1, 2, 3 — easy peasy, nice quick win there. Now is the harder part, what to do and what not to do?

Aiming not to look a total laughing stock, I choose a silver eyeshadow. It's girly enough while still being neutral and matching whatever I'm wearing. Along with this, mascara is an absolute must. The longer those lashes look, the more feminine they appear! Not necessarily feeling the eyeliner today since yesterday's was so... bold, I instead apply my soft pink lipstick. I use some soft pink blush to round it off, but not too much that I suddenly look like a gingham bath bomb. Besides, the pink still compliments my surprisingly still immaculate pink nails!

Hairdryer next, not that it takes long nor adds much to the look. It's only as I sit and dry my hair that I see a little pair of white socks laid out where everything else that I'm wearing right now once was. Surely she doesn't mean to put these on too? Is that a thing people do? One quick Google search, and I have my answer.

'*Can you wear socks with tights?*'

The top result is a YouTube tutorial for how to style this look but instead, I go to an image search. Met with countless photos of girls wearing black tights and white socks, I am convinced that this is a) perfectly acceptable and b) exactly what Mum intended me to do. I follow that expectation and it's only as I put the socks on that I see the little frills around the top. Bobby socks? Now I'm certain that Mum's idea for today's outfit is a 'big kid' inspiration. Few sixteen-year-olds wear socks like this, but that's hardly the most unique or different thing about me.

With half an hour to kill, I sit in front of the mirror just contemplating if I need to add anything. I decide to go against my better judgment and try to put some eyeliner on. The stars must be aligned perfectly today, much like my very impressive performance with the eyeliner pencil. I use a pencil one because it's less messy than a liquid one, and because Mum left it laying out. The flick could still be better, but it is an improvement on yesterday's. Most importantly, I'm happy with it so that's all that matters.

With no indication of what shoes I'm wearing, I simply head down to the living room to watch some YouTube and wait for Mum to return from work. The wait is agonising, but I see the text at 13:22 exactly.

'*Got someone covering my last hour, hope you are ready! 10 mins!*'

I imagine this is Mum's way of testing how serious I am about being ready like a woman — that is to say being ready a lot earlier than you need to be. There won't be anyone covering, she would have always had this earlier finish. Trying to catch me out but I wasn't born yesterday. I was born… hmm, four days ago, so almost.

More 'Girl for a Day videos' help me to pass the time. This one features a group of three brothers. One of them is getting married as a bride at the request of his wife-to-be and the other two younger brothers are his bridesmaids. It's a cute idea, but I doubt my brothers would ever do the same for me. And I'm not even sure I would want them to. I can't even begin to picture Matthew or Kyle in a dress or make-up. All I have to do to picture myself that way is go upstairs and have another look in the mirror. It's a cute idea, but one best kept an idea. I've still got to find someone who actually wants to date me, let alone marry me, before it could be anything even slightly more developed than that.

And disrupting this thought spiral at just the ideal time, the front door bursts open.

"Are you ready?"

"Well, come and see."

My Shoes

I correct my sitting position and re-cross my legs just to be sure as Mum approaches from the hall. She walks in to see me, and I'm tempted to close my eyes and pretend she isn't there. That's just out of habit, I suppose. I open my eyes once more and await her critical opinion.

"Ooh very nice! That dress fits you quite well, even if it does look a bit young. You do need to put the button up at the neck though!"

"Huh?" As I fidget in my confusion, looking for the button, my finger finally comes across a small lump in the white collar of the dress. I thought it was just a dress with a fake collar, but it does in fact have one singular, heart shaped button. This also fixes the collar into place to look more 'collar-like'. Mum watches as I persevere and succeed in buttoning the collar after a few failed attempts. It feels better already, I must admit!

"There we go! That's how the girls wear them to school, that's how you'll wear it today!"

"It's so cute, I love it! Is there anything else wrong with my look?"

"Hmmm." Mum considers possible areas where there is room for improvement as she scans my face almost Terminator style. Her gaze then pans down my dress, down my legs and to my feet. Bingo. She finds her error.

"Oh! Those socks are just something I must have left out by mistake! With the shoes you're wearing today, the white socks won't work that well at all!"

"Ah, no worries! I'll just take them off. I was a bit confused." No lie there, I have written proof (which you are reading at the moment.) Socks haven't become any harder to remove so ten seconds later, my tights are all that remain covering my feet.

"Fab. OK, where are your shoes anyway?"

"Umm... I don't know, they aren't on the bed, and they weren't when I was getting dressed."

"Ahh! They must still be in the car in that case. OK, make sure you've got the essentials in your bag, and I'll go get your shoes!"

Leaving me no time to negotiate the terms or even accept the offer, Mum races excitedly out of the door to fetch my girly footwear. I take my black crossbody bag and open it up to check what is inside. As it's me, these thoughts inevitably become audible.

"Purse is in there already. My lipstick is upstairs, so I'll run and grab that. What else do I need?"

I dash up the stairs to pack my lipstick into my handbag and it's only as I'm making my way back down that Mum returns with a shoebox and giddy look of anticipation on her face.

"Just sit on the stairs, it's easiest to put shoes on here anyways. Come a few further down though, I'm not throwing them!"

I stop at the third step from the bottom as Mum stands around the corner, appearing as if she is blocking me in while I am being told off. She's far too happy for that to be the case though — it's almost scary how gleeful her smile is.

"OK, here you go! Now, open them up and see what you think."

Moment of truth, *my* first pair of shoes. A small lump of tension builds in my throat, forcing me to swallow the nothing. My hands shake, I'm now almost as excited as Mum. The lid lifts off like a case or box in 'Deal Or No Deal' and I wonder if I am lucky. The shoes are covered by the paper they usually put in the boxes to keep them separated and scuff/stain-free. I honestly don't know what to expect as I remove the paper from the large box, revealing the truth.

"Ohh... my... Mum, I *love* these! They're so super cute!"

Inside the box is a pair of white ankle boots. They are leather look, so they don't stain quite so easily and have a little shine to them. They feel super soft from the outside and I can't wait to try them on! Luckily, I don't have to wait either.

"Go on, hon! Let's see them on you. I picked these myself because I have a similar pair."

Much like the black boots I wore on Tuesday, these boots have their zips on the side where they won't be seen by most. On the outside, however, is a little bow design. They look incredibly dainty.

130

What is slightly worrying is the heel on them. The boots I wore before had the most subtle little heel on them whereas these adorable things must have two inches on them. It's going to be my first time in heels, even if most people wouldn't count it as that.

I place my feet gently inside the boots and it's no struggle at all to zip them up. I am expecting them to feel tight as I fasten them, but they never do. Mum takes a step back to allow me to stand up and retreats to the kitchen to watch me walk back and forth through the hall, like a model I hope!

"Those heels are adding the loveliest little bounce to your step! It's perfect! Do you like them?"

"I love them, Mum. Thanks so much!"

"You're welcome, Molly. Now, your coat isn't exactly going to work with your outfit, is it?"

"No, I suppose not. The black will be too clash-y."

"That's my thought with the tights and the boots. The black on your legs offsets it, the coat would drown out the effect. I have a white coat upstairs, please go put it on."

"Your long white one? That's an expensive coat!"

"It'll be worth it to see you in it. It's so long, it may pretty much cover the dress, but you can take it off once we are in the shops. You'll be trying things on all day!"

"OK, one moment!"

It does only take one moment; I've done this before several times. Mum has a posh white coat, it's incredibly long and fantastically cosy. It fits me very well for it not being mine and zipping it up is smooth as silk — which is also what the lining on the inside feels like!

I return downstairs with a girlish spring in my step, thanks to the new heels, and a much warmer, more accompanying coat for this 'teen schoolgirl' outfit!

"That's my daughter! I should have asked you for a photo first!"

Knowing exactly what Mum is hinting at, I remove the coat and stand at the front door, with Mum standing at the kitchen door, waiting to take my photo.

"Big smiles, and then blow a kiss!"

Got it, boss! I'm not the biggest fan of my smile because it often feels very forced. Today is totally the opposite — my smile couldn't be more real! Blowing the kiss is still a little awkward, but apparently I nail the pouting lips look. Unbelievable considering how hard it feels to stop smiling.

"Brilliant, coat back on and let's go! Glad I got one for the Facebook status!"

"Mum! Please don't do that yet, not before I'm out at school!"

"Relax, kiddo. I'm only teasing. Though it would look great online!"

"Well, it can wait. Anyways, should we go?"

"Yep, get your bag and let's go. Our Mother/Daughter Day starts now!"

I can really deal with hearing that on a regular basis — this is going to be fab! We leave the house, and my louder heels make everything just feel more confident and assured — today is my day!

Caring Too Much

There is one detail I'm not feeling totally confident about however, and it is still my short hair. It can't be styled in any way to look feminine at its current length so is best left just air-dried and ignored. Hopefully, I'll be able to find a perfect wig.

Before any of that though, we do need to get to Dundee. As we walk through the usually deserted car park, there's a couple of the mums from the street (Evelyn included) having a chat about who-knows-what. I just hope it isn't a chat about me, but my anxiety creeps up as I panic about her noticing me. She has no idea why Mum asked for her daughter's unwanted clothes and although I'm not wearing anything that used to be Courtney's, it's still a little strange. She may be able to connect those dots.

Thankfully, Evelyn doesn't turn to look at us and the two women are back in their respective homes by the time Mum has the engine running. Would have been an extra awkward window conversation, and she would most definitely tell Courtney who would then tell the whole school and probably tell me how much of a creep I am.

"Ready to head off, then?"

I'm feeling uneasy still at the thought of my cover being blown too soon.

"Sure, let's go. You don't think Evelyn knows, right?

"It won't matter if she does, honey. The truth is going to come out in whichever way it does, and the results will mostly be the same. Whether you get to be the messenger about any of it is sadly a choice you don't get to make. The sooner you stop caring what the world thinks, the sooner you can be yourself."

I know Mum is right, I know she is. I shouldn't be worrying about what anyone else thinks of who I am or how I look, but it's a guttural reaction. I can't help but be concerned about the opinions and perceptions of others. It's just the way I have always been, and it's probably why I don't have many close friends.

In an attempt to shift topic, so that I can keep silently worrying in my own head, I ask Mum an important question about today's activities.

"Are we starting with the wig, yeah?"

That 'yeah' is great for adding the inflexion at the end of the sentence, the voice bounces up a little higher.

"Yes, it's best you choose a wig before we go buying any outfits — need to know what hair colour we are working with. Still can't decide between the two?"

"Yeah, I'm no further on deciding. They're both just so pretty, I just don't know which is prettier on me yet!"

"Well, not long until you find out. So sit back, calm yourself… and probably put the hood up if your concerned about your hair. It's probably an improvement for the appearance anyways!"

"True, true," I concede as I pull the hood up and over. It stops at just about the ideal point for hiding my hairline.

Even for it being during traditional work hours, the road is mighty busy. And every time we have to stop for the lights, or traffic congestion, or waiting to join a roundabout or junction, a new set of eyes is in front of us. They can look in their rear-view mirror and judge me from all angles. They probably mutter homophobic and transphobic slurs under their breath. Then again, how does that saying go?

'If a tree falls in the forest and no one hears it, did it really make a sound?' So by that same token, if I don't hear the abuse I'm receiving from other commuters, is it really happening at all? I'm so far in my own head and just need to chill out and settle my emotions a little. Or a lot.

"Can we put the radio on? I'm thinking a little too much."

"Of course we can, princess! Go ahead, switch it on."

One push of a button, a few turns of the tuning knob, and the music starts to play. The beat and the rhythm of the latest chart hits eroding away at my self-doubt. I tilt my head back slightly until I can feel the back of my neck on the soft headrest and close my eyes for a few minutes. I'm not napping, it is just a coping mechanism when life feels a little too overwhelming for me. I've always relied on music, today is no different.

I don't even know the song that is currently playing, and that doesn't even matter. Anything with a beat and some lyrics is enough to whisk my soul off to another dimension entirely and my worries travel with it.

Five minutes later, my eyes reopen. I take a few deep breaths just to calm myself as another car stops ahead of us. Another red light, another point where the traffic needs to stop and a new set of eyes rest upon my appearance while we wait for the merciful release of the green light.

Across the Tay Bridge and into Dundee itself, this place is truly always being developed. The waterfront of most cities is usually worthy of a postcard and I'm sure Dundee will get there eventually — it just won't be any time soon. Just as they finished building the museum, a new project began beside it and the building site moved fifty feet down the road. It's a nice city; I wouldn't say I want to live here but for a day out shopping, it's certainly pleasant.

And today's shopping is the most pivotal of my life to this point. The car passes by the shopping centres on its way to the multi-storey car park. From there, Mum winds the window down and pays for the parking. We find a spot on the third floor of the car park — it's quieter than the others below it — and with a few more deep breaths, I open the door and press the release button on my seat belt.

I check to make sure everything I need in my bag is in there and once I check again to be sure, I summon enough courage to exit the car. It's only a different city, but it feels like a new world. And it's scary to be out here for the first time, even more so with nowhere for cover. But Mum is here, and Molly is here. It's time to be a big girl, despite the cute, childish outfit I'm wearing. Upon leaving the car, it's strangely warm.

It's actually *uncomfortably* warm. When my body is too hot (temperature-wise, obviously), my back starts to itch and the itch travels around the whole of my body. The best way to prevent it is to leave the coat in the car. My hair may be on show, but the wig shop is the first stop. I only have to survive one walk without anything covering my head. I can do this, I've been through much worse than this, surely.

"All sorted, Molly?"

"Yeah, do I look all right?"

"You look like my daughter, you're perfect."

Looking At Me

The way the multi-storey car park works is actually quite simple. You start outside but on each floor is a lift which will then take you down to the ground floor, usually of a shopping centre. From there, you can visit any of the shops indoor or you can go out to the high street, where more independent retailers can be found. We need to go to one of these independent retailers first for a wig, then to the more established chain clothing stores for uniform and other bits and bobs.

The echo of my heels through a basically empty multi-storey sounds totally different to how it sounded in the car park at home. The ceiling means that it sounds as though a horse is cantering its way through the multi-storey, looking for its owner or just some food. In reality, I'm just doing my best to keep one foot in front of the other and both of them as straight as I can. It's vital that I don't try to clump down on my foot all at once, and instead I start by putting the heel down first and have the toes follow. The middle of the sole of the foot obviously doesn't come into it much, it will go where the toes do! It's this that creates a steady beat as a lassie like me walks through any place, be it home, a car park or as it is about to be, a shopping centre. The hard floors and lower ceiling (not to mention the addition of walls) further amplify the beat. It almost sounds like a drummer warming up for Glastonbury in my head. In reality, Mum's heels are pretty much the same height as my own and therefore just as loud and noticeable. And it's not like we are the only two women who wear heels! Everyone is marching to their own beat, literally!

I feel fantastic as I take each step. It's not just the beat from my elegantly-dressed feet but also the cute swagger of my gingham 'school' dress, the warm luxury of the tights, the feeling of the chemicals all over my face — this is euphoria! The one thing stopping it from being perfect is my stupid hair! I don't know where the wig shop is exactly, but I know we need to be back outside to find it.

As Mum and I walk, not hand in hand but close enough to keep a casual conversation running without needing to catch-up or wait on one another, I can't help but feel curious about how other people are looking at me. I sneak a quick peek now and again at the odd passers-by as we navigate the deliberate one-way system which allows us to leave the shopping centre. As we approach the final escalator heading down to the main exit, I know for sure that I have my first audience.

He's old, he's at least fifty. He's stood there at the bottom just reading his phone, probably reading about football results or football fixtures or football news or something like that. As Mum and I reach a little under half-way down, he raises his head from his phone and his gaze has a new idle target: *me*. He watches as we continue our guaranteed descent, I look away for a second or two and sneak another peek to find him still there — and *still* watching. I don't know if his eyes have moved from their fixation on me at all in between. His stance changes, his phone goes into his pocket, and he folds his arms in confusion, looking a bit like an annoyed teacher. His face doesn't scream 'offended' as we go closer and closer, further down. It more has the look of 'what' about it. He seems genuinely amazed at what he is seeing. I'm not comfortable about being stared at and I just look down and try to focus on where we are going. Mum may have been speaking to me then, but it is lost in my brain as this man overrides my focus. I just want to know what he thinks, but I'm too afraid of the answer to find out. It will forever be a mystery.

The heads of another odd shopper or two turn as we pass by and finally leave the shopping centre. It takes maybe thirty seconds to go from top to bottom, yet that just there felt like years! We are now outside, the subtle breeze a relaxing and assuring sign of this. The wig shop is apparently just across the street and down a block, not far at all!

The worst interaction is yet to come. A group of teenagers, all in drab hoodies and ripped jeans, turn to stare as we cross the road. I can overhear laughing and can't exactly tell what they are laughing at. However it feels like it is at me. I try my best not to let it bother me, I need to focus on choosing what my hair is going to look like! I can't help but feel a little disheartened by the fact that people have been finding my appearance odd — maybe even ridiculous or 'gay' — but I believe in me. I believe in Molly. I am Molly, I am real, and I love the way I look today. So long as I tell myself that and keep my mental armour on, nothing can derail me completely.

"Just ignore them, honey. They really don't matter at all. All that matters is how you feel about yourself."

"Oh, I don't care what they think! I don't even know them! They may even just be jealous!" I say jokingly, but really badly hoping that it's the case.

"That's my girl, you keep telling yourself that. You're made of stronger steel than they are, and you look a lot nicer!"

It may just be my mum saying that, but it's proof enough!

We turn the corner to the left at the end of the street and come across a shop with a white sign. WIIV is the name of the shop, meant to sound like weave but spelled almost entirely incorrectly! I'm not bothered about their grammar, just so long that they can fix the situation on my head!

"This must be the place; let's get you girled up a little more!"

"That's the plan!"

Doll Hair

I've never been to a wig shop before. I've never even so much as imagining one existing. It's not the most obvious shop to ever exist, it's not like everyone uses a wig and it's not like there aren't plenty of online options. But when you need a wig that will pretty much be your real hair, you need to see it up close and personal. The reviews and discussion on the internet will never be enough to make this important decision. And yet, standing here inside WIIV, I can't quite believe how typically 'wig-shop' this place is.

It's small, let's start with that. It's a very small shop floor with a fair few mannequin heads sporting their most stylish hairpieces. They have a few full-body mannequins too which have been fully dressed for more of a complete effect of showing how the wig looks in everyday life. It's not every day you find yourself as just a head! Unless you are King Louis XVI of France or one of Henry VIII's wives, then that pretty much was every day. There is a glossy, black counter behind which two shop assistants stand. A third can be heard in the back — could be cleaning, could be organising, could be causing mayhem — who can tell?

One thing is for sure, this place is not busy. Mum and I are the only two people in here besides the staff. We go up to the counter and ask one of the ladies for help. I decide to read the tag out of just being polite. After all, I will definitely have to speak to this person. The tag reads 'Lee.'

Lee? It's not the strangest name ever for a girl, but I've never seen it spelled that way for a woman. It's usually 'Leigh'. Anyway, Lee's hair is bright blue (like electric blue), and she is wearing glasses. She has a lot of make-up on, her eyelashes look especially thick thanks to the mix of false eyelashes and high-quality mascara. Her complexion is quite dark compared to my own, she looks as though she has been in a tanning bed recently. To each their own, I have never thought about doing anything like that. I just have a fear that something will go horrendously wrong while I'm in there.

Back to Lee, her lipstick is blue to match the hair and the now noticeable eyeshadow as she raises her head to acknowledge us as customers. The WIIV uniform is all black, but Lee is wearing a skirt while her colleague beside her has opted for pretty cosy looking trousers.

She opens her mouth to greet us, and it's only then that I look at the outfit again. At first, the pin which says 'Lee' looks pretty normal. On second glance, it's a lot more than that. With us now being a few steps closer than when I first started taking Lee's appearance in and processing it, I can now read the small print under it. I assumed before that it just said '*WIIV Employee*' or '*Ask Me For Help*' but it actually says, '*Proud to be enby.*'

Enby? Where have I seen that before? Oh, non-binary? Crap, what do I do? How do I address her? Him? Them? Wait, I know what to do.

Just as Mum goes to talk to Lee, I have a brainwave. From all those videos I have watched about transgender people, a reminder from one barges its way into my mind. The soft-voiced woman from my voice training videos briefly mentioned something.

'You should always ask for someone's pronouns when you meet them for the first time or if you are ever unsure. Some people are non-binary, others are transgender like you and me. It's always nice to ask!'

"Hi there, Lee. My name is Molly. I'm looking for a wig that'll work as my real hair."

Mum stands back, amazed that I even managed to say that much unprompted. Lee takes one look at me and smiles. A slightly higher voice than my own natural one replies.

"Hi Molly! Pleasure to meet you, we heard about you from Lola!"

It's such a small business, that Lola is on first name basis. That, or she is here so often that they have no choice to remember her.

"Oh, lovely! I won't need to bore you about myself then!"

"No, please feel free to say whatever you like in here. It makes a nice change from always having to explain myself anyways!"

Lee chuckles at that joke and the voice has a little feminine twang at the end of it. Kind of like how male fashion designers and choreographers sometimes sound.

"Ha, ha, all good! Before we go into anything about my hair, can I just ask you what pronouns you go by? I feel it's always best to ask!"

"Wow, you're very clued up! I go by he or they. If you forget, I won't be offended."

"I'll do my best. I go by she/her but you could probably tell, based on well…" I gesture towards my dress. "Everything."

He smiles again, he's not a teenager but he must be around the same age as Lola. And I do wish I was as good at make-up as him!

"Thanks, and I'm assuming this is Ms Clarke?"

"It is indeed!" Mum says, sounding relieved to finally have the chance to say something. "Sorry, I'm just not used to Molly feeling so confident around someone new. She's never been talkative, eh Mols?"

"Nope, usually I'm silent! But I am really excited about today, and I'm really happy to be out and about like this." I did want to make a point about being happy to see another LGBTQ+ person, but I decide to let that slide since I don't want to cause offence. Some people aren't so happy to be grouped into that, another lesson from YouTube. Why even have traditional school at this point?

"Perfect!" Lee chimes. "Let's see what options you like on the shop floor, and my colleague will have a look in the back for similar styles. Despite the small shop, we do have over 150 different styles!"

"Wow, not bad at all! I promise I won't try all 150!"

"Feel free to! I love experimenting with my hair. This is all mine though, despite it looking like a wig!"

That is pretty incredible, to be fair. I was convinced when I first saw it that it was one of the store's many wigs. Ugh, he is such an inspiration! One day, hopefully, I'll have hair that beautiful. Not blue, but beautiful like his.

Before we get there though, we need to actually try some wigs.

"Did you have any colours in mind, Molly? Does your mum know anything she would like to see on you?"

"Well, it has to be an everyday look for going to school but be easy to style and shape. I want to be able to braid my daughter's hair."

"You're in luck, Ms Clarke. Our wigs are all real hair and easy to style in whichever way you like. We have a lot of colours, both outlandish and not. You can be just like a Barbie doll in here! Where shall we start?"

"Can we start with a blonde please? A nice sunny blonde first."

"We sure can, shoulder length blonde is over there while the longer one is just down towards the window. We have ones that go even longer than that, but it's not the easiest to have for a first wig!"

On the way over to the longish one, we do pass by the black version of the longest option. It must reach down to the thighs; I could never imagine having my hair *that* long.

"Well, you do need one of these first!" Lee pulls a hair cap out from his pocket. "I keep a few new ones on me, you can tell it's new because it's wrapped. We throw them all away, no cross-contamination. They are also totally recyclable, but you should buy a few proper reusable caps with your wig too."

"Noted, I'm not paying anyways!"

"Yeah, mother's treat!" Mum says, sounding genuinely happy despite what today will do to her bank account.

The hair cap is so easy to put on, just unwrap and stretch it around until it fits over and covers all of my short hair (not a lot to cover.) It doesn't feel too tight, but I can certainly feel it on me.

"Perfect! OK, let's put the blonde one on you. Hold your head as still as you can please. Now, you loosen it with these clips, and you tighten it just like so!"

Seems easy enough, will take practice but recently, everything has!

"What do you think?" Mum asks. How does that feel?"

"The length is amazing, is there a mirror?"

"Yep, just around here."

It's only a few steps away and I am in front of the mirror. It's lovely, but it just doesn't feel right at all.

"Hmm, it's almost like I am too pale for blonde."

"Yeah, any other colours in mind?"

"Ginger, let's try a bit of strawberry blonde."

The blonde wig is unfastened and removed from my head, but the cap obviously stays on. Next up is the same length but a very ginger shade. It too is nice, but I still am not feeling like it matches who Molly is in my head.

"Hmmm." Mum pauses for thought. "That one doesn't look bad, but it isn't perfect either."

I take a little risk, by going against Lola's advice.

"Is it possible to see a brown wig in that length, please? Maybe it'll look dark enough to compliment my face."

"Brown is our second-most popular behind our blondes! I'll go fetch it for you, it's just over there. It's also the braided one in the window, braided for a bride was the thinking!"

"It looks gorgeous in the window!" exclaims Mum. "That's the same wig as what's in your hand?"

"Yeah, I braid the wigs for displays when I get bored in here! Anyways, try this one."

I don't know what it is about this one, but it just feels unique as I look into the mirror one more time. The shade is perfect against my light skin, and I can see myself with this hair every day. Molly is a brunette, it's settled!

"This is the one, I love it! It's so soft, it's dark without being too dark and it's great for school!"

"I can't argue with that. Surprisingly enough, we'll take the brown one and a few of those caps you were on about please, doll."

Hmm, I don't know if Lee appreciates being called a 'doll' but if he doesn't, he hides it well. He might just be so used to misgendering, it's quite sad really. I decide not to correct Mum on anything, especially when I'm being spoiled. The wig does not come off of my head, but Lee informs me that I should switch to the reusables after today. He gives us five for the price of four, it's a good deal.

"Thanks for all your help today, Lee. It was lovely meeting you!"

"And you, Molly! Best of luck finding that school uniform and I hope everything works out well for you."

"Aww thanks!"

"OK Molly, we best be heading for clothes now that you have hair you can be proud of."

Proud of? More like obsessed with. It's glorious, and as we leave the wig store, the breeze starts subtly shifting the odd soft strands of hair draping down my shoulders and my 'breasts'. I'm feeling considerably more complete, and I weirdly can't stop thinking about Lee. I don't think it's love, more just admiration of the guy. His hair is dead cute though, and his make-up is on point. Oh god, there's no way it's a crush.

"You so liked him!" Mum teases as we head back up to the shopping centre. "You were smitten!"

"Was not!" I yell, slightly rattled but mostly just embarrassed. OK, maybe I do like him but that's all it is. He's cute, that's all!

'The New Fragrance...'

Every step as we make our way from the lovely wig shop where Lee, that lovely human being, works, I feel pure euphoric joy. My short hair now covered by a cap, and the bald cap now covered by a gorgeous, luxurious, chestnut-coloured head of hair, cascading down my shoulders and stopping just above the middle of my 'breasts'. Every single step, it reminds me by brushing either against the back of my neck or resting against the fabric of my dress. These sentences are things that were just purely fantasy before yet are now a borderline perfect reality.

If it wasn't for my new wig leaving subtle reminders with each step, that familiar and almost addictive clicking from my Lolita-esque boots are another affirmation of just how feminine I am becoming. If you had told me last week that this is what I'd be able to achieve in such a short time, I'd never have believed you one bit. But walking back into the shopping centre in our quest for more appropriate school clothes, the confidence that I had to convince myself was there before is now almost radiant. I want to picture it like one of those adverts you see for perfume or other feminine products.

You know the ones. A woman stands there, either in a provocative, alluring dress or even more provocative, lacey underwear with a fan blowing her hair as she poses, seducing the random man who will be with her by the end of the thirty seconds, no doubt about it.

I walk through the automatic door of the shopping centre and the heating blows my wig, yet it stays firmly in its rightful place — atop my head. It's the long hairs themselves which dance about in the man-made breeze, making me feel utterly gorgeous and desirable for a change. I'm still not aiming to seduce Mr Right though — they were at that wig shop! In all seriousness, I just feel good to be me right now. Everything I have lied to myself about in the past melting away as I finally know what self-worth is.

The creepy staring guy is also gone now, perhaps off to watch some other girl. We don't want to head back up the escalator quite yet though, our stop is on this very floor. There are so many shops selling generic school uniform, so we have options, but Mum knows which ones are the best quality for the best price just through her years of experience of shopping for my brothers and my former self. She's never shopped for a girl before though, not until today. She's almost as excited as I am to start the shopping spree, even if it's mostly quite routine clothing.

"I never thought I'd have the chance to do this, but we've got to go to the teen girls' section to get your new clothes! So, what are we thinking? Skirts or pinafores?"

"Um... I guess I need to try both and choose what I prefer."

"We can always buy you a mixture, but we need to see what will suit you better. Now, I'm thinking we pick up one of each item you need for your uniform then we head to the fitting room so you can try the whole outfit at the same time!"

"Makes sense, I do want to see what it will all look like when I go back to school."

"Trust me, you'll look fab! Now then, let's get shopping!"

Mum whizzes around picking up size 12 skirts, pinafore dresses, blouses and jumpers with not much need for my own input. I suppose I'm here to be a mannequin at this point, a Barbie doll from the back-to-school range! Not that I'm complaining, at least Mum is efficiently covering all bases. With a basket full of options, Mum guides me over to the fitting room with a point and follows closely behind.

The fitting rooms are monitored by a member of staff and are gender-specific. Always an anxious part of this new life I have. I make sure to use the bathroom before we leave the house or only go in private locations like the doctors. In public spaces, I feel so guilty using the women's, even though that's exactly what I am! I shudder to think what would happen if I went into a male space dressed as I am at the moment — how humiliating it would be to be seen there! Much better to try to pass as a woman — I'm harmless after all.

Mum asks for assistance from the member of staff in charge of the fitting area, and after a few seconds of looking at me, a slight smile creeps just at the corner of her mouth. Is it mocking? Is it friendly? Is it admiration? No idea, but she allows us to enter the fitting area with our plethora of girly school clothes.

The Right Fit

As we cross the archway from the shop floor into the dressing rooms, there is an old woman clutching a velvet skirt close to her, clearly intending to purchase said skirt. She sneers in my direction; this isn't exactly ideal.

It gets slightly worse when an outraged mother spots us, clearly I'm not as passable as they would like me to be. Her little girl is about to try on a party dress and as the curtain closes, this woman turns in our direction while we head for the end room.

"OK Molly, it's time. Go in there and take your dress off. I'll hand you through the different items."

This feels super weird. I close the curtain behind me as far as it seems to — it doesn't feel like full coverage — and for once, an uncomfortable chill comes over me. This is made worse by me removing my cosy dress and exposing my torso to the store's air conditioning.

"Ooh, that's cold!"

"Well, here's a blouse you can start with.

The blouse is white, obviously. However, something seems off about it. I put it on just as I would a shirt but can't see past the fact that I can see **through** it. Blatantly and without doubt, this blouse is not suitable for school in the slightest.

"Um, Mum? This looks really… clear."

"Ohh, silly me!" Mum replies, almost laughing to herself. "I handed you the wrong blouse, that one isn't for school! But does it fit?"

"Yeah, I'll button it up and you can see. It's longer than a usual blouse. But why one of these then?"

"Let's just say it's for special occasions and leave it there!"

With all the buttons in, the shirtdress fits well — snug but not restrictive. Mum has a quick peak behind the curtain and gives her

148

approval with a jokey wolf whistle!

"Mum, that's weird!"

"Well, I'm just being honest! The boys will go crazy for you."

"Ugh, I'm taking this one off! Do you have the actual school ones there?"

"Yeah, here you go."

I'm sure she did this deliberately, just as a little joke. But she doesn't seem to be joking about it, even though my bra is clearly visible through it. And is it glittery or am I just imagining it? Best take it off and get on with trying on school clothes.

One thing the see-through dress confirms is that I am a size 12, so the blouses fit absolutely fine as well. They have ones with heart shaped buttons, and ones without as well as having a choice between short and long-sleeve. I opt for the long-sleeve; school isn't the warmest place! And of course, the hearts are a must!

"Blouses sorted, that was very quick! Keep that one on then, and we'll try some skirts next.

The skirt variety is a lot more extreme than the blouse choice. Mum lets me know for the third or fourth time that there's no need to just agree to the first one I try on. It took four blouse options to choose the right one for me. What makes her think skirts will be a one and done?

The first skirt I try is the typical, basic pencil skirt. It fits well enough around the waist, but the issues are due to my legs. The skirt is too long for a modern teenager, and it makes my walk in my heels super awkward. Mum even asks to see me walk without the heels, but it is agreed — the mid-length pencil skirt is not the one.

"Well, we can now rule out every mid-length option. That's a lot of progress already! OK, this one is probably more your length.

The next is a grey pleated skirt, mainly seen in primary school but some high school kids can pull it off without looking silly. Weirdly enough, my issue with this is not the pleated design. Instead, I just don't like the grey school clothes on me. My school trousers for high school have always been black, and I suppose black just looks better. Our school jumpers have always been black, but as my year group are in our last year of high school, we can order leavers' hoodies. Those forms are probably coming out soon, just like me! Even without thinking about the leavers' hoodies, black on black has always looked better to me than the dreary grey.

"Shopping with you is dead easy, o' daughter of mine! That's now a whole colour out of the picture as well. Black and short, that's what we're aiming for! Try this one!"

A short pleated black skirt goes on to the maybe pile — I just want to try my other options first. And soon enough, the perfect one comes along.

After trying a straight-hem, black one and a weird, almost denim feeling one (which we can't have since denim is outlawed at school, bar non-uniform days), Mum hands me a black miniskirt. The material feels quite thick for a skirt, almost like a light jacket, and you can see the horizontal lines of material all the way down the mini-ish skirt. No idea what the style is exactly yet, but I will find out at some point in my girly adventure.

I wonder how I'm going to get into something that looks so small. By flipping it around and inspecting the back, I clock the golden zip which goes a little past half-way down the skirt. Ah, that's how you do it. *Zzzzzip.*

I step into the skirt with a fair lack of belief that it will fit at all, but the material seems to adjust to my body and ends up fitting like a glove by the time I *zzzzzip* the skirt back up; I feel super cute! Not the point of school uniform, but you may as well do it right!

"Mum, I love this one! Is it OK for school though?"

"You're sixteen now, honey. The school can't really decide that for you any more. It's within the guidelines: a black skirt. If you like it, you can wear it to school fine! It's in the store's back-to-school section so it must be fine! Don't the other girls wear stuff like that?"

"Y-yeah, but—"

"Be positive, honey! You look great in it; we should pick up a couple for you! Now, best get you a pinafore as well. Here's a black one."

I remove the skirt, satisfied with my choice, and turn my attention to pinafore dresses. This is not as much of a mystery as we have already ruled out grey and mid-length, so the first mini, black pinafore dress is perfect. I do love how it feels slightly elasticated at the torso as well, means that I can wear a belt with it if I like.

"Fab, and your tights today fit well so we'll just pick up more pairs in that size but with different thickness as well. There is one more thing I'd like you to try though."

"Yeah? What would that be?"

"Well, you need a smart outfit for the meeting tomorrow."

I almost forgot about that, the meeting tomorrow. **THE** meeting that decides Molly's fate and starts the girl's life for real.

"Oh yeah! Any of Courtney's clothes work for that?"

"Well, Courtney might see you. And she might recognise her clothes on the new girl. It could open some awkward questions."

"Good point. What do you think for the meeting then?"

"Hmm a different pinafore, probably pink but with a white blouse. I'm picking up eight of those, they're a wardrobe essential."

Mum leaves me for two minutes while she goes to browse the trendy teen section then returns with a plaid pink two-piece set. It's a pink blazer and skirt combo and it looks way over the top for school.

"We don't want the school to doubt any part of your femininity. Take the pinafore off and give this a try."

"OK." It's all I can really say. I don't have much to add, the outfit totally does all of the talking. It's not a hot-pink, more of a baby-pink shade.

The skirt fits well but is just a straight hem, a little longer than my school uniform choice. The blazer goes on without a fuss, but it weirdly has no buttons at all.

"That's by design, hon. Some women's sets have that. Do you like it?"

"Weirdly, yes. I feel professional but cute as well!"

"That's my little lady! White tights with that one, the black isn't as sweet. And maybe we'll see what we can do for shoes as well. Imagine you rock up in heels! They'll have no choice but to accept you!"

"Heels would be a challenge, but I'd be willing to try!"

"Your first pair of high heels, we must make that happen! Besides, your school shoes are at home already. I saw the perfect pairs in Courtney's stuff, ideal for school and so popular that she won't even suspect it!"

"Right, well I'll put my dress back on and you can go pay! I'll be ready by the time you've done that.

I pass her my new skirt suit and change back into my gingham dress, very pleased with what has felt like hours shopping.

With a minute or two to kill, I go into my bag and check my phone. Just some weird group chat stuff, the lads sending memes back and forth. One of the memes unfortunately hits me in the heart.

It's a seemingly harmless picture but it essentially outlines how much I'm changing compared to my friends. It has a crossdresser on it, and a mocking caption underneath with several laughing reactions. I'm not a crossdresser, but to them I basically will be. Not much I can do but I choose to ignore it for now. The music will be faced soon enough.

Mum returns soon to find me checking my hair in my phone camera.

"Like a natural, already! It looks great!"

I just smile, it's all I can really do with the fear of losing my friends looming over me.

"I also picked up a lot of underwear for you — I just know what size you are and knew you wouldn't want to try it on in public."

She's right there. It's just weird, the idea of being naked in public for even just a second. Despite the curtains and small spaces in this freezing chamber of a fitting area, I still feel as though I could be exposed at any moment.

"Let's see if we can find you some fancy heels to go with your pink set. I know just the place. You can carry these bags!"

Despite the many clothes in them — tights, underwear, skirts, blouses, two jumpers (which Mum just picked up as they seemed quite feminine, and she knows my size) and a pinafore — the bags aren't all that heavy. Must be just because there is no jacket, no coat and there are no shoes in it either.

We arrive at the next destination in less than thirty-seconds. We leave the large clothing store and just opposite us while still in the centre is a smaller shoe shop. Or that's what I think it is.

There are shoes, and they are on display in many colours and styles. Mum stands with me and discusses the type of thing we are looking for.

"We need these to be quite proper, but with a good heel on them which leaves the school utterly defenceless against your wishes. They'll have to allow Molly to attend. Of course, we want a pink that's similar to the suit, or a black pair as it goes with everything.

Black is never going to be an option when pink is on the table. I choose fairly plain looking baby-pink court heels and try them on. Mum reminds me of the style changes.

"They'll look much better with your white tights on, for sure. How do they feel?"

"They're nice, I just don't know if they are feminine enough!"

"Ah, you are looking for something with a bow aren't you?"

"How could you tell?"

"I've seen the videos you look at; you are obsessed with bows! I think we can just go and ask the question, unless you see a pair like that.

There is no pair like the ones I'm dreaming of on display, so I put my own boots back on and (as confidently as I can) I seek advice from a member of staff.

"Hi… (pausing to read the name tag) Jasmine. I'm looking for pink heels but with bows on them. Do you have anything like that?"

Jasmine gives me an uncertain look, but she does inform me that there is a pair like that in the back. I give her my size and she returns two minutes later with a very pretty shoebox.

"There, hopefully that's what you're after." She sounds disinterested, must be some kind of student job. Or maybe she's just bored, even with the steady flow of customers.

Thankfully, I don't need to consult her again as she nails it first time. Baby pink heels, size 7, with a closed toe that is decorated with a pretty baby-pink bow. I wouldn't describe anything as 'sissy', but these are incredibly feminine shoes. They even make my dainty little boots look somewhat masculine. Their rounded toes meant they are a comfortable walking experience, and the ankle strap only adds to the aesthetic. They fit well enough, and we pay before I even give myself the chance to reconsider.

"That's tomorrow's outfit all sorted, and school stuff all bought. One more thing to do, but it's a surprise." Mum teases once again.

"Ah, I still don't like surprises. They have all been lovely surprises but still!"

"Well, you are a surprise as well! I think I am due you a few more in return!"

153

Yeah, fair enough! Not every mother has as strange a child. Not just everyone's child is so odd.

No Going Back

So far, it has been pretty obvious to tell why we are going into each shop. However, the final stop on Molly's setup quest is a lot more random than the others. The shop seemingly specialises in candles and expensive ornaments. From the window displays, it seems really unclear why Mum wants to go in here.

We have a look in the glass cases, some of which contain fancy jewellery while others are home to the previously mentioned expensive figurines and ornaments. It's a collector's dream but it's never been anything I'm into. My largest collection ever was those football trading cards from years ago, but my passions have gone a different way since then.

We are genuinely just browsing things, when a woman in a black T-shirt and jeans approaches us. She evidently works here.

"Hi there, can I help you at all?"

It appears to only be a thing in jewellery or ornament shops. Staff don't tend to seek the communication from the customer, it tends to work the other way around. However, Mum finally drops the bombshell.

"Hi, yes actually. I was hoping that you have availability for ear piercing. As soon as possible, please."

"You're in luck, we haven't had many requests for that at all. Is it for you or your daughter?"

"It's for Molly here. She's never had anything like this done before. Right, hon?"

"Yeah. To be honest, it's a bit of a surprise even today!"

The woman reveals herself to be the shop manager. Based on how many people are visibly working in the shop, it is a 50/50 chance.

"Ah, don't worry! You're in good hands, pet! Gina through there will get you all sorted!"

"OK, thanks!"

Gina's room seems an awful lot like a doctor's office. Really small, cream walls up with a couple of medical diagrams of different angles of the ear and where/where not to pierce. Gina herself has short blonde hair and appears to have every part of her body pierced or studded to some extent. Can't say I've ever wanted to put any holes into my body voluntarily or otherwise. But here we are, I'm sat on this small, soft, black chair and Gina is putting gloves on.

"So I just need to start by cleaning the area and sterilising it, since I'm going to make two little holes and we don't want infections!"

This is actually the main reason why the idea of piercing my skin never appealed to me before. Even now, I am still thinking that clip-on earrings would be much easier. I am already in the chair, so I'll just have to be a big girl and bear it.

The numbing gel is what can best be described as an arctic tundra for my ear lobes. I have no idea why this stuff has to be so cold, warm numbing gel must exist surely! Gina takes her thumb and her index finger and quickly rubs the solution into my skin and all over my lobes.

"OK, now for the fun part! If you're afraid of needles, just close your eyes and go to your happy place. You'll only feel a slight sharpness."

Slight? We'll see about that. The needle goes into my left ear first and I sharply intake a breath, even breathing in through gritted teeth.

"That's it, just calm and let it do its thing. You'll look so pretty!"

One down, the right still to go. Hoping to get it over with quickly, the gun doesn't work right on the first attempt, though thankfully no damage is caused to my ears. It's like firing a blank, no result except confusion and a little laughter. My laughter is nervous however, as I anticipate the second prick occurring.

Another sharp stab, another deep breath through my fake grin and we're just about done. More sterilising cream added to my newly-impaled lobes and then comes the fun part — choosing the first pair!

"Now, you should choose wisely. This set can't come out of your ears for a minimum of 3 months. If you change earrings too quickly, you could cause an infection. If you don't wear earrings often enough, the holes start to close, and I'll need to stab you again!"

I get the feeling that Gina would enjoy another round of shanking my ears with her piercing gun. That clicking is going to be in my next nightmare, I just know it.

Anyway, it is time to choose my first pair of earrings. They can only really be beginner studs, but they come in a variety of colours, both gold and silver varieties. I find a silver and soft pink heart-shaped pair and it's obvious by now what happens next. Codeword is pink — if Molly sees pink, Molly must have the pink!

OK it's not quite that bad — my uniform is at least black!

Mum waited on the shop floor throughout the ordeal so now I can go and show her the results of her cunning surprise.

"Oh yes, very nice! Perfect for you! How was it?"

"Sore, but now it feels so worth it!"

Gina comes out from her strange cave of nightmarish clicking to inform me of something she missed.

"Oh, Molly, be sure to buy some of the cleaning solution. You only need a drop or two on each ear every day, but it will make sure they stay clean and proper!"

Seems like a fairly key detail to miss, like if they missed all the magic at Hogwarts and just described the architecture of the school and the academic schedule. Another task added to the daily routine, femininity sure is exhausting! And exhilarating!

I admire the new addition to my appearance in the small mirror attached to the shop's earring display and am in slight shock. At the start of the day, it was clear I was not a cis-girl. Now, with all of the improvements made and the new gear acquired, Molly is starting to look more and more convincing. No, convincing is the wrong word. I don't need to convince myself of who I am. She looks more and more… I don't know, cute? I look way cuter, let's go with that.

Mum waits until we have left the shop to give an insightful and concrete reminder.

"Well, with those in now, there's no hiding you at all! No going back, you'll see this through for yourself now!"

"Yeah, it's scary but you know I need to be pushed in certain directions or nothing is ever going to be done about my problems." I admit, I have never had much by way of agency. I tended to let life pass me by before, I was a real passenger. No, *he* was. And I, Molly, have now grabbed the wheel. My destiny, my identity — *I* am in *my* own hands. And very pretty hands too!

Satisfied with a full afternoon of shopping, preparation and being thoroughly spoiled, I can safely say that I'm now (physically at least) all prepared to enter the battleground of Grafton High School tomorrow and declare my truth. It starts for real.

Loading the bags into the car for the return home, the sun is setting and giving way to a warm yet moody evening. From the opening in the multi-storey, I can see the glare of the horizon over the ever-changing town of Dundee. In many ways, I am Dundee. Constantly improving, always evolving, and never, ever finished.

I am in true disbelief at how much stuff we have bought today. The bags seem to be never-ending, even though there are just 6 or 7. That's still far more bags than the deceased Ollie ever needed. Being a girl is awesome! Oops, I meant fabulous!

Suit Up

To say that last night was an easy one would be an outright lie. It was tough trying to sleep, far too many fishy thoughts swimming in the complex ocean in my head. 'What if today goes wrong?' 'What if you aren't convincing enough?' 'What if the guys see you?'

To settle these nerves, I'm going to write the answers in my handy little mental health notepad. It's one of those ideas I was given in my ASD assessment years ago. Anytime something is getting too tough to deal with, just write it down and slowly work it through with logic. I start writing, immediately impressed by the little girlish flicks I'm seeing on my handwriting. I haven't even worked on it at all, maybe I have always written this way?

'What if today goes wrong?'

Well, things often go wrong. Not everything will go exactly according to plan, and that's what makes life tricky for everyone. Just be the person you truly are, and it will work out fine.

'What if you aren't convincing enough?'

I don't need to convince anyone at all about who I am. I just need to be myself. I've lived for so long without the need of other people's admiration, I can keep going that way just fine.

'What if the guys see you?'

Sooner or later, they will. And I need to be prepared for that eventuality. If they're really my friends, they will accept me as Molly. If they don't, they aren't worth having.

This is easily the worst question to ponder. I'm not popular by any means, and even having three or four people who don't completely distance themselves from me is a privilege. Then again, being Molly is more of a privilege. I'm sure I can make it work, even if I am left completely deserted by the end of today, or at worst, the start of next week.

"Good morning, Molly! It's the big day!"

I swear just about every day for the past week has been 'the big day.' Still not married!

"Hi Mum, what time is the meeting?"

"Oh, it's in about three hours. You best get moving!"

"Oh sh—"

I manage to stop myself from a verbal faux pas just in time then leave my bed to start getting ready. Breakfast is the usual affair, and the shower is fairly routine even so soon after starting this whole girly adventure. To save time, I even clean my teeth in the shower- I sometimes do this as there is already running water. On to the elaborate getup for today's pivotal meeting with the headteacher.

Today's underwear is all pink, probably one of about eight different all-pink sets. There is an extra little white box on the bed alongside the bra and panties, with the name of a brand that is new to me. My instinct says that it's some jewellery or maybe a hair accessory. Perhaps a new cap to go under the wig? Or… wow.

Inside the small cardboard container is a pair of clear silicon breast forms. They're small, definitely nothing too noticeable if they aren't going to be used by someone who usually has nothing there. On me however, taping apple seeds over my nipples would be a sizeable enough change! These balloon-shaped enhancements will be easy to spot!

As I fasten my bra via the clip at the back, I take one of the forms out of the box. It's very cold and will only be colder when it makes the initial contact with my skin. Oh well, here goes nothing! A brief, involuntary yelp leaves my body as my chest feels as though it's about to turn cryogenic for roughly two seconds. I quickly suffer with the other cup to get it sorted and out of the way — real breasts are hopefully warmer!

Chest hills in and underwear on, it's time to put the tights on. I instinctively grab a black pair from the drawer before I put them back and take white tights instead. Some kind of voice in my head reminds me of Mum's advice that white will look better with the suit.

I turn my attention to the blouse once my legs are encased in the already quite familiar material. Never thought tights would be so second nature to me so soon but it feels like I am nude without them. As for the blouse, this is a perfect opportunity to wear a school one and give it a proper trial run. I button it up as I did yesterday and in no time at all, I'm half dressed!

The skirt is next as it is now so much easier to tuck the blouse in and ensure that I don't look scruffy for the meeting with a tail poking out under the blazer. Not that it would show, as the blazer is quite long and reaches to just under halfway down the skirt's straight leg. Instead of a zip, this skirt has nothing at all. It is subtly elasticated at the top, allowing it to stretch until it is the perfect fit. I can only feel overdressed at this point, and that's before make-up. I opt to throw the glitter at my face before I put my new blazer on. I take a towel from my wardrobe and drape it across my front, preventing any powder from ruining the blouse.

It's a full face of make-up for me today with an extra emphasis on the highlight. I want to create a feminine shimmer on my face that will glow even in the dull and slightly powerless lighting of the school offices and halls. Will I go this far every day? Probably, especially if I am ever going to build a social life as my real self once my fake one falls apart.

Once I've put highlighter under my eyes, on my nose and underneath as well, I opt for the predictable pink eyeshadow. This is an open goal this morning, the outfit is almost entirely pink and white (except for the black lines of plaid pattern) so pink is the only choice for make-up. I frame it with white eyeshadow on the outer section just under the brow, and put a soft, baby pink underneath that so it doesn't appear too harsh a contrast with anything.

Light pink lipstick finishes the look off, and as I inspect my progress, I realise that I totally forgot my mascara. In my rush to correct this error, I drop the brush out of the container and down on to the towel. See? This is why we go for the towel of safety! Brush picked back up, I apply four or 5 coats to the upper and lower lashes of each eye and then, just for a sense of finality, I apply another coat of lipstick. Pucker, pout, and finally set with the clear and cool coconutty spray! It felt like five minutes, but today's face of make-up takes me almost an hour from start to finish!

I don't have much time to admire my appearance — I need to get my shoes on and sort my bag. Where's that peculiar shoebox in which lie the equally (if not even more so) pretty heels?

I can't see them in my wardrobe. They might be here but I'm hopeless at finding literally anything. I'd likely lose my nose and ears if they weren't attached to me! In an attempt to convince myself that I am not going mental, I ask Mum from my room to hers where the box is.

"Oh I kept that box downstairs, because you will need those heels today! Now come on through, I want to see how you look!"

"Not quite there yet, need to sort the wig out."

"Bring it through and I'll style it for you! This is a special day!"

She's right there, this feels like I'm in a bad high-school drama.

I push the door open and confidently step into the room. No need to be ashamed of anything here, and I hope I've done enough to look nice!

"You look fabulous! That's a lot of make-up but I suppose that's what girls your age do!"

We share a laugh like always and I hand Mum my brown wig for her to assist me with. She swaps it out of my hand for a bald cap which I use to conceal my real hair easily and completely. Mum holds the wig in her right hand and brushes firmly through it with the fingers on her left. She takes a comb from her bedside and starts more precisely splitting the strands and straightening them.

"Not got a whole lot of time now, so let's just straighten it like this today. Besides, I don't want to damage it by heating it up too often."

I sit in front of Mum, and this must be how young girls feel when their mothers play with their hair. She runs her fingers through it in between strong combing, which is just on the cusp of being sore. She gently takes two bunches, one in each hand, but let's go.

"Promise me I can do pigtails for you one day, always wanted to do it with you when you were much younger but… he said no and cut your hair short."

"Wait, you wanted to braid my hair?"

"I wanted to dress you up, just as a bit of fun. I did it with your brothers once or twice with no fuss, but your dad was different. He was worried about what it would do."

"When he left, did you dress me up again?"

Mum continues brushing, though her grip is not as firm as it was.

"A few times yeah. You went as a princess for Halloween when you were 3. Too young for you to remember, but I just found it too cute! The other parents were very judgy, but you used to twirl around in your dress all the same. I stopped doing all that when you started school, I couldn't have you being picked on, and I was selfish to want a daughter…"

"Wipe your eyes, Mum. And hey, don't worry about it. The past is in the past. You have a daughter now."

"I just… did I cause this?"

"I don't know, but it's not a bad thing. I *want* this, I *need* this. No matter the cause, this is where we are. I'll be your daughter forever. I always have been, right?"

"Ha, sorry. This is tough for me, and I don't even know why."

She stops brushing my hair and fixes my part, then gently strokes the straight hairs a few times.

"We'll be all right, don't worry! The world has changed. I believe deep down that the world is more prepared than ever for people like me. Especially here. Scotland's all about equality."

"I hope you're right. Anyways, I think we best think about getting shoes on and bags sorted."

As I stand up to leave, I turn and give Mum a hug. This must be so tricky for her, knowing now that she's feeling guilty for being a cause of a problem. If she caused anything, I don't care. I am who I am, however that happens to form in my head.

"Please, don't blame yourself. I love you."

"I love you too, Mols."

It kills me to see those close to me in pain or suffering any kind of problem. My autism makes me sensitive to the emotions of others, and empathy is a natural trait that is as second nature as breathing to me. I always want to be the paper that goes over the cracks, until I can be the cement that fills in the holes. Isn't that what we call a hero complex?

"Your blazer, hon! Mind and put it on!"

In the midst of providing emotional support for my clearly guilty mother while she sorted my hair, I almost totally forgot to don the final integral piece of the puzzle that is my 'Sunday School' outfit. I can only think of movies about rich, private school children whenever I catch a glimpse of the plaid two-piece set.

As I go to leave her room, it's that guidance from Mum which ensures I don't forget it — I'm pretty forgetful, if you haven't gathered.

And now pretty and forgetful!

"Oh yeah, best I wear that!"

Back in my own room, it feels a little like a blast from the past as I put my arms through the sleeves of the pink suit jacket. Everything about it gives the impression that it will be too big, that my hands will be shrouded by the soft cloth — much like many years ago with Mum's clothes. However, this evens out and the blazer fits remarkably well by the time it has stretched fully across my back. Once again, I go to fasten it only to remember that the stylistic choice of the jacket's creator was to make it open all the time, much like a questionable chip shop.

I nonetheless pull the sides of the blazer's open front across myself once or twice — if for nothing else but to see how it would look if it behaved like, you know, a jacket! I can't remain entranced by my own appearance for too long, need to finish dressing.

Ah, the pièce de résistance! The extravagant and oh so over-the-top high heels from yesterday's shopping adventure. A perfect accoutrement to the equally pretentious pink skirt-suit. And sure enough, the box rests on the kitchen table. I thought that was bad luck, not that I believe in any of that nonsense.

I sit down at the kitchen table — much like I did on Molly's first night — to properly and securely put my heels on. Can't have them slipping off or clumping around, not today. It all has to be perfect. *I* have to be perfect today. No excuses, no exception. Anyone who spots me has to have no doubts of my femininity.

Rather than all the sliding around that Mum's old black heels are prone to on the kitchen tiles, these new beauties have a subtle platform to them and a chunkier heel, allowing better grip. The platform is something I didn't even notice, but that is probably how they end up being 4.5 inches instead of the 4 they would be without it. And from now on, I think all of my heels and well, all of my shoes, should have some form of fastening. No more court shoes or easy slip-on pumps, feeling a strap at my ankle is much nicer than nothing at all. The firm yet flexible material on the strap allows me to adjust them to my exact liking. I would compare it to the stats screen on a character creator with how subtle adjustments can make such a monumental difference.

Speaking of stats, it is impossible to ignore the 4.5 inches of height that I have rapidly gained in the last five minutes. Thankfully, I was always short for my age and still am. Then again, that's comparing myself to the average height of the boys. I suppose I may now be one of the tallest girls at school! If I turn up in shoes like these, I will be right up there with the tallest. I stand up and the ground is a lot further away despite my constant attachment to it, thanks to the new phenomenon that is gravity.

I am truly thankful that gravity does exist as this is the only thing keeping me grounded. I'm on the highest high of my life to date with no substance needed except a gallon of glitter, cloud nine isn't even scratching the stratospheric surface of my joy. I sneak the odd look down at my feet as I give the shoes (and myself) a quick warm-up by walking wall-to-wall in the kitchen. It's vital for posture that a lady keeps her head up, that's what my videos say. Yet I can't help but fall into the trance of the bows on the front of these lovely shoes! I never thought I could make this a reality, yet it is now within touching distance.

As the hypnotic heels catch my attention again on my sixth length of the kitchen, my mum walks in.

"Looking good but keep that head up! Confidence and pride are a must!"

See, I wasn't making it up! Anyway, Mum has my bag in her hand, and my phone from upstairs.

"I think the lads are talking about plans this weekend, just what I saw when I glanced at your lock screen."

"Well, I can't exactly do anything about that. Molly isn't going to play football now, is she?"

"Why not?"

Mum's question confuses me, but many things do so maybe not much of a surprise. She was the one who said that everything had to change. I am still formulating an answer when she passes me my phone and I stand against the kitchen wall reading the messages while she inspects my bag to make sure I've got everything. She took charge of packing this morning, as everything has to be perfect, and I had to get ready.

As she reported, the guys are planning on going to five-a-side tomorrow. I can't exactly tag along, not how I am now. Baby pink claws on my fingers and hearts in my ear lobes, it would be very obvious.

I'll sort that reply later as it's time to leave for the pivotal appointment. A meeting with the headteacher and senior school management. To do something that is unheard of to them, and that they have no idea nor suspicions about. On top of all that, it is a school day! One person seeing through my disguise could be all it takes to shatter all this confidence and happy feeling in newfound femininity.

Click.

One step out of the door as Mum follows in my wake.

Click.

This familiar garden path, this old reliable fence, letting my eyes wander to anything that will distract my mind.

Click, click, click, click, click, click, click, click.

Down the steps of the grey garden path and out of the gate, which Mum closes behind me.

Click, click.

Hoping none of the neighbours decide to pop out for a friendly chat.

Click, click, click, click.

One of the street's regular cats, licking its front paw. Despite a cat's lack of ability to judge appearance, its yellow eyes meet my brown ones as it continues to bathe itself on the cracked path. Cracked and rippled long before my own heels make their maiden voyage to the car park

Click, click, click.

I stop in front of the passenger door of Mum's car, somewhere I don't quite recall being in as often as I have this week. Ever since I turned fourteen, I've been taking the bus to school as a "big step" in my social development. I'll be honest, it's simply amazing how powerful earphones can be on a bus full of rabid children. I can also pick my own music, anything from musicals to rap to death metal. Helps to reflect my mood sometimes too!

The door swings open with one firm pull and I step in. I have to adjust the seat to be slightly further back and slightly lower, just to feel comfortable while sat down in this new and peculiar preppy suit. Before sitting down, I brush my skirt to ensure that it's straight and won't ride up when I inevitably leave the car at our destination.

No more clicks, just the sound of the metal door closing over on my Mum's side and the expected starting-up of the car.

Why Hide?

The car pulls away from the street, first reversing out of the space and then advancing on into the day, as I reach into my trusty black handbag. Mum decided that a pink handbag would be too much and that the bag paired nicely with the black lines on the suit. I've maybe mentioned that already.

Anyway, I take my phone and open the group chat.

'*5s tomo?*'

'*Sure how many we got?*'

'*we reckon we have 10, if Ollies goin?*'

'*idk Ollies been away and not replyin at all*'

'*hes reading it all tho?*'

'*at his aunts.*'

Oh yeah, Chris knows where I am! Or well, where I'm not. The chat goes on with pointless back and forth messages and memes. What am I going to tell them? Can I even worry about that right now? Mum clearly notices something is up, and she knows what it is too.

"What are you going to say to the guys then?"

"Um… I guess just that I can't go. I've used one excuse already."

"You could go, you know. We don't have anything planned tomorrow."

"I know but… we've made so much progress and I've changed so much already. Ollie can't exactly just show up, not with the new accessories."

The car motors along at a steady speed as mum drops a bombshell.

"Ollie's dead. Be yourself! Go as you, the real you!"

"Are you kidding?!" Stunned doesn't cut it.

"You could be yourself. I bet your friends would be all right with it, your *real* friends will be."

"Guys can be ruthless. They could do something."

"Nothing is going to happen like that hon, this isn't a movie."

"Hmmm… I don't feel like it's a good idea."

"Let's see how you feel after this. You never know, maybe your friends will see you like this today!"

"Mum, don't even joke about that!" I snarl, quivering with the nerves of what's to come.

Normally, parents' cars can't be parked in the school car park and are limited to drop-off zones. This is probably also the case today. In my panic to prepare for the meeting, I haven't even looked at the time. My phone reads ten to one.

"Oh no, lunch break is in twenty minutes!"

It's the only time that your headteacher has today and I wasn't waiting any longer. *We* weren't waiting any longer."

"Oh, everyone's going to see me! This is bad!"

Mum firmly takes my right hand in her left and tries to soothe me.

"It's all right, this is going to be tough but you're a young woman now, and us women face challenges with confidence. Look at how you were walking in the kitchen this morning. Or how you handled Dundee yesterday. Even think back to the therapist chat or the salon. You've got this, but just pull it together!"

I silently nod my head, check the mirror in the sunshield to make sure I look all right and ask Mum for a final evaluation.

"I'm so proud of you. You look fabulous Molly."

"I feel it. And I feel ready."

"Ready?"

"Let's go, before I change my mind."

The door swings open once more, and I unfasten the seatbelt and step out on to the whiteish curb. Click, it never gets old. Although me writing about it almost certainly is.

Anyway, the symphony beneath my feet continues as I take in the familiar surroundings. They feel brand new, even though I've been coming here for years. I suppose I haven't. We use the back entrance, since it is a lot closer. I doubt the teachers ever use the front doors to the school since they always park their cars behind the considerably derelict building. It's not completely falling apart but it is in bad need of restoration. The metal panels are more rust than steel, a window or two remains broken or boarded up due to previously being shattered and the birds have relentlessly added colour to the whole thing. It's an extreme eyesore.

The inside isn't much better. Though cleaner, it too has the same run-down aura about it. Pastel blue walls with notice boards — looking sort of like an overblown doctor's office. This is what we call the 'crush hall' as when it is full of all 900 GHS kids, it is quite the squeeze. It's where I meet with the guys every morning. Or where I never did.

The echo of my heels deserves a mention here. The distinct lack of people in the crush mean that I'm drawing all possible attention just by walking. Mum suddenly has a shot of inspiration and reaches into her own bag.

"Put these on and wait here. I'll go sign us in and see if they are ready to start." She gestures to a soft blue chair — one of six in the hall. A waiting area for the parents, visitors and any sick kids expecting pick-up.

What are these? I can hear you ask. Mum brought sunglasses. Sun. Glasses. Perfect for hiding the eyes and perfectly pretentious to go with the rest of the outfit. All I'm missing at this point is a puppy small enough to cram into a purse in some sort of cruel iteration of a keychain. The lenses are black (there would be no point in wearing them otherwise) and the legs are a strange rose gold. These are hers; she often wears them when reading a book out in the sun.

I put them on, and this suddenly feels like a spy mission. In full disguise, infiltrating enemy lines and gathering intel. In actuality, I'm just trying to avoid being seen before I want to be. I sit in a chair that isn't even in the line of sight of the gentle receptionist. Even **she** can't catch sight of me for too long.

Two minutes pass as I still ponder exactly what to say. In this meeting, to the guys, to the rest of my peers on Monday — what to say?

"They're ready. Up in one of their offices of the first floor."

"I know where they are, let's do this."

Not so much a confident reply but a strong yet resigned one. Resigned to this being a total curveball for everybody. I don't like causing problems.

New to Us

How to approach this vital march up to the offices of senior management? Stairs I have ascended many times before though never in sunglasses, not once in heels though I have longed in the past for this very moment. It's not the case but my heels echo and create their own crescendo as I walk, Mum beside me, and it almost feels like a wedding. Like I'm about to be passed on to whoever waits up these stairs.

It's the total opposite. I'm doing this to pass myself on to *myself.* My skirt brushes a little higher against my fleece-covered legs as each step is another affirmation. No turning around, time to face destiny.

"Shall I knock first to make sure it is the right room?" Mum asks as we cross the main hall of the first floor to the area signposted with which office belongs to who on the headteacher's crew. The hall is nothing more than a crossing between two corridors and allowing access to the main stairs. The assembly hall is off to the right, one corridor is around the railing (180 degrees turn from when you climb the stairs) and the other corridor, mainly for economics and Geography, is to the left.

In this sense, the first floor is the lifeless heartbeat of a buzzing hive of students. For most of the day laying deserted and suddenly playing host to everyone at the usual breaks. I wish my own heart would calm down, but it's threatening to shatter emergency glass as we cross the threshold into the side room of offices.

The doors resemble that old cliché with the different rooms each holding a marauding beast except the one which is the safe exit. Mum knocks on the middle door as the sign says 'Rector.' I, meanwhile, want to run and scream. I stand my ground; I resist the urge to bolt from the truth and burrow once more into masculine sand. Time to face destiny.

Mr Dean is a stern figure, he's not one for jokes. That said, he is surprisingly easy to get along with so long as you follow his rules. He's not the headteacher, but as promised, there is one deputy head here too. If nothing else, he'll be useful for a second perception of the explosion about to take place. Mum introduces herself as the woman who called on Monday and they remember it well.

"You best come in then. And Ollie? Is he here at all?"

I have seldom seen Mum struggle with her words. She can't quite restrain her own nerves enough to explain the situation. I close my eyes, even though the glasses already obscure them from the judging stares of others. I close my eyes so I can't see what I'm about to do. Throat bone-dry, voice barely tuned, I blow my cover.

"Here… sir."

Once the 'sir' weakly leaves my lips and I have signed my own fate, I can bring myself to open my eyes. And Mr Dean's eyes are open. Wide open. Like Ronaldo against a team of Under-5s wide open. He stammers but does an admittedly perfect job of keeping his composure.

"Well, I suppose there *is* a lot going on here. You'd best come in, folks."

There's always one of two feelings when you are invited into one of these offices: either intense guilt or extreme pride, depending on the situation. The same feelings occur when the headteacher, Ms Waverley, summons you like an authoritarian sorcerer. She sits at the table instead of her desk, coffee in hand. Her white blazer is one of her go-to jackets and she wears slacks almost all of the time. She is one of those people who really doesn't like being strict but can be fiercely misleading if you take her kindness for weakness.

That coffee somehow remains in her hand as I walk in looking like Elle Woods. Her eyebrows raise as if they're about to fly off of her face, her eyes go almost as wide as Mr Dean's, but she quickly realises the mask is slipping and subsequently regains her composure, inviting us to take a seat opposite her on the black comfy chairs.

Mr Dean fetches a jug of water and a few glasses. A drink is much needed for everyone now, but I imagine we're all wishing for something stronger and possibly numbing.

As Mum goes into full 'mum mode' and pours out water for myself, the teachers and then herself last of all, Ms Waverley cuts the silent tension.

"So I understand that you wanted to speak with us about something. And I don't want to assume anything about this. So please, explain the situation."

Mum looks at me, gesturing that it's best I take control here. Talk about 'in at the deep end', this is traversing the Great Barrier Reef with armbands on.

"So I-"

"Best remove the glasses, honey."

Right, yeah. The glasses. I lift them from my nose and allow them to slip off my head into my hands. I then give them to my mum who puts them into her handbag. Glasses off and the full glory of my overzealous eye make-up revealed, I restart the explanation.

"I'm not Ollie. I'm not a boy. I'm Molly. I'm a girl."

The short sentences approach is always best if saying anything becomes as tricky as eating a steak with a paper straw. I down half a glass of water just to try to stabilise my insides a little. But to no avail, my body hasn't paid the heating bill and I quiver.

"Right…so…"

She turns her attention to my mum.

"Ms Clarke, I hope you realise that I'm in no way trying to offend you with anything that is said in this meeting today. And Ollie, please don't take anything personally. This is a totally new thing to me."

"New to us as well," Mum craftily adds.

Mr Dean speaks up to try to make some progress.

"So, the aim here is to do the best thing for your child. Sorry, for Molly here."

I can't help but smile at how quickly Mr Dean has picked up on the new name.

"What can we do?" I ask, worrying for my own mental health as the seconds and minutes tick by.

A glint appears in Ms Waverley's left eye.

"Well, we accept it. We respect it, we celebrate it! We're all about equality at Grafton High School, there is no other option."

That's enough of a relief for now, but it's time to talk about nitty-gritty details. There are many clear obstacles, some which can't be helped and others which won't be amended easily.

"OK, let's talk logistics." Mr Dean is keen to take charge of this one, understandably so as he appears to be the only one with prior experience of knowing a tomboy. Loosely related doesn't even cut it.

I drink the other half of my glass of water, this time a little more civilised but still shaking like a fresh polaroid.

An Intruder?

"So the very first thing to sort out is the exact stage we are at. Have you seen a psychologist?"

"Y-yeah, on Tuesday. Mrs Styles."

"Oh, the school's psych! Well that's a strong start, we'll work closely with her to make sure you are happy. We won't ask for any confidential specifics, but she will be free to feed back to us any concerns for your safety or mental health. Is that all okay with you?"

Ms Waverley's words all make sense. It's obvious that the school want to keep an eye on all pupils, especially those who are such extreme abnormalities as myself.

"All right, we will not ask any further questions about the therapy. We respect your privacy on that one, as well as Mrs Styles' professional integrity."

"Yes. Quite right." Mr Dean adds a fairly nothing agreement, then moves to the next topic.

"So registration. You would like your name to be changed for all classes, yes?"

"Yeah, please."

Mum is now just here to spectate; I've taken the reins of this chat. I twirl a long strand of my 'hair' as Mr Dean explains what this will mean.

"So from Monday, your name will be read as Molly Clarke. Your full name is Molly Kat Clarke, but you'd best change it officially for all other uses as well."

"Deed poll," Mum casually announces the method for such an important change.

"Yes. It has to be deed poll." Ms Waverley's tone is serious but trying not to be. She clearly feels uncomfortable but at this moment, the whole room is a mattress of pebbles.

"OK, I'll do that. So from Monday?"

"Yes, as soon as you return to school, be prepared to answer to that name."

"Oh um, how are we spelling it?" Mr Dean asks.

I respond "with a Y."

"Ahh, I wrote it as I-E!" And then he briefly laughs, which is enough for me to crack a smile. A nice change of appearance from my persona throughout the meeting which has been "Barbie Doll who hasn't studied for a crucial exam."

"Wait. Won't the other kids question that? Do we want her to just be thrown into the fire like that?"

Mum's words carry genuine concern over my safety. She's *worried*.

Ms Waverley thinks she has the solution.

"How's about we hold an assembly? Monday morning, first thing. That way it won't catch anyone off guard at different times and we rip it off like a plaster."

"Oh I don't know, she's awfully timid."

Another false dawn of confidence ignites inside me. Still not enough fire to quell the shivers but enough to accept my fate head on. The light at the end of the tunnel may be that of a moving train, but I'll embrace it, nonetheless.

"Let's do it. And I want to be there."

Why did I just say that?!

"Even better, be proud. Oh and be in your uniform! Do you need new guidance on what that is for our female students?"

"Already got it all! We're prepared, eh Mols?"

"Y-yeah, o-on Thursday w-we went to D-Dund-dee."

"Ah so this has been the whole absence as well?"

"It has, yeah. I couldn't have my daughter in school knowing she was suffering."

"You're a lucky kid, Molly! Your mum is such a great ally!"

Ms Waverley praises Mum and it once again visibly improves her mood. Everyone likes being praised for a good job.

"When it comes to…female-specific things, what do I do?"

"We'll have to ask the girls in your year, unfortunately that is the fairest way. We can't just throw you in there, you may be seen as an intruder. In the meantime, P.E. is off the table for you. You can study in the library instead. In terms of PSE, it's best you attend neither gender-specific class until we work out the best approach. Sorry, we can't do any better than that."

An intruder? That's harsh. I would say I'm more of a refugee, seeking protection from masculinity in the soft feminine form of my true self.

"And what if there are… problems?"

Mr Dean looks me directly in the eyes and tries to smile though it makes it more unnerving.

"We have a duty to protect all of our pupils. Please tell us about any harassment, bullying or anything else bothering or affecting you negatively."

Ms Waverley echoes this sentiment, though slightly rosier.

"You deserve to be treated with respect, regardless of who you are. So please be yourself, and we'll support you."

"Thanks."

That's all I can squeeze out of my drained mind. One word of gratitude. And just like that, the meeting is over. From Monday, I'm going to be attending school as me.

Mum returns the glasses to me without me even having to ask. She knows that I'll need them. Despite it seeming like not much was said, the meeting takes up half of lunch. I cover my eyes once more behind plastic blackout shades and we leave the office, with a final, feeble smile.

Before we can even begin to unpack the outcome of a fairly successful discussion, we need to escape the ever-watching eyes of the students. Thankfully, not many kids hang around the main hall at lunch as they are all eating in the canteen, studying in the library, killing time in the playground or off on an excursion for an alternative to the school's lunch options.

And just as I thought we would escape with no harm done, disaster strikes.

I notice Stephen coming through the main entrance as Mum and I edge closer to the rear exit. I can see him *looking, staring,* at me. He can't know, surely he can't tell! He doesn't know it's me, right?

Red Carpet

"A pretty successful meeting there then, eh hon?" Mum excitedly chirps as we return to the car which we seem almost bound to at this point.

"Sure was! I didn't think it would be that easy or that they'd even allow it."

"I mean, you must really care about this. You agreed for them to announce it at an assembly! Ollie would never have been so bold!"

"Well, he's gone. I feel more sure of myself. I just hope no one saw me today…" I mutter, unable to shift the thought that my friend saw through my disguise.

"They'll see you soon enough anyways, Mols. Don't lose sleep over them finding out early. I think you are ready for it already, and I'm so excited for when you no longer need to hide."

"Best wait til Monday, though. Don't say anything about it publicly before the announcement on Monday."

Mum starts the car as our conversation continues, but slightly shifts focus to the group chat. I take my phone out of my bag and there are no new messages. I suppose that's to be expected with the guys at school and me "at my aunt's."

Yet that same innocent message still bugs me. I can't go to 5-a-side tomorrow, I can't let them see me again before Monday. What sort of excuse can I come up with? I could just ghost it all, but that's a fairly crappy thing to do.

'Can't go, guys. Sorry. I'll be online tonight tho'

I don't owe anyone a reason but at least if I speak to them tonight, I can remove some of the suspicion around it. Plus, they won't see this until after school. I have a couple of hours of peace of mind before they try to crack the puzzle.

"So are we just heading back home now?"

"I was thinking we could go for lunch, like I suggested when I first met Molly. Does that sound good?"

"Food always sounds good!" Mum surely knows me better than that!

"Fab. Would be a shame to get you all dolled up and not show you off. All your friends are still in school too, so no pressure for anyone you know seeing you."

"Yeah, that's true." I must concede. Mum has really thought about every little detail of this week to an almost psychopathic degree. Serial killers don't put this much effort into crafting their plans.

Every time I step out of the car when wearing high heels, I can't help but imagine the red-carpet footage. The camera starting at the feet, admiring the brand on the designer shoes and the long legs. Panning up to hopefully avoid an indecent shot of the actress, they reveal the identity of the star and then zoom out to allow you the privilege of digesting their whole look with your own proletariat eyes.

In reality, we've pulled up outside of Mum's favourite little lunch spot — the same one she and the girls went to at the weekend while Molly was unknowingly preparing to be born.

No cameras, no lights, no adoring fans. A homeless person sits against the wall of the neighbouring newsagents, reading. A colourful piece of graffiti stains the otherwise greyish walls. The first letter smudged; the others read 'YT'. Not to be confused with a social media star, this 'YT' likely means 'Young Team' — code for chavs, neds and other miscreants to live by. Beside this is obviously a phallic design — you can't go anywhere without seeing a prick.

Mum is a regular to this cafe, despite its age, and it shows as the owner is there to greet her. She fails to hide her confusion at who is with her, and the sunglasses are still on my face so she can't even make out any resemblance with the eyes. I still like to think my face is young enough to give the game away but the owner never reveals this to be the case. I silently continue to tune my voice — I've been adjusting it since my red-carpet moment.

In a way, this is another one of those. That's only because of the maroon/burgundy tones of the carpet in the entrance of the cafe. It soon gives way to dark brown, moody laminate but this is a sharp contrast to the clean white walls and floral paintings all over the room. The tables are finished in similar dark oak to create a real sea-to-sky horizon look in this tiny eatery.

As I'm taking in the scenery, I'm caught off guard by Mum calling over to someone.

"Sarah! Hi!"

Sarah? As in Chris' mum? I know she and my mum are good friends but surely this isn't co-ordinated. I can't exactly flip my lid and be a diva on my lunch date debut so I'll just bottle that worry and put it with the others on the dreadfully overstocked and creaking shelf.

"Hi Kat! And you must be the girl of the moment!" Sarah says, pointing to me.

I remove the glasses this time without prompting and try my best to maintain eye contact while putting them away in my bag. Unsuccessful, I simply offload them to Mum who stores them in her own inventory. I do my best to politely introduce myself. Sarah knows me from the few times Chris invited me up to play games but that was Ollie. Molly is a fresh face, a new person. The new girl.

"Hi there!" I aim to sound cheery without sounding psychotic and without being formal. We are still Scottish and I am still sixteen after all. I assume she doesn't need to hear my name — Mum definitely shared that much with her if she knows about any of this at all.

"Shall we take a seat then?" Sarah says, inviting us to sit opposite her in oak chairs, with cream floral cushions on the back and the base.

Ladies' Lunch

As I have just removed the sunglasses, my eyes adjust to the full colours of the surroundings and the complete appearance of the surprise lunch guest!

Sarah's a quite familiar face so I don't feel nearly as ashamed, embarrassed or even uncomfortable around her. She is likely more nervous being around me at this point. She won't want to say anything to upset or discourage me, especially not with Mum there proudly showing me off like a prized festive ornament.

Her hair is styled in a black bob, effortlessly straight. It looks as though it was done professionally and expensively. Her round face fixes in a subtle smile — a natural resting happy face plastered on. Must be a nightmare when she's having a bad day. She wears a purple blouse and white, flowing trousers, which dance at her ankles as she sits down. For this time of year, she can't be warm!

"So get your orders in, ladies! My treat!"

Such a generous gesture, but Mum insists on splitting the bill anyway. To be honest, I would be adamant about doing the same but it's free for me either way. We decide on the food and drink orders then Sarah puts the spotlight on me.

"You look fabulous! Where did you get the suit?"

"Oh, er, we went shopping in Dundee. But I don't remember which shop because we did go to a few different places."

Mum chimes in with the correct shop name: "H&M."

"Ah, very nice stuff in there! You'll have to learn your brands though, all part of being one of the girls!"

Sarah's cracking us up with her good-natured banter. It's nothing offensive and actually quite a useful thing to remember.

"All the girls know their brands? I just thought they bought stuff 'cause it looked cute on them. That's the way I look at things."

Sarah smiles at my innocent and truthful answer. Without her mouth moving, her whole demeanour is saying 'So much to learn, girl.' Rather creepily, this exact phrase is said just once the waiter brings us our drinks.

Mum's driving so she can't have anything alcoholic, and I'm obviously too young. This doesn't stop Sarah from satisfying a need for gin. The young waiter places our Cokes and the gin on the table with a 'there you go, ladies.' If life was a cartoon, I'd be swooning right now. My heart flutters with joy, even if the waiter is just being customer-friendly.

The food follows a few minutes after. A panini is my usual go-to lunch at high school so I opt for a small helping of spaghetti carbonara. May as well have something a little more special! Mum and Sarah both choose sandwiches instead. Boring!

Eating, drinking, pointless chatter, mutual compliments, light-hearted jokes — this almost feels like any other day at a lunch table. If it wasn't for the Italian music playing subtly in the background akin to those on the gondolas in Venice, I'd say it is just like any school lunchtime. Except my friends in this case are my mum and one of my friend's mums. Oh, the jokes that could normally be made about going for lunch with Chris' mum — the lads would have a field day except for poor Chris, of course. Though I guarantee that if they ever knew the full story behind it, I'd be the one struggling to find the funny side.

Sarah's only had half of her gin so it's even more concerning to me that her next question sounds so preposterous! I can't believe she asks this sober.

"That waiter is about your age, Molly. He's a cute one, eh?"

"He's a good four or five years older than my sweet daughter. I don't know if she should be going for men while she is just a girl."

They talk about me and my potential future relationships as if I'm not at the table with them. They shoot suggestive looks and glances between my own eyes and the waiter, who bends over a table on the other side of the cafe as he wipes it down in preparation for new guests. I'm not even looking his way, or I'm not noticing it if I am.

"No, I think you would like a boy closer to your age. A high school

181

sweetheart for you!"

The older ladies at the table laugh and I play along. It is pretty ridiculous to be talking so openly about my sexuality. But Mum's comment has to be the worst one.

"Well, your Chris is almost the same age. A few months older but that's a lot better!"

Sarah responds, "True! You never know, Kat, maybe Molly could go to prom with Chris in the summer!"

I need to say something to switch the topic of our chat from this frankly horrifying idea they're hatching together, but without sounding offended. Besides, I don't think I am offended. Between mouthfuls of pasta, sips of Coke and little remarks here and there, I've had a really pleasant time for the most part. My stomach reacts to the Chris comment but it doesn't feel particularly awful. I can't actually like the sound of that idea, can I?

Being at prom with one of my closest friends, all dolled up and presumably there as his girlfriend? I suppose that's better than being tortured and tormented. Still, very weird to hear it so openly suggested.

"Oh, I'll pass! I don't think I'll be ready for a relationship anytime soon. Still working out this whole girl thing."

Mercifully, that's enough of a comment to distract the women at the table from further arranging a marriage. Chatter flips from fashion to work/school, from the weather to the holidays and then to a crazy reminder.

"The boys will be back for Christmas next month, won't they?"

"Oh yes, that'll be fun. And they can meet their new sister!" Mum says, pinching my cheek like an American parent on *Toddlers and Tiaras*.

"I'm sure they'll love you! You're a good laugh and you're still you!" Some more motivation from Sarah is a refreshing change from the tongue-in-cheek teasing.

With that comment, lunch comes to an end. My head is more filled with thoughts than the ocean is water. The chemical make-up in my mind is throwing my psyche to and fro, rocking me through a hurricane which shakes in my core.

I grab my bag from the handy storage space (under my chair) and we say our goodbyes to Sarah. She promises a similar lunch date soon and waves us goodbye as we part outside of the cafe. Now that I've eaten here, I'd say it's more of a bistro.

Back in the car, no new messages await me on my phone. The lads aren't out of school yet, so that's no shock.

"I told you that cafe's good! Did you enjoy that?"

"Yeah, it was lovely. I just hope she doesn't tell Chris about me."

"I don't think she will. I'd be shocked if Chris talks to her long enough to hear about it, really."

"That's kind of sad," I admit.

"Well, boys typically spend time with their dads over their mums. Girls prefer time with mum. You've always had me, and only me."

"And that's been perfectly fine by me." I smile, doing my best to show all of the gratitude inside me as I do so. "You're the best."

I squeeze Mum's hand the same way I have done since I was much younger. She's always done the same to me as well. Hugging is awkward in a car.

Plans, Poses and Panic

"So I'm thinking that once we get home, you can fix your make-up and I'll take a photo for your eventual Facebook profile pic change. And my proud announcement, if you don't mind me posting about you."

"I don't mind, it will all be out in the open anyways. I'm just worried that Matt and Kyle won't know before the rest of the world does… it feels unfair on them."

"I know that you don't like being a burden to anyone, but there are some things you just have to do for yourself. Why not see if you can video chat them this weekend? They'll see you for you before anyone else does on Monday."

"Oh, maybe. Won't they be busy? I don't want to distract them from coursework…"

When you are atypical like myself, every single little event is weighed up with hundreds-and-thousands of problems sprinkled on top. I can't even make up my own mind, just my own face. Even that's still a learning process as well. Certain things feel insurmountable right now. Chief among them is everyone's reactions to my newfound identity.

Then again, it's only fair to give family first dibs on hearing any life-changing news. I'm glad they aren't here to witness this awkward phase runs its course. I'll be out for better and for worse way before Christmas rolls around and Matt and Kyle come home from good ol' Englandshire.

"Family love is unconditional. Your brothers are going to protect and support their little sis, trust me! I raised them right!"

I fidget with my phone as Mum reassures me, something she has had to do far more often recently. I know it is very much like wildebeest seeking safety by following gazelles, but Mum is the best guide I have for femininity and womanhood.

Before long, we are back home in the warmth. Just in time too, as grey clouds have rolled over to cover the pleasant shimmer of the November sun. And true to Mum's instructions, I head upstairs to sort the subtle wear-and-tear on my made-up face. The liner needs redone, the eyeshadow begs for a little touch-up and my lips are nowhere near as glossy or girly as they were this morning for the meeting, so that also needs addressed. I remove my wig and start brushing it out like Mum did this morning. It's amazing how quickly the elements and just daily life can damage a spotless appearance!

Anyway, about half of a rock-and-roll album blaring from my phone later and I am once again satisfied with my glittery visage. I delicately pop the wig back over my bald cap and do my best to replicate the shape it held before. Pleased with the efforts once more, I leave to take part in the photo shoot Mum wants to perform on me.

She still wants me to stand in the kitchen for the photo like before — the natural light from the window is the usual reason but the clouds have obscured that. I think it's now a combination of a force of habit and Mum wanting to show off her kitchen at the same time as her daughter. "Now I want to see you pose a little! Confidence is a must if you're going to be accepted on Monday. You'll maybe even be on stage at the announcement, so you can't be shy about how you look! Especially when you are so pretty!"

Being called pretty is the best motivation I can get at the moment. It always causes a little sweet flush in my brain whenever I hear someone compliment how I look that just was never there before. Maybe because I was never here before?

I've seen many YouTube videos by now of all of those 'try-on hauls' and they contain many montages of multiple photos and numerous poses in each outfit like a nineties teen show clip in a shopping mall — sometimes even complete with camera-click sound effects.

Mum's phone makes no sort of sound at all as she snaps away. That's just Steve Jobs' invention at work. Most smartphones are silent all the time now anyway or hooked up to a watch or some glasses. Even my own phone only leaves vibrate mode if I'm expecting a call. However, I do my best to recreate the poses I see most often on those videos.

To put that into slightly more detail, I start with a simple stand-and-smile against the blue wall. Then I pucker and pout my lips for a shot or two before subtly moving my hands to grip my waist. My left hand then moves from my waist up to hold up two fingers — for peace, of course! I move these fingers closer to my face, forming a chevron near my left eye. Mum just gasps, amazed at the striking moves I'm showing off. They are striking for someone like me, who often fails to smile. The last photo is a cheekier one — my tongue sticks out and I stand a bit more side on. I am tempted to put my middle finger up like all edgy teens do — but Mum raised me better than that. I think so, anyway.

"One day, we'll have to get you into a proper studio. If that's how your personality comes out now, you may have a future as a model. With enough… changes, of course!"

Mum didn't want to and doesn't want to outright mention the end-goal changes. Not yet, we are barely through the first level of this somewhat self-imposed challenge. We can't be thinking about the 'H' word or the 'S' word yet.

My phone buzzes on the kitchen table. It's the group chat replying. The guys are obviously out of school now. I'm thinking about saying a different 'S' word. But Mum raised me better than that, so I'll keep it in writing instead.

That Fake...

$\mathbb{I}$ pick my phone up and hesitantly tap the bubble to open the chat head for the 'Fitbaw Lads' group chat. I see a couple of the guys in there replying and planning everything for tomorrow's session. Then the first question appears as a direct reply to my message from earlier:

'*Y u not goin Olly?*'

The guys have often written my name short-hand in texts because the minutes saved over typing 'y' instead of 'ie' could add up to days apparently. You can practically hear my eyes rolling, huh? My sarcasm is limitless, much like my fear at this moment.

Mum sends the pictures from the kitchen photo shoot over and I'm extra careful to lock them in a hidden folder. If I don't do this, the pictures are all too easy to find. Guys like to steal or 'borrow' each other's phones from time to time. Even if you look at the Truth or Dare game with Shawn, you see that I'm not above observing his phone activity either! Well, Ollie wasn't. No part of me now wants to be quite so mean.

Shawn's another obstacle which I'll have to address later. I can't pull my gaze from the group chat at the moment. So engrossed in the developments that I haven't even removed my heels despite there being nowhere else to go and no other reason to still be wearing them. I mean, they are adorable, but they will cause blisters. I do take a quick second to pull up a chair, my manicured nails hovering over the screen in between taps to ensure that the phone doesn't lock. A staring contest with technology that I'll never win.

My mind fixes on what to say. Do I say anything? They know I've seen the message, that honestly looks worse now. OK, think! A tiny part of me wants to just come clean — I'm a dreadful liar! The hand of common sense rushes to cover the mouth of moral victory, or more accurately to grab the fingers of truth. What sort of excuse is there?

Illness won't work, the lads are relentless whenever one of them is unwell and won't come out. My issue isn't that I won't come out. My problem is that I *have*.

'*Soz guys Mum's sayin we have plans.*'

That is seriously the best I can do. What follows is a bit of mockery and rude words but nothing nearly as brutal as if they knew what is really going on.

Just as I think the drama has all boiled over, the smaller group chat titled 'Game Guys' — just me, Chris, Stephen and Darius — dings and pops up. It's Stephen's turn to rock my steady soul once more.

'*Guys did u see that girl today?*'

Darius responds with his usual wit.

'*There are lots, who?*'

Chris throws in a laughing emoji and a quick note of how he agrees with Darius' sarcastic comment.

'*Oh you guys should of seen her—*'

Interrupting to specify that Stephen isn't the most intelligent of the lot. I would usually reply to any grammatical error, but I'm too hooked on conversation to notice. Anyway, the full message.

'*Oh you guys should of seen her. Sunglasses, make-up, big tits. Looked about our age, maybe a little older.*'

OK… that's not necessarily a bad thing for them to say. Except for the fact that Stephen is now definitely talking about me. I'm so worried, I can't even fully appreciate the 'big tits' comment. Am I even supposed to appreciate that? It's like validating to hear and absolutely disgusting to be objectified like that at the same time. But I should have known, objectification is second nature to lads.

'*Again, could have been anyone in our year by that*'

I don't know why the other guys are being so pushy to find out every detail here. Conversations like this happen all the time.

'*Not in uniform*'

'*Oh then i didn't see her*'

Chris wants to push the conversation on a little further by asking for further detail. I'm surprised his questions aren't along the lines of 'where were you on the night of the murder?' And just then, they kind of do sound like that.

'when did u see a girl like that?'

'she was leaving crush when I came back from my fag. U guys were at the table'

Cue immature laughing at the use of the word 'fag' for a good few questions and some interesting banter about Stephen being a homosexual.

'sounds like a proper slut'

'wonder if shes a new student'

Stephen is then teased relentlessly for crushing on a girl that he only caught a fleeting glimpse of. I too would join in on the poking fun if it wasn't *me* that he's talking about.

'aw stfu u kno what i mean'

*'yeah ur gonna **** over her'*

*'u wanna f*** the new girl!'*

This is where I step in and finally join the truly intriguing and captivating conversation.

'We don't know if she is a knew student yet.'

'y else would she be there?'

I finally have my go at mocking Stephen

'You imagined her? Idk man lol'

'I wouldn't imagine a slut like that. too many clothes.'

Yes, this is one of my closest friends who has just unknowingly called me a slut twice. I can do nothing about that, not yet. I'll bide my time — it's actually going to be kind of funny when I can finally avenge that.

Again, it's possible that comments like that are just for 'lad points.' He may genuinely have a love-at-first-sight type crush on the new girl. I just doubt it, the lads lock their gazes on to anything with breasts and a pulse.

Darius' next message is honestly the worst one yet.

'she may be a tranny lol u know nothin bout her'

Resisting the urge to climb up on my soapbox and deliver the words which would bring an end to this conversation and any remains of a social life I have; we all just send laughing emojis in while Stephen swears at us all. Another typical day in the world of teen boys. Ugh, honestly.

'Anyways, playin Xbox later?'
Finally, back to normal.
'Yeah sounds gd.'
'I'm in.'
'Be on at 8'

That shouldn't be too bad. As long as they don't talk about me, I'll be fine. My restraint when typing is naturally much stronger. Something may just slip out of my mouth if they push anything.

Unlikely Distraction

Mum opens the kitchen door with her usual grace, likely just coming in for a drink. She spots me still sitting at the table and is obviously confused.

"I thought you would be away upstairs doing whatever now. Something wrong."

"Just group chat drama. I think Stephen saw me today, but he doesn't know it was me. He just said about a new girl in sunglasses with quotes big tits."

"Ooh, that's nice to hear the first time! It's okay to appreciate that the first time it's said or when you've known someone a long time. A stranger says it to you, kick him in the balls."

"Mother! How could you be so violent?"

My faux shocked expression and my exaggerated tone leave no doubt that I'm joking and we laugh and joke about it.

"Well, maybe Chris and Stephen will be fighting over you by the time you come out to them!"

"Muuum! That's weird to even think about!"

I'm not wrong — anyone would be freaked out by the thought of their best friend crushing on them. People who don't find being attracted to their friends weird are likely in relationships with their friends. For an outsider to that world, I just can't shake the unsettling thoughts. Or any equally chilling worries about Monday.

"Anyways, I'm not going online til later. What are you doing?"

"Well, no idea really. Ironing's done, washing's on and we both had quite heavy lunches so no need to do dinner. We have snacks in if we get hungry later."

"So you're just going to sit around watching TV?"

"Yeah, most likely. That's my usual Friday night sadly. World of a

191

grown-up, hon!"

"Hmm, this is going to sound weird."

"It won't be the strangest thing I've heard this week, not even close. Go ahead, Mols, what's up?"

"You said I needed a more feminine education. So… do you want to watch a film?"

"You want to watch a movie with me?" Mum's surprised face hurts. Ollie was an awful son; I'm going to be so much better.

"Sure, why not? I've got no plans."

"OK, you should maybe go and get changed, while I pick a film out for us. A proper chick flick." Mum's face lights up, filling me with a similar glow. My good karma is growing by the minute — it has been ever since I shed that dreadful, rough skin I had.

"Awesome, back in a tick."

"Oh and hon, the voice—"

"Thanks, I'll fix it."

I cut off her instruction halfway through, knowing exactly what she is going to say. I take my heels off once I'm upstairs for two reasons. I want to practise stairs in heels as much as possible and they are just too cute! Part of me wants to put them back on once I have changed but best not.

Come to think of it, I've no idea why my voice matters if I'm about to watch a movie. It's not like I'm starring in the thing! Ah well, it's all good training and habitual practice.

Tonight's nightie is shockingly not pink! It's actually zebra print with a pink outline on the cuffs and a pink neckline. The nightie itself is almost full length and is super silky and soft against my body. Such a contrast between the official-feeling blazer and this laid-back animal dress but it feels equally as cute! I pop today's suit and tights in my washing basket, hoping it won't be the last time I wear it but also looking forward to more dresses. Maybe it'll do for job interviews! I can't bring myself to remove my make-up yet, so I just head back downstairs knowing Mum will appreciate my gorgeous pink toes being on show over any socks or slippers. The house is always warm enough, the living room is at least.

I return to the living room with Mum's joking high-pitched 'ooooh', raising my self-esteem and it causes me to lift the hem slightly and wink at her before allowing the gown to fall back to my ankles. Mum hasn't changed yet, she's still in her jeans from today. She's not the most feminine coach I could have but she is still the best.

"Are you not getting cosier before the movie as well?"

"I'm perfectly comfy in these, hon! Now come on, I'll hit play."

I perch myself beside Mum, smoothing my nightdress out as I do so to stop it riding up and forcing an indecent angle. On the small table, Mum has put a few bags of chocolate and a bag of crisps. Alongside this is a bottle of water — always a refreshing drink — for myself and an orange juice for her.

"There is also hot chocolate, but we'll save that for later! Can't go too crazy, even if it is Friday!"

With that, Mum presses play and the title screen of tonight's movie disappears.

I can't help but take this moment to reflect on how 'Twilight Zone-y' this past week has felt. All from the moment of dressing up to being caught by Mum and then her accepting me. The doctor on Tuesday who unpacked my mental state and added the word dysphoria to my vocabulary. Sharon and Lola's helpful guidance comes to mind as I flick a stray hair from off my nose. My nightgown hugs me softly and my lips remain soft and cool as they have been all week. I can't see how pink my face is but my nails and the cuffs of the gown are reminder enough of how far I've come. Upstairs, a full wardrobe and three full drawers of feminine clothing with make-up stored in my bedside drawers. Even just a week ago, none of this could be seen as even a shred of a possibility. And Monday morning marks another apparent impossible dream becoming a sudden reality.

Anyway, movies are supposed to be distractions. All the progress marked and appreciated mentally, I put my thoughts away and cosy up on the couch to watch this film that is certainly new to me. Mum and I are very similar in that we can never quite just stay silent if a movie is on. We watch the movie but we also comment on anything that's going on or pass any funny commentary that we come up with. It makes us a nightmare for the local cinema, not that I've been there recently.

The movie is about a bride-to-be and a wedding and the mother-in-law sucks. Mum teases me about being a bride someday for a handsome groom and we are both very critical of the fashion, especially the wedding dress scene. In all of the chatter, one thing is very clear — Mum is happy to have a daughter to plan a wedding with. Knowing her usual love of planning and decorating, she may be planning it **for** me instead! I might not have a say!

The movie is nothing special — no real standout character, twist or plot for me — but this isn't a film review.

We have such a good time stuffing our faces and watching the movie and just chatting that we don't really want it to end. The movie finishes and so I show Mum a few of the 'try-on haul' videos I've been watching to hear her opinions on how girls my age dress. It's my turn to set up the video while Mum leaves the room to change into her pyjamas. I can hear her clattering in the kitchen for a few minutes and she emerges with two mugs of not-too-hot hot chocolate. A fabulous Friday night treat!

Mum has me in fits of laughter as she judges the fashion of girls my age today. A few of the best bits included 'her skirt is at her arse', 'she looks like a Calypo,' (referring to the woman's tan) and my personal favourite, 'she's showing more skin and bones than clothes!' I don't think I'm going to be allowed to go around advertising myself like that in the future. To be fair, I don't think I'd want to either.

We discuss the many different outfits in between sips of milky hot chocolate and the odd chocolate button.

"I promise you that when we go shopping for beachwear, you'll be a classy lassie!"

"Beachwear? I don't know if the beach is my scene, even now…"

"Nonsense, honey! We just need to get you a suitable swimsuit, and work on your tan lines. You'll be a beach babe in no time!"

We enjoy ourselves so much that time seems to disappear from the island of relevancy it often so proudly stands on. Its overbearing presence on our lives vanishes with it and I lose all track of time. This is no problem, unless of course I agreed to do something else at this time. After all, it's only five past nine. Oh.

"Shh-yugar!" (nice save) "I was meant to be online an hour ago." What is really strange is that it feels as though fun time is over and I'm away to do some kind of chore. An obligation which I must fulfil. "This was fun though! We should make this a regular thing!"

Her genuinely warm smile tugs at my heartstrings. Mum must have enjoyed it as well. I'm going to be the best daughter ever.

For now though, it is long past game time. I definitely have some explaining to do…

Mask Slipping

I head upstairs as if I am heading to class on a Tuesday morning. It was not long ago that I would excitedly dash at any chance to relax with some online gaming, and it was all even better when the guys were on. Now though, I just don't feel as motivated. I think it's more just my nerves. Molly has never, never spoken to the guys and has only been seen by one of them.

I settle into my chair and turn the console on. It's probably best to just log on and blame connectivity and internet issues, so that is the approach that I'll take. I hop online and don't even wait for an invite to the chat. I click on Darius' gamertag, 'Sniper Ghost', and join the conversation. The TV emits a sound to let me know that it has worked and to alert everyone else that I have now entered the 'room.'

"Hey, look who's finally here!"

"The skiver is back!"

"Aye about time!"

I honestly am unable to tell you which one of those three things from each guy is said first, they are all sort of released in unison like the workforce of a bankrupt company. My head attempts to formulate a response, but instinct takes over.

"All right, guys!"

"Whoa, what the hell is with the voice?!"

S***! I haven't dropped my voice down again to the normal pitch that they are all used to. I unplug the headset and proceed to cough for a few seconds. I test the voice for the ugly 'male' pitch I need then try again.

"Is that better?"

"Yeah, your mic sucks though!"

"I know, you sounded like a bitch just there!"

"More than usual!"

It feels like a stepladder of insults, but this is just how guys behave around each other. I've known and lived this life for far too long, but I know I have to endure it just a little longer.

"Yeah, yeah. Let's just play some damn games!"

"Invite sent."

And for about an hour, things just feel entirely normal. They feel like nothing has changed, Ollie's corpse reanimating and convulsing, perhaps even zombifying. He thankfully isn't coming back; he's just bleeding out. Slowly. Agonisingly. Violently. *Thankfully.*

In fact, if it wasn't for the consistent, silky, stripy affirmation clinging to my body or the ten, fluorescent Barbie-pink reminders whenever I look down at the controller, it would all feel just as it did last Friday. And the Friday before that, ad nauseum. After tonight, no more. Ollie no more.

I also find it a bit peculiar that despite playing for so long, none of the guys have asked me about being absent. I just hope I don't jinx that…

"So, Ollie, why are you skiving?"

Damn you, Chris. I have the perfect comeback for it stored in my mind, practically dancing on my eager tongue. I can hear the outraged laughter now. Just ball up all of that courage and fire back with 'I was on a date with your mum!' But that wouldn't be very ladylike of me and would provoke many uncomfortable questions. If Chris' mum has mentioned anything about lunch today, he might be able to join the dots and solve my delicately crafted puzzle.

"Ah, my auntie booked us a holiday for a few days so I've been doing pretty much nothing."

See, I know how the guys think. I know how they'll react. It will be something along the lines of calling me lucky or mocking that I was 'spending time with my aunt.' But I would rather that than the torrent of abuse I would receive if they knew the truth. My brain wants to hijack the conversation — overthrow the common sense in my head — and just confess. Molly in my mind is still firmly in control, Ollie's lifeless body is her marionette for the moment. Selfishly used for her own means then discarded back into his shallow, fiery grave.

"Yeah, whatever. You guys just wish you had a week like mine!"

This comment could ruin everything. Has Molly let go of the strings and opted for the incinerator too soon? "Because I have been doing absolutely nothing!"

Sure enough, the conversation would turn to the anonymous puppet master.

"Well, you missed it today. There was this total slut in the crush…"

More sexually-charged conversation. Do these guys ever have a night off from this? Does *any* guy? This time however, I am interested. Perhaps my own 'dolly' ego is fishing for compliments, subconsciously liking the idea of living out that life. I poke the bear for more information, and it delivers. Chris and Darius want to change the topic, making fun of Stephen's continued horny lust over the new girl.

"I'm just saying! She was fake! You could just tell she was a slut."

"Are you saying you liked her?"

What am I doing? What am I saying? The mask slips a little further, revealing the made-up eyes of the mastermind. Why do I care if Stephen likes me? I don't like him! Again, I feel like it must just be a deep lust to feel attractive. Any sort of praise will do, just like a pet.

"I'd f*** her of course. But we all would. If you guys saw her, you'd say the same."

Oh wow! I didn't expect hearing that to trigger any sort of response but there is a slight tightening feeling between my legs and a jump inside my stomach. In this strange in-between state of playing with the marionette and gauging their reactions, I'm somehow liking the disturbing lust. I can see them drooling, longing for the 'fake slut' to give them what they want.

We wouldn't all have sex with her, we aren't all attracted to her. Maybe those three are but Kat didn't raise a narcissist. It's tough to justify that based on my desperation for praise in this moment, but I don't believe I'm self-centred. I'm making a mental checklist of what the guys think about me now, before they can finally match a face and name to the glimpse they either caught first hand or heard an account of.

In trying to take in everything that I just heard, I can't quite untie my tongue, loosen my lips or bring back my brain power. I sit in silence until prompted to say something.

"Your mic again, Ollie!"

And the games, the conversation, the banter all continued as if nothing has ever changed. Those naïve fools aren't even aware that their friend is dead and that their 'slut' is the delightful demon who has overtaken his mind forever.

Mum knocks on my door to remind me to take my make-up off and to oil my ears. She says all of this aloud and I panic, knowing there is a high chance the lads heard it.

"Oil your ears?"

"What the f***?"

"Did I hear make-up?"

Nope. Too much to justify, too much to explain, too deep a hole to attempt to dig my way out of. Practically a trench, so I opt to dispose of Ollie in the canyon of my own creation and leave the chat. The charade is over. The gang have removed the mask of the monster. And now, I'm just a freak to them. I can't bring myself to stay and hear their incoming insults. I can take a joke, but not about that.

Judged

Headset removed and lying on my bed beside me, I frantically race to the settings screen, my fingers never having moved quite so fast. I would be a top 100 player if I could do this when it didn't matter as much. I leave the chat, blocking out any ongoing mockery and placing temporary traffic lights on their ill intentions. If they want to say anything to me now, they will have to do it by text.

Worried tears fill my eyes. An ounce or two of regret slowly creeps into my mind before being persecuted and destroyed by the she-mon I have become. My phone buzzes, the notification says 'Messenger' but doesn't say who, or what. This means multiple people. I see no other option than the nuclear one, so I uninstall the app. They can say whatever they want as long as I can't hear or see it. You can't catch a witch who refuses to turn up for the hunt.

I set my console to 'Appear Offline' and then retreat to my new comfort zone — femininity. My throat is dry with anxiety, my whole body shudders. I think I just came out to them. More specifically, I think I was just **found out** by them. They're not the most intelligent but they can't be that thick!

I foolishly think that I've escaped only to find that Facebook will still inform me of waiting messages as I idly scroll through girly posts and the odd update from family.

In this situation, there are two possibilities. I can either ignore this current narrative, likely driven by the amused and bemused tapping of former friends. Or… I can just *stop* it. I can just edit my profile, post about coming out, delete everyone who disagrees and carry on living my true and best life.

If you haven't worked this out yet, thinking straight is not one of my strengths. I stop swiping through outfits on Pinterest and head to the special council for feminine strategy — or my mum, as you know her.

"Mum, I eh… think the guys heard…" I have accepted my fate and my dreams of being a girl coming to fruition yet I can't help but panic at even the thought of what is being said about me. If it were Victorian times, I'd be tied to a stake by now. If I was in a less tolerant country, I'd be shackled to a wall in an asylum, slowly having my mind erased and rewritten like starting a new save game. I'm so fortunate to be where I am and to be cared for and protected by such an amazing person. Yet, it feels like the witch's luck has run out.

"Oh f***. They did?" Mum's language is honestly shocking at times.

I recount the conversation and the fateful turning point while Mum gently massages my hands, trying to eliminate even just a tiny bit of stress. Tears aren't falling yet. I'm just so tired of hiding that I can't even properly take in the fact that there's no need to any more.

"OK, I think we just play it cool. Ignore any messages or anything like that. Once we speak to your brothers tomorrow, we might be able to just fix Molly's Facebook."

"Won't the school be annoyed if we do that?"

"It's not their news. It's not about them. Or the lads. Or even me and your brothers. It's all about you. You could change the profile now if you like, but I think we should at least tell Matthew and Kyle. We wouldn't want to shock them."

"It'll shock them anyway," I bluntly reply. Then I consider what Mum really means. "They deserve to know before everyone else does."

"That's what I meant. They'll be on FaceTime tomorrow night. It gives you all day to prepare yourself to become their little sister for real. Exciting, eh?"

"Sure is." What's that? A smile? The worries are there but they have been put into perspective. We were and are just prolonging the inevitable. But from tomorrow, everyone I know will know. And come Monday, even those who never knew the person I was will be all too familiar with the girl I'm becoming.

Another night comes; another disturbing dream coincides.

I awake in a dark hollow. So dark that there is almost no light, the only glimmer the result of an oil lighter left to burn on the cold, solid, concrete floor. I want to feel the warmth, but I can't reach out for the handcuffs. Small silver chain which should, in theory, be simple to break. However, my weakened muscles can only just keep me sat up. I have no idea what led me into this mess but I'm also thankful that the darkness obscures any knowledge of the damage on my body. I could try to burn the chains on the oil lighter's flame, but my legs are also chained together, with much thicker and denser steel.

Another source of light appears, revealing what I have mostly worked out. I am in a cell, likely a prison cell. The uniform of the burly and shady individual who collects me from my cage confirms it. He has no name and his eyes are hidden behind his hat. His dark blue uniform looks more like a doctor's getup than anything to do with the police. He can't have a badge; it would reflect in the harsh glow of his torch.

Only as he unchains my wounded frame can I comprehend the full situation, though still too dazed to hear anything the mysterious man mumbles. I can see glimpses of a black-and-white stripy garment but as the chains were touching my bare skin, I know this must be a top, or a dress. Hopefully the latter, I doubt they've given me underwear. I want to look around and take in my surroundings, but the man doesn't like that idea. He takes a blindfold out of his pocket and covers my eyes with it, tying it in a tight knot which almost cuts off the circulation. From the clicking, one of us is wearing heels. I assume that's me composing a little song of despair as we walk, arms still cuffed with no sign of release.

The blindfold is removed as we reach a grand, wooden door. There is mumbling and muttering and hushed whispering on the other side, but that all ceases as I am led in.

A courtroom. Old stone pillars framing the typical dramatic scene. Dark brown seats and desks stand out on a shiny white-ish floor. My eyes sting from the contrast, and I almost long for a return to the darkness before anyone has even spoke.

I still can't understand anyone's words, they all speak in a foreign and likely imaginary tongue. A man in a black cloak pushes me forward towards the stand at the front. When asked to state my case, I can't even feel a tongue inside my mouth. My lips may not even be there. I look down to confirm the full situation and yes, they were my heels. The only bright spark of a truly traumatising situation.

I am forcibly removed from the stand and a few bald men surround me. They grab me by my arms and start displaying me. They toy with me like a doll, I can't even feel anything except abject terror and humiliation.

The droves of the public who were once totally unintelligible were now chanting loud and clear.

"Tranny! Tranny! Tranny!"

The judge uses his gavel for the first time in what I mistakenly see as a change in his threatening demeanour. But no, they revert back to their unknown language and groan a little more until sharp, vicious claws dig into my forearms and I am dragged away. I try to scream but it's no use. I must be unable to do anything, the opposite of a lucid dream. It's an on-rail dream — sit back and endure the ride!

Just as the beast with the claws lets out a mighty growl and spins me around, likely sizing up its silent yet shrieking prey, the sweet relief of tearily waking up cuts it off.

"Tranny," I almost unconsciously whisper. A quick drink of water restores a fraction of my senses. I look at my phone, just 4.05 a.m. A long night to say the least. I choose one of many 'Let's Play' videos to drift off to sleep with and the irony isn't lost on me as 'Prison Simulator' appears in my recommendations. No, not that one. I sit upright for two or three videos, the last time I remember seeing on the phone screen before my exhaustion defeats my fear is 5:27.

Cut Off

I wake up bolt upright and stiff as old brakes. The dreaded phone screen won't release me from a cycle of having to settle my thoughts back into one place so I can continue to sleep. I slump back down on to the pillow this time at 6.52 a.m., deciding that lying down will likely be better for sleeping. I know, shock!

The next stint of sleep is the last. It's not a remarkably long one, the clock reads only 8.49. With very quick maths, that's about six hours. My sleeping pattern is abusive at the best of times so even this is a victory. The amount of times Ollie went to school with four hours of sleep or was simply too tired to even go is a lot higher than it should be. He had no idea that it was my doing or that I'm getting comfortable in my new cutesy consciousness. He lies in his grave, it's my time.

I don't go back to sleep but I also don't make the best use of time. My instinct is to check Facebook for any updates but then I'm thrown back into my topsy-turvy reality. The messages just say 9+ but I can't bring myself to read any. I can't leave the groups without seeing what they have been saying about me — about the freak.

Instead, watching more YouTube and writing a few disturbed thoughts into my self-help notebook is really all I can do. The writing slowly forces my mind to accept that there will be no further sleep today, that this is me awake. Semi-ready to face the conundrums of a new day. Anyway, what to write?

They know. They know about me. I'm no longer a mystery, no longer a riddle. My absence once conspicuous now totally transparent. The charade was fun while it lasted but now they know.

I put the pen down and take another sip of water which acts as a liquid slap across the face

So what? So what if they know now? They had to know soon. So what if they think you are weird? You think you are weird. You think they are weird. Everyone is weird. They won't hurt you physically, you won't give them the chance. They can only talk sh** about you and everyone does that anyway. You can read those messages or you can ignore them. It changes nothing.

A scribbled psyching-up. I take a few deep breaths through gritted teeth like a weightlifter attempting a new personal best then tap the blue F once more. I close my eyes and tap the bubble.

New messages from each of the guys, and the group chat is booming. I start there, just to see if there is any widespread damage.

'So who's all comin?'

Oh yeah, they want to play 5-a-side today. Maybe even 7-a-side if they have enough players. I'm afraid I can't help them there; football really isn't my thing. I can tell you every team's name, show you their badges and name their best players but all of that is leftover knowledge from my old life. Now, I don't think I ever want to be seen on the pitch again. I wouldn't be missed.

A bunch of one-word replies confirming attendance follow the request for a roll-call from James. James isn't one of my closest friends but he often organises the football meet-ups on account of his popularity and his footballing ability. And yes, you're correct. Ability is totally irrelevant here but try telling him that. Very much the team captain when there is no team to lead. Just a bunch of lads with nothing better to do on a Saturday afternoon.

'Anyone know if Ollies back?'

I sense a rush of blood and adrenaline similar to what I felt last night as the lads unknowingly hit on me. A moment of misdirection and poor consideration led me to deliver a killing blow to the wounded boy in their minds.

'He won't be back.'

I send the ominous news and subsequently leave the group. A few of the guys must believe I'm dead but my worries turn to the few who know that I am still alive.

Chris is the first to be struck by the truth hammer. He generally questions everything from last night but I have no idea if he has seen my latest announcement. Any excuse, any lie — that's all out the window.

'*I'm a girl.*'

Then to Stephen:

'*I'm the fake slut from yesterday.*'

And lastly Darius:

'*I'm trans.*'

Then I just…leave it to burn without me. I light the match and escape from the scene while my social life descends into Dante's seventh level of infernal Hell. I think twice about blocking them, imagining some fantasy world where what I just said doesn't matter to savage teenage boys.

I block Stephen but leave the other two be. I don't even really know why, maybe I'm genuinely worried he's attracted to me or maybe he'll kill me for making him feel that way. He will never be able to live it down that the subject of his lust is one of his closest friends.

Anyway, that's my friend group totally eviscerated. I think that calls for breakfast.

Girly in Grey

When I enter the kitchen, Mum is sitting at the table. She's flicking through one of the leaflets a local supermarket has posted through our door earlier that morning. She has a mug of hot water, her usual tonic.

"Oh, finally awake are we?"

"I've been awake for a couple hours already, just lying upstairs relaxing." I want to explain the night I had and the strange nightmare, but a yawn cuts me off mid-sentence and I'm not desperate enough to rescue the point.

"Well are you remembering what we're doing today?"

Let's see…today…well it's all a bit lost in the whirlwind of the morning I've experienced but I know that she means talking to my brothers.

"The video call! What do I wear?"

"Well it's not a formal event but we don't want to do things by half. So maybe we can dress you like I would have if you were Molly while all three of you were running around here."

"Sounds a bit odd."

"Hon, you wore barbie socks and underwear to the doctor's. I don't think you're above being my little girl today. Being their little sister. It might make it easier to take."

"How childish are we talking? I can't dress like a baby."

Mum spits her water over the magazine, clearly amused by my comment. She takes a minute to compose herself then explains.

"No, we can't and we won't do that! I mean a cute pastel outfit and I'll put your wig into pigtails like you promised I could. Something that leaves no doubt, we don't want them to take it as a joke."

"Oh right, that makes more sense. But will they not see that as going too far?"

"Yeah, I suppose they will. OK, I'm still putting your hair up but we'll tone it down a bit."

"That's probably easier for them to take. I don't want to go too far with them right away.

"They'll be fine with it honey. Family have no choice but to love and support each other. They might find it weird, but they have time to accept it before they come back next month." Mum ruffles my hair, not my wig yet, and then lets me grab my cereal and retreat upstairs. I am in the middle of a video!

Weekends are a great time for a bath, so I reward my courage and no-effs-given attitude with a luxurious one. I realise I can actually practise my voice in there, so long as I close my mouth when the soap is on my face or spilling down from my hair.

"Hiii you two!"

I think that would be a very cutesy and friendly greeting for Matt and Kyle when they meet their little sister for the first time. It's my usual greeting when we speak (not that often with all of their university stuff going on) but in a higher and happier pitch and elongating the vowel. Not a radical change as it's still the same words. I don't want them thinking that I've changed too much. Yet I think that is inevitable.

I know that I must have been in there near enough an hour, but the water is just so soothing for both body and spirit. I spend the last ten minutes trying to sing along to my playlist in my adjusted voice but the high keys are too much for me and my voice breaks. I'll get there one day, it's a process.

I wrap the towel around my smooth-again frame and feel the new familiar sensation of my skin stinging. A few drops of blood from fresh razor nicks can be seen on the yellow towel, but they're nothing to cry about. All they need is a little oily moisturiser and they'll mostly disappear. If every little cut needed a plaster, I'd be more paper and adhesive than person. I suppose this is just part of the new way of life.

I return to my room and start brainstorming for an ideal outfit. This is my first real look at what Courtney has donated, unaware of who the recipient is. I know that all of my underwear is mine, nobody should ever give used lingerie away. Yet I keep the towel wrapped around me — it's so uncomfortable when I am not completely dry before dressing.

Hanging up in my wardrobe are some skirts of all different materials but none longer than knee-length. Clearly, Courtney and I have quite similar taste. Shame she will likely never want to hang out with a freak like me. Oh well.

I opt for denim, it's very easy to pair with well, anything. A denim mini skirt with flares down the sides is the lucky winner. It sort of reminds me of the skirt I was caught in just six days ago. The flares are new though, I'm just really intrigued for how they will feel and look on me. The skirt is more of a washed grey than the blue I wore before, but a cute skirt is a cute skirt. I take it off its hanger and lay it on my bed.

A T-shirt is the obvious choice for pairing, and I find the perfect one in less than a minute. It features an American flag graffiti-like design sprayed on a grey wall, just a shade or two lighter than the skirt. The red and blue really stand out along with a black slogan '*Obey*'. That's almost dystopian, but it also looks great. I'm a little surprised that I haven't opted straight for the prettiest, preppiest or pinkest thing available but cold air on my near-nude body means the outfit has been chosen.

Today's lingerie has to be white, or it will show through the thin cotton of the T-shirt. Thankfully, a lot of my new underwear is exactly that so no problem there at all!

Compared to yesterday's multi-piece and many button bonanza of an outfit, today's is so straightforward. It has a total of one button (on the skirt) and the bra to fasten, the rest is just throw-on material. I do just that with the T-shirt and tuck the tail into the skirt but something is missing…oh yeah, my breasts.

It's moments like this where I feel more like a product than a person. Adding all these little extras to cover natural imperfections but my brain loves them. Feeling my bare legs just touching each other is not new but it does feel like I'm a tad underdressed. Underdressed for what? I'm not going anywhere! I still insert the breast forms, if anything to prepare for a future where weight on my chest will hopefully be permanent.

I look at myself in the full-length mirror in Mum's room — the first time since coming out that I've truly styled myself. I obviously still need to do make-up and sort the wig — a new daily routine — but this is a strong start. A cosy feeling builds inside me that one day, I can maybe be happy with my appearance every day and not just in fleeting instants like this.

Fri END ship

I sit in front of my now very familiar make-up setup. My phone camera practically knows a second function as a mirror now — it automatically opens on the right zoom and light settings for me to begin glamming myself up a little. This is the part of my appearance that is non-negotiable.

Even after just six days, make-up feels so second nature that I feel naked without it. It may sting my eyes when I keep it on for too long but that's not too huge an expense. No one should see Molly without her make-up, not even me. I'm a sight for sore eyes before any glitter makes contact with my face but with enough perseverance and 'painting', I can almost start to look cute and pretty.

The go-to pink shades won't work today, not with the grunge-y outfit I'm wearing. The pink shining on top of all the muted, laid-back grey would be like putting neon signs in place of the beacon on a lighthouse. It would be bright, sure, but it wouldn't be of much use. I could go for red eyeshadow, but it can appear like a health condition and again, maybe too bright for today's clothes. Silver eye make-up is the obvious choice. It's enough to draw attention without being over-the-top. I wonder if this is how I'm going to view getting ready every day now.

You all know the routine by now and it makes no sense to change anything up for the usual. As I spread the blotches of foundation with my bronzer brush, I could once more see the face of a pretty girl forming on my phone screen. I never grow tired of the fascination in the transformation. Even halfway through the ritual of powders and creams, the appearance changes drastically.

With the base set, I can now add the silver glitter to my eyelids and apply yet another 3 coats of mascara. Three coats always just feels right. One or two never feels sufficient, four feels excessive. I wonder how much of the mascara actually washes off and if enough make-up can permanently make my eyelashes black without adding more. I would think that it's a bit more complicated than that.

One part of today's look is noticeable on-purpose. I want my lips to stand out today but I'm not really sure why. I won't be kissing anyone, but dark, gothic lips will look way better with a cute grey ensemble than with the usual feminine palette I rock with. I also don't think I've had dark lips before so a quiet day inside is the perfect chance to try something new. Besides, I'll want to use several different looks at school.

As I line my thin lips with dark red, I exaggerate the outline and make them appear a little fuller at first though I then chicken out. I am just not used to seeing my lips that shape and don't want anything I do to look stupid. I wipe it off, give my face another once-over with the bronzer to cover up any stains around my mouth and then apply the dark red (almost burgundy) to strictly just my lips and it looks a lot more natural — as weird as that sounds.

Just as I take the lid from the chair and close the tube of lipstick, I hear a knock at the door. Not to worry, Mum will answer that. I'm so in the zone of my daily routine that I fail to notice the sound of running water from the bathroom. Mum must be in the shower. Ah well, not to worry. I'll just go answer it instead. It's a weekend so it's probably just the postman or maybe the window cleaner. Either way, not the end of the world if someone sees me like this. Unless it's a certain someone.

I open my bedroom door and make my way downstairs barefoot. I plan on putting something on my feet but I need to answer this first. Only as I look through the obscured glass window on the door can I see who it is. My heart drops down a few floors inside my body and I know once more that the music will have to be faced.

I close my eyes and open the door. To tell you the truth, I don't know what his face initially shows. I have no idea what his automatic expression is when he first sees one of his best friends in full make-up and skimpy clothes. Even worse, my wig isn't even on my head yet as that comes after make-up in my daily doll-up routine. If I do it the other way around, I could miss parts of my face with the make-up or even end up staining the wig. Not worth the hassle in any case. Though it maybe would save some face here. I could maybe pass as a cousin with long hair. Without that, it's obvious what's going on. He can see it all in front of him.

"What the f*** are you wearing?"

Shawn is holding a ball under his arm. He's wearing a hoodie and jogging bottoms, likely with a football shirt underneath. Everything about him suggests that he too is part of the 5-a-side group today. He came along with me and the guys before and they all seemed to get on with him. He has always been a much better player than me but so was everyone else when it came to football. I guarantee you I do better make-up than any of them though!

"S-sorry. I should've told you before. I'm trans. The guys will know by now."

"You're a girl?! Nah, come on! I know we like a joke, but this is too far. Look at the state of you."

Ouch.

"It's true."

"Nah, have you like lost a bet to them or something? So now you need to go to football like that?"

How dense can he be? He's right that this is way too much effort for a joke, but then can't accept that it must mean it's not a joke! A small part of me has an awful idea of going, the rest of me conflicts it and somehow, common sense prevails.

"I won't be going anywhere near football today. Maybe never again. I'm a girl now."

He stands there, mouth agape. I can see a hint of anger in his eyes as his open mouth closes.

"I don't know what the f*** you think you are doing but I'm not going to be friends with a little crossdressing fag. If you think you can just be a girl now and we'll all just accept that, you've f****d up. I'll be telling everyone about this, you freak."

I don't know if it's just that I am resigned to the ill fate that awaits me when everyone finally does see, but I actually respond with the perfect answer to his pointless threat.

"Well I can go sort my hair and set my make-up for you to get a nice photo to show everyone, then. It doesn't change anything. So f*** off."

I slam the door in his face with the adrenaline pulsating through my entire body and my fingers and hands continue to shake as I hastily lock the door behind me and in front of him. Well, that will be the last time he visits, I suppose. He boots the door and storms off, his loud, parting shout a mix of threat and false bravado.

"Faggot! I'll batter you!"

What could he possibly do? What power does he have to tell me who I can and can't be? What I can and can't wear and what I can call myself? If he wants to be violent, I can accept that. I don't want to fight anyone, but I won't let anyone deny me the right to be myself. I've already ended one male life. I don't mind defending myself against another.

My deranged babbling on the stairs is interrupted by Mum. She comes out of the bathroom with a towel wrapped around her and asks a simple question of concern.

"Did you slam the door?"

I take a deep breath and try my best to explain the situation.

"Shawn was at the door. I don't think you need to worry about me seeing him any more."

No tears — I think I've dried up over the past week. So emotionally cold and deadpan now that I feel almost unbreakable. The look of heartache on Mum's face is telling.

"Go sort your hair, honey. Then you can tell me what happened."

Ignoring Messages

On my way back upstairs, I try to gauge whether Mum is angry or not. I know she won't be once I tell her what happened but it's always awkward when someone doesn't know the full situation and tries to fill in their own blanks. I cover my hair with a bald cap and follow this with the wig, secretly longing for the day when my own hair will be at this lovely length. Don't get me wrong, I love the wig. It's beautiful. I would love to just be able to show off my own natural locks though. It will be a while until then, my hair isn't even near my shoulders yet.

The cap is the main problem: it's just a little too tight. There's a bit of pain when it first snaps on to my head but by the time I've put the wig itself on over it, I can't really feel any pain. Part of me wishes that Shawn waited just five more minutes before coming to see what has become of his friend. He might have had a different outlook if he saw the whole picture. Or like I said before, he might not have known it was me.

I brush my hair out nice and straight in my hand. The expensive, top-quality wig stays straight for longer than cheap substitutes. I line it up correctly on my head and lower it down. It doesn't need adjusted at the straps, since I used it yesterday and it shouldn't need tightened or loosened possibly ever again.

I finish this interrupted get-ready session with the setting spray. I would have usually spritzed this before but for the unexpected argument. Another spritz, this time of perfume, and I'm all set. I head through to see Mum and explain what went on.

"Cute outfit. So what happened at the door?"

A deep breath or two as I perch myself at the bottom of Mum's bed while she sorts through her washing.

"It was Shawn. He came to get me for 5s."

Mum's worried look appeared once more.

214

"Oh. So you answered the door to him?"

"I thought you were downstairs at first, so I ignored it. But I heard you were in the shower, so I just went and answered it. Thought it would be the window cleaner or the postie."

"He didn't hurt you, did he?" She's almost on the verge of tears — she always liked Shawn.

"Nothing physical, but I won't be seeing him again. He called me a fag and said he's going to tell everyone today."

"So they'll all know? How many usually go? All from your school?"

We're both guilty of this when we are worried, we bombard each other with questions before even allowing the other to even process the first one properly.

"I'm not worried about any of that. I told the guys this morning so they can now say and do whatever they want. It doesn't change how I feel."

"Are you going to be OK at school? What if they try to hurt you?"

"I'll deal with them. Please, don't worry."

I don't want to sound like Shawn but I'm also not afraid to fight back. Usually, it wouldn't be worth it. Now, every single fight would be justified. I'll know exactly why I'm fighting.

"Maybe we need to look at those self-defence courses. We'll look at different things like that tomorrow along with trying to find you some new clubs and activities to try."

"Sounds like a good idea. It certainly can't hurt. Well, can't hurt *me* anyway."

Despite my attempts at cheering her up, the fear won't leave Mum's face. She's always been a bit of a hypochondriac when it comes to her children. Too much Facebook news will do that to you. And to be fair, I can't really mock her for overreacting. It's sometimes my very nature to struggle emotionally. Ollie or Molly, my ASD persists.

Knowing that staying on this bleak topic won't help either of us, I ask a simple derailing question.

"What time are we calling the boys?"

"They're going to call us in a few hours, group call. I'll let you know once they call so keep an eye on your phone and your ears open."

"Will do!"

I leave the room with a cheery smile in spite of the recent happenings and occupy myself with a little more training. For today's exercise, I'm going to do some heel training combined with voice and mannerism practice.

I take flat, nude sandals with a black toe strap from my wardrobe of (still) mystery clothing as they'll be what I put on later. Socks would be another option but the sandals look cuter and it's a new thing to try. They won't be much use for high-heel training though so I also take a plain black pair of court heels as they don't appear to be anything special. I wouldn't dream of using my fancy pink heels for training the same way top basketball stars wouldn't use their $15,000 sneakers for a pickup game or daily practice. You save the best kit for the big occasion. Or for when there's someone to impress.

Unlike NBA superstars, I won't be doing anything even slightly athletic in my heels. I would maybe stretch to trying dancing but even being transgender doesn't change someone that drastically. I'm likely still as flexible as a steel plate with the turning circle of a cross-channel ferry. For now, I just need to focus on not falling on my backside. Or frontside. Or any side.

At the same time, much like the simple multitasking of walking and chewing gum, I'm saying simple sentences in my girl voice. I branch out to try some of my common school phrases too, but certain words are still so hard to keep the girly sound on. In particular, French is going to be tough to feminise just due to my already adapted, deep-voiced accent which I've been using and honing for years. I try some social phrases too, not that I'll need them the way my social life is heading. Simple greetings, 'how are you' and most importantly, a laugh. The laugh is critical — I laugh a *lot*. Natural for such a funny femme like me, I suppose.

I don't just do this for three hours. I'm not *that* crazy. It's better to practise in stints, particularly the walking. The longest I need to walk for in a school day is about five minutes. As long as I can last ten minutes in heels and endure the pain, there should never be a situation where the heels win the battle against my feet. I eventually want to reach the point where it won't hurt at all. This takes a long time — shockingly.

Throughout all of my practice, I do my best to avoid looking at my phone. Much like avoiding a spoiler by refraining from logging into social media, I'd rather not know what is happening in my miniscule friend circles. You know those nature documentaries? The kind where they show the vicious predator basking in the searing sun before cutting to the innocent, unsuspecting prey? You know a chase scene is next and you also know not to place much hope in the chances of the smaller, more vulnerable creature escaping. That is my friend groups now. I'm the itty-bitty field mouse and they are venomous, bloodthirsty snakes.

However, I finally sneak into the lair of the predator. I tap into Messenger. I don't even know why I'm doing this. The notifications still have the eerie '9+' beside them and a quick glance makes me aware of at least seven different people messaging me. Each of the three lads, the football group, Matthew, Kyle, Shawn and finally (and most concerning of all), the school leadership group. What could they possibly want to know? Have they been told already?

OK, I need to explain. I'm sort of the 'deputy head boy' at the school. More accurately, Ollie *was* the deputy head boy. It basically meant that his opinions on what the school should do carried weight. Charity initiatives, prefect duties, school events, new rule suggestions and gauging the unrest of the students — it all fell on the shoulders of ten unlucky students who were all naïve enough to sign up. There's a head boy and girl, there was a deputy of each too before Ollie's timely passing and then two 'captains' for each of the three houses of the school. Captains and houses — this isn't Quidditch. Just another poor attempt at trying to make school relatable and 'hip' in terms of pop culture.

Thankfully, the leadership team are only asking which house is on prefect duty this week. I check and it's not us. Prefect duty isn't bad but it isn't great either. That phrase could describe school overall, to be honest. How will they cope with the news that their deputy head boy was only an enigma? Merely a shell for my true self to hide in. I guess we await that whole show on Monday.

Next, why are Matthew and Kyle messaging? Disappointingly, the answer is just a reminder. Both brothers in different ways letting me know that they'll be calling in around five p.m. — just before they have dinner most likely. They are not living together; they actually are at separate universities though they are at most just an hour away from each other even in heavy traffic. The wonders of group calling and the modern miracles of technology mean three people can call from three different places all at once. Remarkable *eye roll*.

I catch sight of the clock in the top corner of my screen, and it says 16:51. Nine minutes until the moment of truth. I change into my sandals and head through to Mum's room.

Little Sister

"Having fun with all the training, Molly?" Mum's opening gambit as I return to her room. My steps are taken very gingerly — the consequence of three hours in stiletto heels. "I could hear your real voice breaking out from that deep ruse you have at the moment. A lovely voice, too. Maybe we'll get you singing lessons."

"Hmm maybe." Martial arts/self-defence class, singing lessons, dancing — how busy is my after-school life going to be? I think it's really cute that Mum fights my corner and believes — *truly believes* — that her little girl can do anything. Singing has always been just a hobby and I've never been too interested in proper fighting, but Molly will give everything a go. Especially if it's for protection.

"Anyways, the boys are calling soon. I saw messages on my phone."

"Yeah, I saw them too. Are we doing it from here or downstairs?"

"Hmm… I think for big news such as what we have, the living room is best."

For a moment, I remember how these announcements usually go. Myself and my brothers all summoned to the living room usually to hear about a relative's death or some other depressing news. Hopefully, my news isn't quite so sad for Matt and Kyle.

With that, I hesitantly, slowly and oh so sheepishly hobble my way down the stairs behind Mum, who is carrying her tablet. We'll use that for the call.

"Heels in moderation from now on, I think!" Mum giggles, taking delight in my misfortune. Schadenfreude.

"I just need more practice. I'll get used to this."

"Well, you still have to be careful. If you keep your heels on for too long and too often, your heels and feet can actually get stuck like that. You'd only ever be able to wear heels."

"Oh, that sounds like hell!"

"Being a lady isn't all rainbows, Mols. So it's good to practise but don't go too far. No point in hurting yourself."

And just as Mum's lecture threatens to drag on any further and begin dismantling other methods to my practising madness, the ringing starts from her tablet. Once again, time to face the music. Time to come out of hiding, once more.

"OK, I'll start the call and set up your news. Then you just be yourself. Your real self."

Too nervous for words, I nod and even muster a quick thumbs up. Mum clicks answer and I escape to the kitchen to overhear the conversation and listen for a cue of sorts.

"Hello, boys!"

"Hey."

"Hi Mum!"

"How are you both?"

"Good, yeah."

"Bit stressed with uni work but nothing new!"

"That's good. It will be worth it when you make lots of money for your mother!"

I can hear the laughter of all 3 of the closest people in my life. It's always nice to hear from my brothers but am I still going to feel that way once they hear from their newly uncovered sister?

A few minutes of casual chatter about what they've all been up to is the followed by the question I dread.

"So, where's Ollie?"

"Ah he's probably just pausing his game or something. Might even be doing homework!"

More laughter. Laughter which I am about to decimate much like a wrecking ball crunches and tears at derelict walls of abandoned factories.

"Well I think I can hear… yep, just coming now. Getting a drink."

Nice cover, but I also can't help but pick up on the lack of pronouns. Not wanting to say 'her' because that will scare the boys but also rejecting use of 'him' to protect my feelings. They also wouldn't work, Mum never uses 'they'.

I take a deep breath and close my eyes as I take the short yet perilous walk from one room to the next. Judgment day has arrived. Every day is judgment day.

"Here, the boys are on it. Come sit down and say hi."

I still haven't opened my eyes yet. I know the layout of the room to every little detail so can easily position myself on the couch beside Mum without breaking anything or hurting myself. Usually, the issue with coming out has been that my heart drops deep down below its recommended slot. This time however, I can feel my pulse so evidently in my throat. As I take a seat on the couch, I know I have entered the tablet's view. I open my eyes to see four staring back through the screen. No laughter, just bemusement.

"Hi... g-guys. H-how are y-y-ou?"

Whew, I manage to get one simple sentence out in my own voice! It hasn't really helped Matt or Kyle though. I could read each expression on each face for 1000 straight days and be no closer to accurately depicting what they are feeling right now.

"Hey, Ollie?"

"You're looking... different?"

"Y-yeah. So I k-kind of decided that I want to be a... girl now. From now on."

The faces aren't really giving much away yet. Neither of them laugh — they clearly know when a joke is a joke and when it's too much effort to be one.

"R-right. I see. Well, that's obviously your decision. And f*** what anyone else thinks about that. It's your life, be who you want and do what you want."

Mum interrupts Kyle's comforting advice to scold him for his foul language but his point still hits exactly where he wants it to. Matt also adds to this.

"Yeah, we'll love you no matter what Ollie. Oh, wait. That won't be your name now surely."

"It's not." I wipe a tear from my eye then decide to make a game out of this. "Any ideas what I'm going to be called now?"

This is so worth it for the hilarious antics which come as a result. For two brothers, they obviously think the exact same thing to begin with.

"You've probably kept the 'O' at the start. I'll guess Olivia."

221

"Ah bast***! I was going to say that!" Matt is clearly annoyed by Kyle's faster guess. "I guess I'll say Orla then. It's like the second most common 'O' name I can think of unless you've gone for something mental."

"Language, Matthew!" Mum isn't fully on the screen any more. Nevertheless, she polices our conversation.

"Yeah. I mean is it like Oceana or something?" Kyle asks

"What? You mean like all the islands and that?"

I can't let that stand, being a geography student.

"That's Oceania!" I correct him, doing my best not to disrupt the flow of my guessing game entirely by correcting him. "And you guys, I have an 'O' in my name but it's the second letter." I feel like Jigsaw, minus all the murder weapons or psychotic setups. Maybe more like The Riddler.

"The second letter? It could be anything. There's a Corrie in my journalism classes so I'll guess that."

Kyle now has the joy of guessing second. "I was never going to say Corrie. Hmm… I'll say you're now a Josie."

"Nope. Need another clue?" I'm so smug right now. I definitely suit the role of a quizmaster.

"Yeah, go on then."

"OK."

"Right, think about this. The whole of my old name is *in* my new name."

"I've got it! You're Holly!"

I take a sharp breath through my teeth to indicate just how close Matt was to getting it just there.

"Surely you haven't called yourself Dolly. That's such a stripper name."

"Kyle Clarke, I do not want to hear that!" Mum jokingly reprimands one of the boys again. "My daughter has young, innocent ears!"

"Guys, it's Molly. My name is now Molly."

"Ohhh!"

"If you'd have just said that it was the street name of a drug, I would have got that! Not that I've taken any, of course. But a fair few folks here do."

Now we are all laughing. The impromptu icebreaker I accidentally stumbled into setting up has actually eased a lot of the tension surrounding what would have otherwise been a hostile situation.

I would go more into the conversation but there isn't actually much more to be said about it. I hate being the centre of attention so talking about anything else and just pretending nothing has changed almost makes it feel as though nothing has. It's only by looking at my own picture on the screen do I feel wildly different than before. When I'm not focusing on my appearance, I'm still just me. I'm the same sibling I have always been to them.

We all chat for several hours about really any old rubbish. One of the closing remarks brings the conversation back around to me.

"So you'll both be back next month, yeah?"

Both boys confirm at pretty much the same time. Matt adds a very good point to round it all off.

"Yep, we'll be back for Christmas. I'll have to ask the Missus what to get you though, 'cause I have no idea what girls like!"

Matt is married, but always called Leah his Missus even before their big day. The last time I wore the big suit. Gross. Anyways, it's quite cute, even if I've never properly met Leah. I obviously saw her at the wedding, but I barely *saw* her. If that makes any sense. I wouldn't know a single thing about her. At least she never met Ollie either. It's always easier to meet someone for the first time when they haven't met the 'you' you were before.

And just like that, we end the call with a heartfelt goodbye and a 'see you next month.'

The rest of this weekend passes with no real special events. On Sunday, there's a bit of organisation of my school bag and making sure that I have all of my uniform laid out and ready to finally wear. I am still deciding over which shoes will work best and whether to start off with a pinafore or a skirt. I probably won't be able to choose until Monday morning, if I even can by then.

All my books say 'Ollie Clarke' but there is nothing a little pen can't fix. Rather than simply edit what is written there, I simply draw three lines through the name of the deceased with a thick, black marker. I then take a simple black ballpoint pen and delicately write out 'Molly Katherine Clarke.' I have 6 different jotters but it's a job worth doing right. It feels like one of the final scraps of evidence is being erased. One less line to trace back and find the shadow of my past. He's gone. Every little step, though seemingly insignificant, adds up to create the whole effect of my newfound persona. The truest reflection of myself on the world. Molly.

I continue to ignore my Facebook messages. Their hate will fall on deaf ears and blind eyes. But no one's eyes will be blind to me come Monday. No, no. Come Monday morning, no one will be able to ignore Molly Katherine Clarke as she is unveiled to the waiting public. You can view it as a princess' coronation or as a witch being burned at the stake. Either way, it's bound to be eventful.

Like Any Other Girl

Monday morning arrives, unencumbered by nightmares or strange dreams from the night before. The darkness of sleep gives way to the equally visually unimpressive beige walls of my bedroom. I check the time on my phone and find that I've beaten my alarm by ten minutes. I can easily lie here for those ten minutes and bask in the glory of my victory but instead, I take the perfect opportunity for a head start and sneak into the shower ahead of my mum's usual slot. I won't need too long anyway. My body is pretty much completely shaved, and the stray hairs won't matter under my tights. Do other girls take shortcuts like this?

The sweet smells of my soaps waft pleasantly under my nose on the steamy vapours following my quick shower. I turn the water off and wrap the two towels in the appropriate places. No more time for dress rehearsals and playing dolls with my own body. Everyone is going to see exactly who and what Molly is and what has happened to Ollie. Confession time, the jig is up, and a million other witty one-liners from police dramas. I check the weather from my bedroom window to see that the rain is back. It's not remarkably heavy but the shades of grey and black in the sky suggest that it's only going to worsen throughout the day. Hopefully not a sign of what today will be like but the sky looks almost hopeless. If I must be all the hope that today carries, then challenge accepted.

On rainy days, trousers have always been a smart choice. I don't wear trousers even if he did. I won't be wanting to spend much time outside, so it won't matter if my tights aren't enough to keep the cold out. I wonder where I will end up in the intervals today. I never had any friends — that much will likely be confirmed today. Mentally prepared for a social disaster, let's get ready for my school debut!

Today's underwear really doesn't matter. If it does, something has gone horribly wrong. No P.E. and no other reason to show it. Call it stupid or call it brave but I opt for bright red/orange bra and panties. The colour sparks that final boost of confidence within me. If any part of me is starting to feel hesitant, the fiery tones of my lingerie assure me that I'm going to set this day ablaze and torch through whatever is thrown my way. It almost looks like wrestling gear as well which is even more apt for a fight like today.

I choose a thicker pair of tights to hide any of those pesky growing hairs and razor bumps. The fleece lining feels nowhere near as luxurious as pure nylon massaging my legs but sometimes, you just have to be sensible. At least fleece doesn't tear nearly as easily as nylon so you can be a little rougher about forcing them into the right place.

The three items before this one feel like wallpaper but now is just the second time wearing a blouse. I'm not the best at buttoning this thing up yet. The buttons being on the other side seems like such a trivial change and yet, I still go for the incorrect side more than once. As I reach the second button from the top, Mum knocks on my bedroom door.

"Are you decent?"

"Ish." That's the best I could come up with to explain but Mum takes her chances and opens the door.

"Ah, halfway dressed. Not bad, not bad. I hope you're going to button that blouse up all the way though!"

"Of course! I'm not a slut."

"Good girl. Remember to put your boobs on though."

"Oh yeah! Nearly forgot them!"

"Hopefully not too big or small for the bras. They aren't always the same size across different shops and brands."

I take the chance to put the breast forms inside the cups before continuing to button the blouse to the top as Mum leaves me to get on with it and goes in the shower. The chill on my chest will never quite feel right from the first minute but as my body heats the forms up. Something, something… residual heat something science. I don't exactly know but that's my best guess.

It's only as I lift the hanger holding my school skirt that I realise I haven't eaten. I usually eat before getting dressed but I guess today is just unusual. That or I have a new normal routine now. Not one to drop a job halfway through, I remove my skirt from the hanger and pull the gold zip down. I wiggle my way into it which is entirely unnecessary thanks to the zip. However, it just feels right. I liken myself to one of the many girls in my YouTube suggestions who squeeze into skin-tight dresses by slinking their rear ends and shaking their hips. I'm simply exaggerating to feel more feminine in my movements and adjusting my voice as I dress.

'Zzzzzip' and the skirt is on. Now, where's my school tie? I hope it hasn't been thrown out with all my old clothes. After a minute of panic searching for a small yellow piece of fabric, I decide to throw my jumper on instead and worry about the tie a little later. My school jumper is plain black but has little feminine touches which differentiate it from a boring old 'boys' jumper.

The material is softer and there's a little vertical linear pattern stitched throughout. To add to the cuteness, there's a white trim below the neckline, creating a clear distinction between the girls' jumpers and the boys'. I remember when Dean Abbott came in with his sister's jumper on one day back in third year. Man, he got some serious stick for that. Yet that's nothing compared to what I'm doing and that's all I can think about as the jumper goes over my head and my arms slip through the sleeves. Now dressed, I can grab a quick breakfast. I check the time and I still have well over an hour before we need to leave the house. I don't have the wig or the make-up on yet but why would I do that before eating? Again, it just doesn't make sense.

With the extra time and a little paranoia over spilling milk on my uniform, I opt for toast instead. I sit at the kitchen table and tuck into my jammy breakfast, with a glass of fruit juice to make it two of my loose five a day. I scroll through Facebook as usual and even have a look at my messages, to see a concerning one.

'If I see Olly im gonna punch the gay out of him'

It has three 'thumbs-up' reactions. Breakfast threatens to re-emerge, but I hold it down. What can he honestly do? I don't even talk to him; he's just one of the wider football group. Still, it would be wise to tell Mum. Do I want to make this morning worse for her? Nah, I bet it's all just empty threats. I don't even bother to look at who has reacted. It's only going to disrupt me doing my make-up and fixing my hair. I pop my dishes in the sink and head up to start my favourite ritual.

The dilemma that I am faced with is that I could go all out and be very dramatic to try to impress people. Or I can go for a more natural appearance and hope that it looks nice enough. The latter is a safer bet, so I'll go natural, at least for the first few days.

You know the words by now. Primer, foundation, bronzer and blusher. The base of my strong, feminine face. The next issue is picking a colour for the eyeshadow. My lipstick is going to be a soft pink — I know that much already. I choose a sparkly brown which isn't too noticeable and then move on to mascara. Eyeliner isn't the most appropriate for school and I am still a learner.

I delay the lipstick a little longer so I can go and clean my teeth, using the chairback as spillage protection just as I did before. Enjoying the clean feel of my whole body, I start sorting my hair once I'm back in my own room. My own hair is almost completely dry so it's a quick once-over with the towel and then onto the bald cap. That is of course followed by the gorgeous brown wig. In front of my own eyes and displayed on my phone screen, a brunette school girl is brought to life. One coat, two coats, three coats of lipstick and one of lip gloss — it's done. I almost want to sign my own work with my name like Monet or Picasso but that would look really odd on my face. Time to hear a second opinion.

I knock on Mum's door in a reverse of the conversation we had just an hour ago.

"Are you decent?" I ask and almost make it to the end of the question without giggling at the clear parody I am attempting. Mum knows exactly what I'm doing so responds just as I did.

"Ish." She sounds like she too is holding some laughter back. I walk in to see her brushing her hair out though she is fully dressed. She turns to face me and gushes.

"Oh my! Molly, you look fantastic! This is so meant to be, my daughter!"

"Muuum!" I retort in total embarrassment at my blushing. I then remember the other reason to be through here. "Oh yeah, where is my tie?"

"I kept it through here while I threw everything else out so it wouldn't go with it. Here." She stands up and takes the tie from one of the cubby holes in the middle of one side of her wardrobe which hides behind the sliding mirror door I am checking myself out in. "I'll do it for you. Do you want your hair up?"

"Hmm not today, thanks. It's going to rain so my hood will be up anyways." I graciously accept her offer and stand in front of her as she ties my yellow tie. I wait until she has finished and then tuck it under my jumper. One last look in the mirror and everything looks right.

"OK, shoes, bag and coat and I'll be ready."

"Not bad timing either, we've got ten or so minutes before we need to leave."

Mum's blind optimism as to how early I am ready is almost a curse. Her phone rings from an unknown number but she picks up. She never receives calls this early so this must be something other than a hoax call. She puts it on speaker.

"Hello there, is this Kat? O-um-Molly's Mum?"

"Yes, it is. Molly is here with me? Who is speaking?"

"Oh sorry, it's Ms Waverley. The headteacher."

"Ah yes, how can I help you?"

"Well, we would like Molly to be at the morning assembly today, front and centre! So if possible, could she make her way down to school a little earlier so we can run through a quick plan?"

"Oh, we can do that. It's good that she loves her make-up so much, she's basically ready to go now!"

I can hear a warmth to Ms Waverley's tone as she responds to Mum. "Aw that's fantastic. You must be so proud. Anyways, can she be here in the next fifteen minutes. I know it's only quarter past eight now but if she gets here around half past, we have plenty of time to decide what is best to say. She'll also avoid the crowd in the crush."

"No worries at all, Ms Waverley. I'll have Molly with you in fifteen minutes at most." She turns her head towards me and says, "Molly, you best get your shoes and coat on and grab your bag."

"I'm on it!" I cheerily comply.

Now, which shoes to wear? It's raining, it's dark and it's cold so… ah! These will be perfect! Black ankle boots with a two-inch heel on them. Enough to make a satisfying click but nowhere near drastic enough to cause any damage. I'm just glad I'm not all that tall. Boys adding two

229

inches to their height would start looking like goliaths. Good thing I'm not a boy. My school coat is the one real pop of colour in my outfit. Instead of my own black coat, I needed something that would stand out a little. Or a lot, judging by my choice.

It's odd because I never saw this coat on Courtney at all. It's baby pink and very thick, with a fur trim on the hood as most feminine coats have. It zips and buttons up — because one method of fastening the coat just isn't enough. I do a final check of my bag to make sure I have packed everything that I need. I add my phone, my purse and my soft pink lipstick to the bag then close it. The moment has arrived. I'm going to school again for the very first time.

Mum suggests taking a photo of me but we really don't have time for it this morning. That and the rain will ruin the picture. She stands me up in the kitchen as she has before and snaps a quick few on her phone then hurries me on out the front door. She locks the door and follows behind. I'm hyping myself up in my head as I make the short walk out to the car. Each click of my heels seems to synchronise with my all-too evident heartbeat. I try to tell myself not to be nervous but it's never that easy. I'd be surprised if anything ever was…

Morning Announcement — Introducing...

I continue to try to amp myself up — trying to spark the last little drops of confidence necessary to finally reveal myself to the whole school. Mum makes casual conversation with me but we're both clearly having issues surrounding 'normality'. Little passing comments about the weather and such. She then asks me what subjects I have today in a bid to make it sound like nothing has changed and surprisingly, it kind of works.

"So what subjects today?"

"Hmm it's Monday so... double geography, German, French, Modern Studies and then double history to finish."

"Ah so it's a fun day for you!"

"Mum, every day is fun in sixth year. I literally chose all my favourite subjects since I don't need to worry about doing English or maths any more."

"Yeah, you never liked those."

"English was fine, the teacher was just a total... clown." Clown was not my first choice of a word to describe her but I'm trying to be nicer with my words. "And maths was just really tricky. I'm glad you sorted extra lessons with that tutor."

"It was worth it in the end, you finished with a B. Is that right?"

"Yep, really proud of that one."

"You're a clever girl, honey. I think you can honestly do anything you set your mind on. Even knock them all dead this morning."

The car pulls up outside of the school at the drop-off zone at precisely 8.27 a.m. so it's a quick goodbye and Mum's car reverses out of the zone while I walk around the silver fence which blocks cars from running over the students. I'm in half a mind to keep my head down and keep my identity totally concealed as if it was Friday once again. If only

I had those glasses with me today, I would so be wearing them. No, that attitude is wrong. I need to face the day with an unbreakable spirit and previously unseen resilience.

I'm actually very grateful that Ms Waverley suggested this early arrival. There is no one else in the crush hall yet, no one here quite so early. I still can't just hang around and wait — I have arrived early for a specific reason. But do I check in with Mrs Lidell or just carry on upstairs and meet with the school leaders? Surely they know to expect me so I choose to walk upstairs and greet Ms Waverley and Mr Dean as well as two people you haven't been introduced to yet.

My guidance teacher, Mr Francis has joined us and he is with the other deputy rector, Mrs Roland. I don't know much about the latter as we have rarely if ever even spoken to each other before. I suppose as Molly, the same thing could be applied to Mr Francis. However, he has helped Ollie out of many little tricky spots before his very timely passing. Bullies, schedule clashes, references for university, extra-curricular opportunities which would look great on a personal statement — he has been a lifesaver in the past.

"Ah, hello there, Molly! You'll know these two but I thought it would be a good idea to have more than just myself and Mr Dean on this one." Ms Waverley's pride clearly glows in her eyes — she may even be more excited about this announcement than I am.

"It's a pleasure to meet you, Molly. We'll go over the tiny fixes that I can make as your guidance teacher in due time. For now, we need to put a plan together for this assembly. Let's all pop through to behind the curtain in the hall and we'll brainstorm." Mr Francis with the sensible plans as ever.

The assembly hall is almost separate from the rest of the school. Located on the first floor, we walk through a set of double wooden doors which lead us down a left turn away from the modern languages and maths corridor. There's a discreet side door in this new corridor — this is where music store a lot of their equipment and it also allows access to behind the curtain of the large hall. It could easily be a sports hall but for its unbelievable height and the fact that both side walls are paned with glass. We don't bother going this way to reach the 'backstage area'; however, as no one is in the hall yet, so what exactly would be the point of hiding?

Instead, we enter the grand hall and walk up the two steep wooden steps to climb on stage. The hall itself has space for the entire school to attend the announcement — and this is clearly the plan this morning.

"OK so my thinking is to start with regular news and expected announcements like the UCAS applications and any upcoming trips or special events. That way, people don't click that something is unusual right away. Then, we're going to introduce you and you will walk out from behind the curtain and say a few words about yourself and your experience. Just explain who you are in your own words."

"I'll do my best." Ms Waverley certainly has ambition this morning. It may be a little much but it's better than being dull or apathetic towards it. I won't let her down.

"Do you want to practise a little speech just now?" Mr Francis' suggestion sounds like the logical approach.

I can't really paraphrase what I say to him. It's all a bit stammered and wavering. I'm doing my best to keep my voice at the right pitch which results in me choking on a few words. My emotions riding higher than Pegasus, Hercules' famous animal companion, isn't helping either. I can't seem to keep still, swaying my body around but also keeping my feet rooted to the floor exactly where they are.

"Just speak from the heart, Molly. Tell your story."

"OK, Mr Dean. I'm just in my own head about it is all."

Mr Francis suggests I remove my coat and put my bag backstage with it. I drop the cargo off on a side table where they normally keep props and microphones. I don't need a microphone… is what I'd like to say. When Mrs Roland offers me one, I don't turn it down. Everyone has to hear this and I don't back myself to be able to keep the volume up naturally.

"You look feminine, you sound like a girl. Are you a girl right now?"

Ms Waverley's question might throw me off but instead I stand back and hit it for six.

"Of course I am. I'm a girl, now and always."

"Good! That energy is exactly what you need!"

Was she just trying to aggravate me to psych me up more? It has certainly worked. Passion bursts out of every glitter covered pore. I'm ready to do this.

The clock at the back of the hall reads quarter to nine as I keep going over rough points in my head and reciting them aloud to test my voice.

"I'm Molly Clarke. I'm a girl." Repeating these two short sentences is key — they are the two most crucial ones that I need to broadcast to the masses.

"Sounding good, Molly. Are you ready to disappear backstage? We're all going to start filing the students up here and settling them for the big reveal. From the moment we give you your cue, it's all on you."

"I understand. What is my cue?"

"We're going to invite the new girl on stage."

"I see. Makes sense. That lets me explain the situation without prior knowledge." Yes, except of course that I'm fairly certain most of my year group will already know by now.

"OK, off you go. Feel free to write a speech if that's better for you."

I never tend to write speeches. Quite ironic considering you are currently reading my literal diary. It's full of speeches and inspirational advice and also plenty of utter nonsense. Much like my own brain, to be honest.

I close my eyes as I begin to hear the teachers leading students into the hall, row by row. I can hear all sorts of immature jokes, general chatter and the banging of chairs against the hard floor. I can't let anything break my stride this morning. This is the single hardest thing I will ever have to do. At least, I hope it is. I think back to that line from *The Simpsons Movie*. 'This is the worst day of my life,' says Bart. Homer follows up with, 'Worst day of your life so far,' in a bid to bring about optimism that sounds entirely backhanded.

My thinking about animated movies from over a decade ago (feel old yet?) is disrupted by more clutter and bustling from the assembly hall. The curtain doesn't block out nearly as much as I thought. It's been a while since I did violin, so I don't fully remember how being here feels. The last time I was up here was for the speeches for the head boy position — before I killed *him*. The kids were all very silent and respectful, but this is a whole different kettle of bananas. This could go any way imaginable. Deep breaths, just keep breathing. Smile, breathe, count to ten. Smile, breathe, count to ten.

Mr Francis joins me backstage, clearly worried about my feelings.

"Do you need me on stage with you?"

"No, I think this is something I need to do alone. It's better if you are down there making sure the kids behave." It feels odd giving orders to a teacher but he respects my wish and fulfils it.

"Knock them dead, kid."

I think he might be the best teacher I've ever had. Except for the odd P.E. lesson with him, he doesn't actually teach a subject. For guidance, he's top notch.

I hear Ms Waverley's booming voice welcome the students to the morning assembly. She opens with the usual reminder of respect and repeating the school motto. 'Effort in everything.' Almost nauseatingly clichéd.

She runs through some of the usual notices from the bulletin. There is a new one about some of the local residents complaining about the rubbish being dropped on the street outside the school. I'm sure you can imagine what the speech for this one was, almost word for word even. Then, I need to do everything to stop my heart from ascending into my mouth or falling into my groin. No, no. You stay put!

"So, the real reason I have gathered you all here today is not just to read some notices. We actually have a new student joining us. Now, I wouldn't usually put such pomp and circumstance into a new arrival. However, this one really hits home to me why I do this job. See, you all come to school to learn but you also come here to grow as people. This young lady's story is one of the most inspirational cases of personal development. I would like her to come and introduce herself to you all. I would like you all to show complete respect and appreciation for what she is doing."

Here I go. One step closer to the curtain, the nerves won't settle. Another, they won't sit still. Another, they jump and shake and wriggle around. Ah, this will just have to be the way it is. I close my eyes as I round the curtain and enter from the right of the stage. Complete silence. My heels are all that can be heard, and they echo as if someone is chiselling the cliff face away from Mount Everest with a pickaxe. How can it sound so distant yet be so close?

I naturally stand behind the podium despite not even having any written words. All of my cue cards are in my head. I'm improvising the retelling of my life story in front of the whole school. I don't clear my throat. The risk of my voice dropping from the ideal pitch is too high.

"H-hello everyone and thanks to Ms Waverley for such nice words. So, I've been introduced as a new student to Grafton High School, but this isn't exactly true."

Up on the stage, I honestly don't know what happens but I just start to walk away from the podium. The microphone is still in my hand; my eyes are fixed to the clock on the back wall. I allow them to wander just a little bit just by locking eyes with each of the teachers. I can't face seeing the students' reactions so vividly yet, especially when the juicy detail isn't out there.

"The truth is that I have been studying here for over five years. I have met quite a few of you and made new friends. Some of you have known me even longer than those five years — those of you from Pitton Primary School."

Confused murmurs threaten to flood the assembly hall but Ms Waverley silences them with a 'shhh!'

"You knew me, but you also didn't. You knew Ollie. You knew the deputy head boy. You knew a quiet, shy, reserved and very timid guy. Some of you liked him, more of you didn't."

"I know so much about Ollie because I *was* him."

More baffled whispering fills the hall and is silenced once more, alongside a warning that anyone caught talking will be given a punishment exercise or detention.

"I have been living with gender dysphoria for longer than I can remember. I have been living my life as someone that I never was. I've been lying to myself."

In the corner of my eye, I catch a boy being removed from the hall, laughing on his way out. He must be third year at most as his tie is black. The yellow ties are for senior pupils.

"Last weekend, I decided to stop living that lie. I started presenting myself as a girl and immediately felt a lot happier. I was absent all week as I worked on my appearance, my voice, my walk, and everything else you can think of. Changing everything about the me that you all knew in order to become someone entirely new."

I walk from one side of the hall to the other like a singer or a comedian would while they perform. But these are no jokes.

"As this new person, I'm no longer Ollie. My name is Molly. I'm now the girl I've always felt like on the inside. It's nice to finally show you all the real me."

A thought dawns on me. It's probably a good idea to show just how serious this all is with one simple action.

"Of course, Molly can't be the deputy head boy of the school for obvious reasons. I therefore will gladly give up this position. It doesn't fit me any more and I would argue that it never did."

I sense that I should probably wrap this up soon. I have only been speaking around three minutes but it's definitely enough.

"So long story short: I'm transgender. That may offend some of you. I honestly don't care. I would love it if you could all respect this choice that I've made, even if you can't all accept it. I'm Molly now."

I was so caught up in finishing the speech just there that I didn't even notice the heckling from several people. They were all sent out while I was speaking but again, I don't care. I hand control back to Ms Waverley who instructs me to stay on stage.

"Thank you, Molly. And thank you to the majority of you who politely allowed Molly to share her feelings with you. It takes a lot of guts to come up here in front of the whole school and announce such a remarkable development."

"She's a guy! She's got a cock!"

I know that voice. Did Pete just shout that? The laughter of several lads and even a few girls at the back of the hall confirms it. My heart is covered in iron chains and a thick veil of impenetrable haze. There's no way they are going to break me, not on this.

"You can stay behind for that vulgar comment, young man. And everyone who finds it funny is welcome to join him. We prioritise respect in this school for a reason. Anyone else in Molly's position would demand the same courtesy and common decency."

"Ugly!"

"Tranny!"

"Freakshow!"

"Fag!"

The hall erupts into chatter which forces Ms Waverley and Mr Dean to start shouting at the students.

"*Right!* Whoever is calling this girl such horrible names will be staying behind. The rest of you, you have classes to go to!"

I stand proud. I'm not broken, not even bruised. Their words bounce off me as if they were plastic bullets being fired at a Panzer tank. The hall empties save for the few younger kids who clearly regret what they've done and most of my peers.

I instead decide to femme it up even more. I attempt my most feminine walk down to beside Ms Waverley to ask her what I should do.

"Well, I think it's best you stay here. Most of those staying behind are from your year group so it might be good for them to meet you more closely. Don't worry, Mr Francis is going to join us."

"Indeed I am. That was fantastic, Molly. I had goosebumps. Have you ever thought about public speaking?"

"I do enjoy it, but I don't know. Glad I did a good job." Flattered and flustered, I accept the compliments.

Once the younger hecklers have been given their punishments, only me, the two teachers and the sixth-year kids remain. I notice that most of the football lads haven't stayed behind. Pete has even snuck out as well but there's no way he's going to avoid detention for what he shouted.

"OK, so now that we're not doing a big announcement, maybe you would like to ask Molly a few things?"

"Yeah, I would. What kind of joke is this?"

Ugh, Sabrina! She's so tightly wrapped that she may as well be a cheap penny sweet.

"It's no joke. I am now a girl."

"Uh-uh. No you aren't. You can't just throw a skirt and some make-up on and start calling yourself a girl."

"Pfft, whatever. Anyone else?"

"So is this because you like guys?"

"I honestly don't know, and I don't need to tell you either."

"Yeah, right." Harry rolls his eyes.

Mr Francis almost acts as a bouncer at this point.

"This conversation isn't really getting us anywhere if you won't show Molly basic respect. She'll be in the library this morning while you all process what she has said."

That is my cue to leave. Was it a disaster? Depends on who you ask and what you think the aims were. If the aim was to win a popularity contest, then it is a catastrophic failure. If the aim was to come out, it can't be seen as anything other than a rousing success.

"I want to assign someone to be with Molly in there this morning as well. Are there any volunteers?"

A few seconds of nobody raising a hand and then someone finally does. Slightly unexpectedly, too.

"I'll go with her. As the volunteer leader of the LBGTQ+ group in my local youth club, I think I'm best to do this. I also believe that no one else is going to fight me for this position either."

She is right there. No one seems even the slightest bit bothered about her handling of the situation.

"Ah, thank you, Chloe Maxwell. You and Molly can head up to the library now. I'll tell your teachers, girls."

So I leave the hall with Chloe following.

"Wait up!" Chloe shouts from just outside of the hall and so I do. Now what do I know about Chloe? Oh yeah, pretty much nothing. We are in one class together — history. For the most part, we have only ever spoken about the subject itself. I would never have pictured her taking an interest in any of this. She hadn't once told me before about her youth club volunteering or that and why would she? She didn't want to know Ollie and Ollie didn't feel like he needed to know her, so a mutual class discussion was about the limit.

Yet here she is, essentially my buddy for the morning at least.

"We have a lot to talk about. You have a lot to explain. But I'm different. I'll listen to you."

She makes eye contact with me and smiles. I smile back. In what has been a pretty dismal morning for my social life, this may be the one single silver lining to the ashy clouds in the sky. The rain patters off the glass windows on the wall opposite the storage room. Another one of these all-glass walls.

"We're off to the library. Let's go."

At Arm's Length

'I'll listen.' It's an odd thing for someone to specify. I liken it to a pilot saying, 'I'll fly the plane.' It's pretty much expected that everyone should at least acknowledge each other's basic rights to be themselves. Yet, Chloe's the only one who is showing even the slightest crumb of understanding and sympathy. I'll do my best not to get too caught up in the negativity of everyone else's reactions. The onslaught of name-calling this morning was almost depressingly expected. My own dreams last week confirmed as much and now, it's all my peers who appear to speaking that made-up language. Their false pretences of being even slightly agreeable on the surface have all but died this morning. I guess it's pretty much 'lone wolf Molly' going forward. I'm even cautious about how close I allow myself to grow towards Chloe. I've had to accept that if this is the life I want, the baggage that comes with a social life can't be checked in for the journey. I'll have to pick one up on the way, however I manage to accomplish that.

Anyway, Chloe and I walk up to the library. All of the main staircases run through the heart of the school, so you end up looping and spiralling around each floor to access the stairs for the next level. That is of course unless you go via either of the side staircases. They run through tight corridors and lie at the end of other tight corridors but they're a nice shortcut if you are at the end of a corridor for your next lesson. The sides of the staircases are split by a thick wooden rail and black metal pillars. The idea behind this is so everyone keeps left on the stairs to avoid causing a collision or delaying everyone reaching their next lesson. Chloe and I immediately break that rule.

See, I just don't feel comfortable around her right away. You will eventually fear the oven if you burn your hand every time you open it. If the same neighbour keeps watching you, you'll grow afraid of them. I am scared of any social interaction. Any occasion I choose to open my mouth could be an open invitation to have anything shoved down my throat before I have a chance to protest or say my piece. My eyes may be deceiving me or I could be overthinking things (perish the thought) but Chloe also appears to be concerned. She's likely still a little doubtful over the legitimacy of the speech I just gave in the assembly hall. Seems too far to ever be considered a ruse yet some people just don't have the same levels of trust. I know that my own trust has plummeted since I first saw those hurtful words on Messenger and since my long-time friend ended any hope of things being 'as they were'. A cycle of unfeeling is a vicious one.

We walk up the stairs side by side and at the same pace but about as far apart laterally as we possibly could be. Chloe walks with her arm rubbing against the wood on the far side, her gaze fixed looking outside the window at all of the nothingness going on. I walk facing straight ahead on the opposite side with my own bag running along the wooden banister as we climb. We join a little closer together once we are on the second-floor landing but still not at any sort of distance where anyone would think we are friends. Her eyes still won't turn towards me, my eyes are only sneaking glimpses to see if she is still looking away. The tension in this interaction with one person is oddly more evident than the pressure of the announcement in front of hundreds of kids.

In the dark corridor on the second floor (I call it that as the lights never seem to be on) we find the English classrooms. There are six of them, each manned by a different teacher who is eccentric in their own way. I'm glad I no longer have to endure the subject or those who teach it. In the middle of the corridor is the library. It makes sense to put the book storage by the place where the most reading will be done. Supermarkets don't typically place the butcher's counter beside the stationary. It's in a useful place for any class to use it as well, almost slap bang in the middle of the school once you take the fourth floor into account — even if the fourth floor only contains a greenhouse and some science equipment. I can't even remember why I've seen that area of the school having never done any science since second year.

Chloe breaks the silence — and my endless monotonous train of banal thoughts — as we cross the threshold into the library.

"Even though we were sent here by management, I think we'd best check in as if it was study."

"Makes sense."

It's all I can say in the moment. All it contributes to a conversation is equal to that of a 'mmhmm' or a head nod, but it is more than nothing at all.

Chloe walks up to Mrs Ellis' desk with something close to a smile and greets the long-standing librarian.

"Good morning, Mrs Ellis. Ms Waverley has sent myself and Molly up here instead of our regular classes this morning. I don't know how long we'll be here. Could be an all-day thing but we'll sign in anyway."

"That's quite all right. Sorry, you and who?" Mrs Ellis is a nice librarian, so I'm not offended by such a genuine question. I feel a tickle of pride in my throat and so do my best to introduce myself.

"I'm the new girl. Molly Clarke. I had the announcement this morning."

"An announcement? Oh, right. The announcement. My apologies, us librarians don't typically leave the work desk once we're here for the day." She ends her cheery explanation with a smile and a laugh though she doesn't have to explain herself at all.

"Oh, that's OK. I'm glad someone told you about it at least. Is my name on the register?"

"Ms Waverley gave me an updated one this morning and switched the template so you're covered there too. She informed me on Friday so I could change your name on the library system and the computers. You'll need to change your password again so here's the code right now. I had to make a new login. Your USB stick means you obviously haven't lost any work. That's why we tell everyone to bring one — we never know what school server storage is going to be like."

"Thanks, I'll go set this up." Seems like way too brief a reply to such a detailed explanation but I don't know what else to say. Mrs Ellis passes me the small, laminated card which has a username and temporary password on it. It reads:

mclarke7

uw7Vp6Y4

You can always change the password, but you need to login first.

Chloe has already gone to sit at the far corner of the computer area. I go to put the card in my trouser pocket then remember a key issue with that. I suppose muscle memory is trying to kick in every now and then. I instead pop the card back on the counter and leave it there while I sign in. I have both a bag and a coat with pockets yet this is the easiest solution I can come up with. Common sense and a lack thereof. I scan the register and it only takes a few seconds to see the name 'Molly Clarke'. The register is organised by surname so it's not like anything has really changed about that small detail. I just wonder if every class's register has been updated the same way. I tick the box beside my name in the column marked 'Morning' and place the pen back down on the sheet. I then go to leave the counter and head for a computer chair but stop myself just one step later. I return, pick up the card with my login information on it with an embarrassed smile and then walk towards a seat. The soft carpet of the library almost silences my heels, the silence is almost therapeutic.

Where should I sit? I don't want to be rude and sit on the opposite side of the room, but I don't know Chloe nearly well enough to consider sitting right beside her. As I go to take a seat with one computer separating us, Chloe tries her best to put my nerves at ease.

"I won't bite, you know."

Must be her way of saying 'please, take a seat next to me.' She's very blunt about most things, she doesn't like to dance around topics in history. You ask for an answer in class, and she will give you it. She won't give any more detail than she needs to, it's almost like she too feels like she needs to hide from something. Or hide something from someone. Surely we all feel that way sometimes.

"Oh, sorry. I didn't mean that against you. I just... long morning." I graciously accept the offer and take a seat at the computer to the right of where Chloe is sitting.

"Yeah, I can imagine. Self-inflicted though, at least partially." She's not wrong, but it sounds a lot colder than I imagine she means it to. "I've got some homework to do. It won't take long. Keep yourself busy in the meantime and then I've got a few questions for you."

Again, not much emotion to what she is saying. Very matter-of-fact as usual.

"OK, all good." To anyone else, it must sound like two computers are trying to chat to each other. I put my earphones in and choose some music for studying then take my German stuff out from my bag. German is the subject I've been doing for the least amount of time so it's the one I tend to spend more of my allotted study time on. I've only been studying it for a year after having studied both French and Italian — the former of which I have been doing for many years. I'm not sure Eminem and German are quite the best mix but the clever wordplay is enough to airlift me from the ocean of my own problems and help me focus on preparing for today's '*Deutsch*' class.

My music is so loud that I don't hear someone else enter the library. It's Sabrina. You remember her, right? Tightly-wrapped girl, takes everything far too seriously and clearly quite offended by my presence if this morning is anything to go by. It's only as I see some lesson notes forcefully placed on top of my sheet of German verbs that I notice her. I turn to acknowledge her and thank her with a nod. Her lips move but I'm too lost in the lyrics of a rap song to pick up on what she's saying right away. I remove my earphones in case it's something she needs me to hear and only hear the last couple words.

"…for you."

I heard nothing before this but now I see Chloe turn towards Sabrina — and she doesn't look too pleased.

"Enough. Leave it."

She doesn't say it with much anger but there's enough of a threatening undertone that Sabrina scampers off out the library and back down the hall and stairs to Geography. Chloe puts one earphone of her own back in and turns back to her work. I can't respond to what she has said because my knowledge of the context is so shallow. I have no idea what Sabrina said and I'm not going to interrupt Chloe in the middle of her work to ask such a pathetic question. The last thing I want is to be caught up in any feuds or drama and I know I have no option but to accept the inevitable when people do kick off. But until then, I'm choosing to ignore the possibility.

I rewind my song just 30 seconds to hear the clever bits of wordplay that I missed in trying to hear what was going on around me and read the new notes sheet which the "lovely" Sabrina "gave" me. Ah, just a sheet with questions about a population pyramid. This will take about ten minutes if I type it and double if I write it instead. I type most of my work if it's not in a foreign language. Typing in French, German or Italian (when I studied it) is a chore on school computers since only 'The Administrator' can change settings like language and other technical details.

Geography questions are all fairly routine; not much changes once you know the general way to answer something. It's nowhere near as expressive as other subjects I do. Even in history or Modern Studies, you can express your own opinions in your own words. Geography has a list of buzzwords that must be in each answer, almost like sorting papers in a filing cabinet and sometimes just as thrilling. I love learning about the world — both its past and its present.

As I finish describing the population pyramid of a developing country — Senegal in this particular question — I remove an earphone. I anticipate that Chloe will want to speak soon so I remove the one nearer her just as my song finishes its first chorus. I do so subtly in case she isn't ready to talk yet and thinks I'm any weirder than she must already consider. If I can make it look like it just fell out, it can't be as weird as actively removing it and looking like I want to say something. I'd have to weigh up pros and cons if someone offered me the chance to never have to speak again at this moment.

"That's that taken care of. Biology homework done. OK, are you free to talk?" Chloe's words are exactly the ones I've been waiting for yet I can't help but feel reluctant to agree.

"If I'm not going to bore you."

"Quite a few things bore me. You can make it interesting." That's an intimidating response at best.

"How so?" I don't know what answer I am looking for to this question. It's not flirting, it's not offence and it's not an offer of anything. I'm just intrigued as to what she means.

"By making it interesting." She's almost annoyingly sharp in these social situations and this is the first one I can remember us having. It's without doubt the first one that has taken place outside of the history classroom.

"Oh, right. I'll do my best."

"Good." She stops speaking to put her biology books back in her bright blue bag. I follow suit and pop my German and geography stuff into my own large black crossbody. She'll likely be offended if I keep working on anything while she asks whatever it is she wants to ask. By that same token, I pause the music and remove my earphones, placing my phone on the table beside the keyboard, where my books were just removed from. The phone is still in its black case — making my phone more feminine was far from a priority last week in amongst everything else that needed to change.

"So, what do you want to talk about?" I ask this knowing the answer already. She obviously needs help with something in history *eye roll*.

"You, of course. The same thing everyone will be talking about today. And tomorrow. And by the time the kids all tell their parents, you might even expect to make news headlines on a local level. Depending on how overblown the story gets, you might have to appear on TV somewhere. What you've done is almost unheard of — no one comes out that way at school. Very few guys admit to being transgender at all solely because of the humiliating consequences of such an act." Despite a lot of emotive language, Chloe's tone never changes. It almost sounds like a news report on a sub-par radio station.

"You really think it will go that far? I mean, I know it's a big deal to me. But why should it be a big deal to anyone else? Why does it even matter to anyone else how I choose to present myself to the world?"

"It matters to me. What you're doing matters to me. Your actions up on stage this morning struck me. I don't quite know how to feel about it."

You and me both Chloe, you and me both.

Taking Time to Process

"Why do you care? I'm not trying to be rude or provoke you, but it's not like we even speak outside of history. We likely don't even think about each other. We're just two different people who happen to be in one class together. I honestly didn't think you would care. I only thought a few people would react in any way — I didn't expect the level of complete rejection this morning from the entire year group."

"Well, do you regret anything that you said this morning?"

"Of course not."

"Do you regret asking the register to update your name and gender on the system?"

"Absolutely not."

"Do you regret any part about how you look today?"

"I wish it was nicer outside so I could wear cuter shoes."

Have I just caught a glimpse of emotion from Chloe there? The corner of her mouth slightly raises as though she is amused by what I have just said.

"OK, I understand. I guess I just have such a hard time believing you because of my own experiences."

"Your experiences?" I'm taken aback, does Chloe have some huge secret about her identity?

"Not me. The kids at the youth club. Those kids are a mixed bag. Some of them are just happy to be themselves but don't know a name for it yet. Some of them have been disowned and given up for adoption as a result of who they are. I've had a few cases where people came along just to be obtuse about it and spread hate. While I'm not part of the LGBT myself, I feel very strongly that everyone should be free to be who they are and not be mocked for it. That's why I didn't know if you were being serious. I'm not completely sure yet but you are convincing me."

"Thanks, I guess. I don't even really feel like I'm part of any wider group. I just feel like me. I just feel like a girl. I don't know how else to explain it."

Chloe locks eyes with me to deliver her next point. "You don't need another way to explain it. If this is who you are, that's the way it is. I'm not going to gatekeep every part of who you are. I just… I'm sorry. I'm sorry for doubting you. I'm sorry that I didn't think you were completely genuine and I'm sorry that you are basically the school's biggest weirdo right now."

"You don't need to apologise. Everyone felt the same way and I imagine most still do. People will be thinking that I'm playing a prank or flat-out lying to hog some shallow attention and they'll be thinking that for as long as they wish to see the world that way. I'd say that you are in fact way better than the rest. You agreed to come here with me, and you were honest enough to just ask me some difficult questions. Please, don't feel sorry for me." Chloe's face still doesn't show a lot of feeling, but her words sound less cold now that she feels mistaken.

"It's all a weird situation. You are at the centre of it all, but it actually impacts everyone. Think about what was being shouted at you this morning."

"Yeah, people were just making fun of something different because they wanted to impress their friends. I'm not new to that."

"It's easy to see it that way but…" Chloe pauses to flick some of her violet hair out of her eyes and off to the side of her face, then carries on without forgetting where she is in her sentence: "…everyone feels odd right now because of what you said and what you did. Everyone who ever knew you as Ollie at any point now has to reassess every moment they associate with you. Everyone has an opinion of you — some are bold enough to let you know about it. There would have been many others in that hall who would want to support you. I want to support you."

"Why? Again, I don't want to cause you any hassle because of a decision that has nothing to do with you. My gender is something you have no control over. You shouldn't feel any responsibility for that."

"I know. But I do feel responsible. I feel like I can help you and so I have to."

"Are you sure?"

248

"I volunteer to help people like you. Why should I ignore you? Because you're not in my group? Because we don't talk outside of class? We're talking now. I feel closer to you now than I ever did to who you were before. I'm not saying we'll be besties or anything like that. I'm saying that I'm willing to help you integrate."

My eyes widen at the thought. Integrate? How can I trust any other student again? How can I just try to smooth this over like nothing has happened? I'm my own biggest hypocrite. I long for people not to care about the choice I've made then decide to hold myself back and become a lone wolf because other people dislike the choice I've made for myself.

"Is anyone going to want to speak to me ever again?"

"People might stop caring eventually. Some people might come to like Molly. They need longer than a three-minute speech and one day of knowing about you before they decide how they really feel. Remember the reason we are here. The rest of the sixth-year students are taking time to process what you said this morning."

"I thought that was just Ms Waverley coming up with a reason to stop me being abused."

"It might have been. It definitely could have been a part of the reason but not all. Any abuse you received and will receive is still a result of people processing who and what you are. It's almost unheard of. Remember that."

"So what do you suggest I do?" What am I doing? Why am I asking for advice? I can't allow myself to start trusting someone.

"Keep your head down today. I'll speak to people during break and lunch to try to calm them down. They might listen to me now that I've heard more from you than they have."

"Where do I go while you do that?"

"Hmm… you honestly might be safest in here. But failing that, you'll be a priority for safety today. You know how people end up on high-alert for security. That's you right now. Is there anyone at all who you could stay close to?"

"No one I can trust with that."

"OK. Stay with me then, Molly. My friends can meet you properly."

"Last chance — are you sure you are fine with me being a burden?"

"You'd likely be a burden anyways, even without being transgender.

But yes, we'll stick together today and even try to understand each other a bit better. Who knows? We may even be friends soon enough."

"Friends? What are they?"

I see it! A smirk! Chloe does actually have feelings and visible ways of showing emotion! I can't tell whether that's a smirk out of pity or I actually have made her smile. And I also don't know which I would prefer.

"Anyways, we'd best get back to work. But just come with me at break, girl."

"Will do, girl." The most awkward conversation possible but somehow not a disaster.

All Eyes on Me

The remainder of the time in the library is spent doing exactly what I was doing before Chloe and I had our chat — more German. The verbs, the nouns and the general structures are all far more complex than romantic languages. I can't imagine how difficult it is to learn English as a foreign language with how many different words we have for the same concept. I also wonder if they'll eventually have a class where I can study the unknown language the kids were all using this morning. The kind where instead of a qualification on the certificate, they reward you with an antisocial behaviour order at the end of the course. A criminal record if you put in enough work for extra credit.

Not everyone is speaking gibberish today. I may even actually be able to make a friend, or at least an acquaintance. Someone who will just acknowledge my existence without feeling like they need to unload all of their own frustrations on someone else for an entirely different and unrelated reason. Someone who will just co-exist with me. That's honestly how low the bar of my expectation is positioned currently. If just one person doesn't hate me by the end of this day, Molly's social life is off to a quick start!

'Rrrrrring!' The bell to inform me that destiny awaits. Am I fated to be a loner or will people start to understand? If not that, will they realise that my gender has no power over their life? If not that, will they at least keep that to themselves. That bar sinks lower and lower to the point where I may need a shovel for it. Or a bulldozer for how much dirt I'll have to uplift.

Chloe turns to face me as her computer finishes shutting down — my own has been closed for a few minutes.

"Time to go meet the girls. I'm actually kind of excited for you."

I remove my earphones once more and return them to my bag. I take my pink coat from the back of my chair and put the small password card into the top pocket. In concentrating on working hard and then socialising even harder (metaphorically), I forgot to fix my password so I'll need to use the temporary one next time. Judging by Chloe's opinion, I'll likely be in the library for longer than just this morning. It's like quarantine but where I am also the disease itself. People are too afraid to catch beautiful I suppose!

I hang my bag across my body, as the name of the style suggests, and double check that I'm not leaving anything behind at the desk. It likely won't matter — the library is locked most morning intervals for Mrs Ellis to have her lunch. It's an incredibly early lunch but she doesn't normally get the chance at everyone else's lunchtime since the library is a retreat for the introverts. Shockingly, not somewhere Ollie would usually go as he was accepted by a few sad, fake, callous boys. Those uppity brats won't take to Molly the same way, arguably ever at all. They might be afraid of catching something from a girl. Like manners or a fashion sense or interesting conversations or prettier faces. They really would be spoilt for choice!

Satisfied that I have packed everything away and that my coat and bag are both with me, Chloe and I leave the library walking slightly closer together. Don't get the wrong idea! Interval means that the corridors are packed with kids all heading the same way. While we wait for the pool of younger students to clear ahead of us, I can hear the murmuring roar of judgement. All eyes are on me in some way or another. The kids behind me gaze at the back of my head. I can hear a young boy turn to his friends and say, "Look, there's the crazy girl from this morning!" The pupils directly in front of us turn their heads to sneak quick looks at my face and therefore stop in their tracks. Chloe is having none of this and she orders them to clear a path.

"Move, idiots!" Her almighty roar stuns the corridor into complete silence, and she forces a small route between (and in some cases through) the many children as we head for the main stairs. Much less chance of being attacked on the landings than in the claustrophobic side passages at the ends of the halls. I follow in her train, considerably impressed by her no-nonsense approach to overcoming an obstruction. We head down the stairs and back to the first-floor landing where Ms Waverley spots us.

Not hard, I sort of stand out.

"Ah there you two are! Everything all right up in the library?"

"Yeah, it's all good." That's my contribution to this riveting discussion. Chloe has far more words to say.

"The library is a good spot to keep her hidden while everyone works out just how they are going to welcome Molly to their classes. I'm just wondering if there has been anything said about Molly. Any threatening language you've heard? We were going to head to the cafeteria and start trying to wear down a few of the girls."

"I haven't heard much of that at all. Just a lot of childish name-calling, pointless rumours and ridiculous speculation."

As if they are listening in on the conversation, a fourth-year boy walks right up to my face.

"You don't look bad for a gay-ass tranny." Clearly this moron doesn't see who I am talking to.

"Well young man, I think you've earned at least a detention for that. And I'll be informing your parents too, to see if they accept you using those words."

"Aw what? Thanks a lot, fag." The fourth year goes to storm off, but Chloe pulls his arm back.

"You're going to apologise." Chloe's eyes fill with rage. How can she be angrier about this than me?

"I don't have to."

"And I don't have to let you leave until you do. So apologise. I don't care if you mean it. You are clearly seeking attention so you're insulting the new girl. And look around you! Your big mouth has got you all of the attention now! Everyone on this floor can see us and can hear us. So before you are given your detention letter, you're going to say sorry and then run your embarrassed, irrelevant self away with your tiny tail between your legs. Understood?"

I imagine she likely grips the poor idiot harder. Ms Waverley certainly isn't stopping Chloe's tirade and why should she? This guy was asking to be knocked down a few pegs. He yelps.

Chloe releases him and Ms Waverley turns her attention to issuing the punishment. Ms Waverley mouths a quick 'thank you' to Chloe and the volume on the silenced first floor slowly subsides as chatter picks up.

But hey, maybe they'll be talking about some different things. There is no conversation as we head down into the crush hall or through to the canteen. Just before the sitting area, I ask Chloe to stop for a moment.

"What's up?"

"I just wanted to thank you for doing that. It's one of the coolest things I've ever seen anyone do."

"Oh that was nothing. I just wasn't going to let anyone treat you that way. I won't let anyone treat anyone that way if I can help it. What I did back there was for both of us. He insulted you, and it offended me."

"Well, thanks anyway. So where is it your friends sit?"

As I look out at the tables I see them. The guys. They are definitely looking over and back to each other, likely exchanging witty jokes or popular memes to talk about me behind my light-pink covered back. They also aren't the only table doing this. Every eye in the room is on me at some point. Every single person can't resist a look. Some are bewildered, some are amused and by the brainless looks on some boys, a few might even be turned on. Maybe someone is finding something out about themself there too.

"The girls and I sit right there," she says while gesturing towards round table right beside a large grey pillar. Again, it feels as though the entire school stands upon these relatively small and thin poles of metal. And sure enough, there are three other girls from our year group. The tables sit eight people, but the four girls each like to place their bag on the seat beside them. It stops anyone from intruding on their sacred circle — something I'm clearly allowed to do today. A girl with a blonde ponytail and glasses waves to Chloe and she waves back with what I would call a smile. By Chloe's standards, it may be the grin of a psychopathic murderer.

"Chloe, over he-"

She stops when she sees who is with her- that being me. Not to be deterred, Chloe encourages me to follow her. It's a habit I'm almost worryingly proficient in despite spending just one morning learning it.

"Don't worry about it, I'll smooth this over and we'll at least prevent them from hating you." We arrive at the girls' table with three confused, unimpressed faces greeting us.

"Hey girls so I don't need to explain who this is, right? She literally did that this morning."

The blonde girl, who is named Sasha if I can recall, is the first of the trio to speak. "We know who she is. But what is she doing here?"

A ginger-haired girl sort of echoes that sentiment while the black-haired girl just looks at us with a smile. I don't think these girls mean it in a nasty way so what can I say to try to win them over? I could tell them a joke but that never works. I don't know any magic tricks and they won't understand any sophisticated French I can throw their way. I'm going to have to try (ugh) friendly conversation. I can't let Chloe take the wheel all day, I'm not a damn Sim!

"Look, I know it's tough to put this all together and deal with it. That's been my entire last week and I still don't feel much closer to having it all figured out. It's our last year at school, and my old friend group is a gang of immature, sexually-frustrated, stupid guys. I'm not asking you all to be my besties and have sleepovers and make daisy chains. All I ask is that we can at least get on with each other. It feels weird for everyone involved; I totally get that. But can we at least all try to get along as peers? We'll see from there if we actually like each other but I don't want my last memories of school to be filled with hatred over who I am and how I dress, and you girls surely don't want that either. So can we at least be friendly to each other? I'd really like to get to know all of you better."

Chloe mouths something which looks like 'good job' and she seems vaguely impressed. Grace, the black-haired girl, is the first to reply.

"I've got no problem with you sitting with us. It might actually be kind of cool to learn more about you, Molly."

Chloe looks at Sasha and the redhead to see if there are any protests.

"I don't know, Chlo. It could be too much trouble for us all."

"Yeah...she'll attract a lot of attention. She's sort of doing that now."

"This is the perfect chance to show Molly that she made the right choice in joining the fairer sex. We should be treating her with respect and common courtesy. Let's not hate someone before they give us a reason."

The girls are somewhat reluctant, but they ultimately have to concede to Chloe's great point. Chloe invites me to take a seat between

255

her and Grace as we keep our bags on us. It's the default position for mine anyway as it's much more hassle to take off than it's worth and I may also forget to pick it back up again.

Grace asks me a simple question. "Do you know all of us?"

I can only answer honestly. "I don't think we have ever actually spoken to each other, but I know that you are Grace. Lovely name, by the way."

"Why thank you! Yours isn't too bad either, Molly."

"Thanks!" I turn to the blonde girl. "I may get this one wrong because again, we've never spoken to each other. But are you Sasha?"

"I am indeed. It's nice to meet you." Her words sound kind, her voice sounds disinterested. A bit like Chloe earlier this morning.

"And... I'm sorry, I've no idea what your name is."

The red-haired girl lets out a friendly giggle. "That's OK. Had you not announced your name to the whole school, I probably wouldn't know yours either. I'm Holly. Pleased to meet you."

What are the odds of a Molly and a Holly at the same table? I could mention the weird detail that Holly was almost the name I chose, but I can't just throw that out there for nothing and freak everyone out even more than they already are by my presence.

"Our names are quite close!" It's a simple topic to start breaking the ice with one member of the table. Grace and Sasha's faces are firmly fixed on their phone screens.

"Yeah. The funny thing is that my dad wanted to call me Molly but my Mum preferred Holly. My mum loves Christmas!" Small world!

"Who doesn't?" I jokingly add. It sort of works? I don't know. I'm picking up that she found it funny, but it hasn't made me seem any less weird.

Well, all of that drama at the start of the break and the long plea for a chance to sit with the other girls really ate into our interval today. The bell rings to signal the end of the break and the start of third period.

"Well, we've got biology. Chlo, are you still in the library?"

"I think so. Molly still needs my protection!"

All the girls laugh, including myself.

"You're not so bad."

Holly's parting words as she heads for PE are some of the warmest

I've heard all day. The other four of us walk up to the second floor together, my input on the conversation still very limited. I'm just dipping my toes into this strange new sea, so don't blame me for being cautious around others so soon after coming out so publicly. Our coats and skirts are slightly soaked from being outside. See, the canteen runs on a one-way system where you can only leave out the back. Going out of the rear doors leads you to the playground and if you follow the path, it snakes you around to the front entrance for you to make another ascent to wherever your next class is.

Grace and Sasha split from myself and Chloe on the second-floor landing. The other girls hug Chloe but obviously just simply say 'bye' to me. That's honestly much less awkward so it's fine by me.

"So… what did you make of my friends?"

Retaliate

For the first time, I honestly feel like these girls may be potential friends. Not people who begrudgingly accept your presence if you stick around long enough like a stray cat. Not guys who keep you around just to be the butt of the jokes or the one who almost always ends up in goals at five-a-side football. Not people who lie to your face and say they'll be your pal no matter what then turn their backs as soon as you remove your own mask and feel bold enough to live as your real self. Holly, Grace and Sasha might grow closer to me — and I may grow closer to them with time too. I can't let my guard down at all yet my back is covered by more stab wounds than skin at this point. I enjoyed being at their table though, that's a start.

"Your friends are pretty cool. It was nice to feel like I was just like any other girl at the table, even if they aren't convinced yet."

"It will take a couple of days. Join me long enough and they'll start talking to you. Grace seemed like she wanted to ask you something about it all."

"Yeah… I don't know. It's hard to believe based on today but I don't like talking about myself."

"You can share as much or as little as you like with me, Molly… I'm trained to understand what people like you go through."

That slight pause before she explains her training is suspicious. Is there more to why she wants to help me? I don't think I care if there is. I certainly don't want to force any uncomfortable details out of her. Just because I stood in front of the school and told my life story doesn't mean that it's suddenly time for everyone to release the secrets that they hold.

Chloe is closer to me than anyone else. That is both by design and by complete accident. After all, there was no contract binding her to my side today and join me in 'Molly Quarantine.' Yet, she chose to come with me to my temporary classroom in the middle of the school where I'm essentially being kept under protection. At first, I thought it was a case of her just wanting to be out of class. I now feel really guilty for doubting her — and she has told me that she feels the same from when she doubted my announcement. It's a mutual guilt relationship. Not ideal, but better than nothing.

Subjects are so loosely organised for me today that neither German nor French have even sent any work my way. I already studied German this morning so I'll spend the next ninety minutes or thereabouts on French. It's my favourite and I have a lot of freedom with what I can learn, being the only student in the whole school doing French at the most advanced level. Quite often, I use French to vent my real thoughts. I can practise the right structures and use a wide range of words that would otherwise go undiscovered. How else would I know the French for 'transgender, target, hated by the whole school and isolation?'

Chloe taps my shoulder as I'm jamming out to some rock music. The first time, I don't really feel it so the second tap is a double. OK, I doubt that one was accidental. I remove the earphone closest to her, as we are sat in the same place as before.

"Just a heads up: an English class is coming into the library. Think it's some first-year kids picking library books."

"Do you think that even those kids care? They didn't even know Ollie."

"Ollie was deputy head boy. Believe me, the whole school knows who you are. Even in the loosest sense, they know who you are. Or well, were. Your old picture is on the notice board outside of the leadership team's offices, mind."

"Oh yeah! I totally forgot about even having that photo done. Well, I guess they'll be removing that soon."

"I love how laid-back you can be about all of this. You've flipped your own life upside-down with a smile."

"I've flipped my life the right way. It was upside-down until last week."

Chloe has some reply ready, but she is cut off by the voice of one of the English teachers. And of course, it would have to be my old English teacher. You know, the clown I referred to earlier. Her name isn't that important to you, I am aware. However, for three years, the name 'Mrs Poulson' haunted my existence and hacked away at my happiness. Apt for today, but she always made me feel like a target. Once she started the mockery, a few students would pitch in and pile on and that's how I grew to hate her class.

Anyway, here she comes with a ragtag group of S1 kids. English in first year contains a lot more 'reading time' than later years, when exams become a bit more pertinent than taking in stories for leisure. Her voice still rings through me as if I was a cave. She instructs her class to go and find books for their reading time. Seems like she's phoning this lesson in, but that means nothing to me. She's… walking over? Her class are all at the opposite end of the classroom, where the books are neatly organised into genres on high shelves that are embedded into the walls and firmly fixed to the carpeted floor.

"What are you two doing in here?"

"Ms Waverley sent us here because of Molly's announcement. We are giving the other kids time to process everything that went on this morning." Thanks, Chloe.

"Ah I see. Well, hopefully you're working hard."

"As ever," I reply, even trying to sound cheery while talking to a past foe. I should keep my mouth shut more often. Those two words in my not-yet perfect voice mixed with their teacher going over to see us has turned the heads of a couple of the rugrats in first-year. They're pretty interested to see the 'crazy girl' and they're not hiding it as well as they'd like to believe.

'That's her!'

'It's him!'

'The old deputy head boy!'

'She was the one on stage!'

'Why is she here?!'

'Mrs Poulson! It's the crazy girl!'

I've never felt more like I came directly from a horror movie. I am the new Leatherface, and they'll probably call me 'Glitterface' or something. Molly Myers maybe? I'm not a fan of horror movies so I'm already out of puns.

"Class, that's enough!" One shout and the crowd falls silent. First time I have ever been grateful for Mrs Poulson speaking, ever. Like scolded dogs, they stand in shame. Some in fear of poking their bear of a teacher. Her fierce roar is no more pleasant when you are sitting less than a foot away from her, even when you aren't the target of her grizzly, rage-filled scorn. She turns back to us and says, "Well, good luck with everything." She may as well have said anything else there for how much that means in any case. At least she doesn't seem annoyed at me for anything — a welcome change of circumstance. She returns to her class to order them around some more and to try to keep the noise spewing from them to a minimum. Chloe and I exchange a small laugh at her misfortune, and it feels good to be on this side of the laughter.

"She was actually quite nice there. I never liked her class." I obviously make this comment very quietly so just myself and Chloe can hear.

"Oh, she was such a difficult teacher. Always made me feel like I'd made a mistake."

"Oh yeah, that's her style. Glad we aren't dealing with that any more." We? Why am I talking to Chloe like we have known each other forever? She was in the same class as me for English, but we didn't sit anywhere near each other and didn't team up for any group work either. I actually faced her in a debate task once — it was close, but I came out on top with my charismatic delivery. Maybe public speaking is in my future... once I have something to say that's worth saying and a platform to spread my message.

"Yeah, it's a nice change. I think we've only got nice teachers now." Chloe just said 'we' as well? Is she... does she... want to be friends?

"I like all of my teachers, anyway. Do you?"

"Yeah, especially the art department. They're so understanding and helpful and proud to be themselves, too... kind of like you in a way, Molly."

"Me?"

"Well...yeah. We've only just really spoken for the first time this morning but... I'm really liking this. Even if the other girls find it too weird, I can see us being friends. With all my volunteering in the youth club, I've never felt like those kids are my friends. I relate to their stories but like a trusted adult and ally instead of just a friend. You're different.

261

And I like it."

"Aw well, I'm flattered. I'm really enjoying hanging out with you too. You've been such a massive help to me today, all out of choice. Having you here is the best part of this quarantine period." What did I just say? Best tone that down. "As a friend, of course. Please don't think I'm flirting."

"Ha, ha, I was about to say, 'easy tiger'. I think you might turn out to like guys instead, anyways. You just haven't met a nice one yet!"

"Nice guys? They're a myth!"

I sure don't know any of them.

"Ah well, you never know. Anyways, let's get back to work. Oh, in fact, maybe we can do some history together. We can prep for the next class?" I didn't expect Chloe to be the forward one here. Also, prep for the next class? Is she saying we should actually go to history?!

"Um…yeah, sure thing! I'll just finish my French work and then we can look at it in fifth period. I think we're still gathering sources for that 'Causes of the American Civil War' essay anyways so makes sense to team up."

"Great! Speak soon, Mols." Chloe pops her earphones back in with a smile on her face. I do the same, giddy inside. How can anyone want to be my friend? Is this actually happening?

After another 300 words on the random topic of 'Transgender People in Society' (no idea why that's on my mind), I can just about hear the bell ringing. It is however the rush of bodies outside of the library that lets me know it's the start of fifth period. I save my French work and while Chloe is finishing her music questions, I reach into my coat pocket for the small piece of card from earlier. I go into 'settings' and then 'profile'. Scrolling down to 'change password' I click and enter the temporary security key that's on the card.#

'Hi (M)Ollie? Please enter your new password.'

Why the brackets? Is that really how they have fixed my name on their server? Ah well, I'll get around to sorting that. What should the new password be? Hmmm… I've got it

'HighHeels0902'

Good luck guessing that, potential hackers! Chloe looks over at my screen once the password screen disappears and can't help but laugh at the name display.

"Brackets? That's a new one! Didn't realise that is how you were spelling it!"

"Ha, ha, yeah it's an old-school influence. I must actually be part computer, after all!"

"Hey, that would explain all the languages just being stored in your brain!" Why does it feel like I've truly known this girl for years as opposed to hours? Her humour is so like mine; she just picks up what I put down and vice versa.

"True, true. I should probably get that fixed, though."

"I wouldn't worry about it. Only you can see that info. Well, now I can too but that's because I'm a nosy bitch!"

"Aw come on now, you're not a bitch."

"So I'm nosy?" Chloe's expression turns all serious

"No, not at all." I'm scared I might have just spoiled everything.

"Ha, wrong! I'm the nosiest around. Thanks for not calling me a bitch though." The smile returns, and confusion floods my brain.

"Oh um… you're welcome?" Human interaction is hard. Conversations are hard!

"Aww did you get all flustered? That's kind of cute. Anyways, let's get on to history before I flirt with you any more." She's flirting? Nah, must just be another thing girls say to girls. And to be honest, I'll feel better about it all if it's not romantically charged. Girls always post 'love you' on each other's pics and Facebook statuses, so maybe this is just a rite of passage in the journey towards the superior gender.

Just as we start organising our history books and set ourselves to compare our findings and resources thus far, another class enter the library. This time, they are here to gain access to the laptops. These students are the Modern Studies class that I'm meant to be in right now. That I would be in if I wasn't being kept separate from them all. There are some fifth-year kids in the class but it's mainly other sixth years. And they aren't so quiet or subtle about making their presence known.

"Oi oi, it's fag boy!"

Ouch, Stephen. Ouch. We used to be pals. I know I blocked him on Messenger, but you see now exactly why I did that. A couple of the girls in the class — including Sabrina, the teenage witch — find this very amusing. I'm not going to cause a scene in the library, even if they are trying to goad me into it.

"Wearing a skirt, heels and make-up won't hide your dick!" This shout comes from a fifth year. Why is no teacher stopping this? Simple. In the senior years of high school here — S4 to S6 — you generally gain more trust and teachers won't necessarily accompany the class wherever they go. Fetching laptops independently is one of those things that a teacher trusts older pupils to do responsibly. Had they been sent to the laptops in the science corridor, I doubt they would cause so much of a disturbance. Oh and the librarian? She's supervising a first-year class while their teacher is absent. Anyway, the more vulgar comment gains a few more chuckles.

At times like this, you ask yourself some questions. Am I just going to sit down and take all this abuse or am I going to put on my girl panties and fire back? Am I going to revert to being a passenger in life or am I going to take the wheel once more? Am I going to show Stephen up to his peers? Yes, and I have the perfect reply.

"To be fair, Stephen, you weren't calling me a fag when you were drooling over me on Friday, were you?"

"Sh-shut up!"

"I have all those messages. 'Oh there was this fake slut with big tits and make-up and a pink skirt on'. What was it you said? She'd 'get it'? And now that you find she's above you and she doesn't want 'it', you've got to act disinterested. So why don't you lot grab your damn laptops and leave us alone? We are trying to work."

Silence. You could hear a pin drop right now. I'm a little breathless from the conflict but I'm tired of absorbing punches and not swinging back.

"Ew. What the fuck, Stephen?"

"Stephen likes the tranny!"

OK, not an ideal outcome. But it does get them to move along, grab their laptops and high-tail it on out of our isolation station. A teacher from the classroom directly across comes in to usher them on out and then checks on Chloe and me.

"You two should be working."

Chloe stands up to respond, doing her best to keep it polite.

"We are trying to. If Modern Studies didn't send abusive, horrible students for laptops, we wouldn't have had to spend the past five minutes trying to get those kids to leave. We've got our history stuff open, and we are working. Just please, try to keep other kids out. We'll be gone next period; they can cause their chaos then."

"Oh, my apologies, Miss Maxwell. Please, do carry on." As Mr Irrelevant closes the door, I praise Chloe's efforts.

"You sure put him in his place."

"Could say the same to you about Stephen. Awesome work, girl. That guy's a dick."

"Guess we make a pretty good team."

"Yeah... I guess we do!" Chloe chirps. It's the most excited I've heard her yet. "OK, what have you found for research so far?"

"Well, this passage from publication one is really handy for getting to the meat of the matter with slavery and states' rights. Seems that the two go hand in hand, but I reckon slavery dominates."

"Sure does seem that way. The second book was pretty scathing towards the South's fascination with slavery. And that's fair enough, of course."

I'm sure you can tell that the excitement is over with for now. Unless you want to know beat-by-beat exactly what research we complete, I'll just leave this part here. Besides, I'm sure Stephen will be Mr Popular come lunchtime. A smile of malicious intent creeps across my face. The thought of anyone else being the focal point of all conversation within school premises today is a glowing beacon at the end of a dark, twisting tunnel.

Girlfriends

"OK, I think we actually have a pretty good base of knowledge and sources now. Thanks for your help!"

"Thank you, too. It was also really nice to have a study buddy."

Aw, Chloe just called me a 'study buddy'? Buddy is like close to friend. It's tougher and tougher to see her as anything less than that right now. Although we have only truly known each other for five periods and one morning interval, we seem like kindred spirits in an odd way. I can't quite hit that nail on the head, but we are certainly understanding each other. It's also nice that, at least on my side, there's no romantic or sexual pressure. If my old form was to speak so closely with a girl, the whole world would be 'shipping' us. I don't hear anything like that yet. I do ship us. I think we can have a great friendship.

We pack up all our books ten minutes before the lunch bell — may as well sneak an early lunch while we have the opportunity. Something concerns me about the next move of the day.

"So, you know how you said we were just preparing for the next class?"

"Yeah, what about it?"

"Whatever work you all end up doing, could you please make sure it reaches me down here? I really don't want to fall behind."

"Oh, you won't fall behind, Mols."

I have to say, I love it when she calls me Mols. I don't know how she'll react if I call her Chlo, but this is the perfect chance to find out.

"How so, Chlo?" It sounds kind of natural yet also kind of forced. Like a fake cry during a wrestling promo.

"Because you're coming with me to class."

"I'm what now?"

"It's just us girls in history class, remember. Ollie was always the

266

outsider to the world of girl talk in history. Why should you miss out on that now? You're as much of a girl as the rest of the class. Dare I say, even more feminine than some of them. Would you say Kendall is more of a girl than you?"

"She's got the right parts." This answer is obvious, surely. To outsiders, it doesn't matter what someone wears. When it comes to identity, the majority define it as the parts about us that can't be so easily swapped. In some cases, these are impossible to replace too.

"True, that's what everyone else says. To me, you're every bit as much of a girl as me. And we are both more feminine than half of that class. So, trust me. We'll blend right in, even if it's a bit turbulent at first. We've started winning Grace over already, remember?"

"Oh yeah, Grace is in the class. And I'd guess that we are three of the four most feminine girls in that room. Maybe Meghan has us all beat, though!"

"Meghan is really girly. But so are you! And you're still learning. I guarantee you can be the most feminine student in this whole school, if you want to be that. No one does what you have done without immense motivation and intense drive."

"OK, you're right. We'll go to history."

I stand up and put my coat back on. I drape the bag around my body again as Chloe puts her backpack on. I check the time on my phone and pack away my earphones. One last check that I have logged out, and I'm ready to go.

Chloe and I walk much closer to each other than before. Like almost hand-holding close. It's not romantic, it's friendly. Whereas before our walks were silent, that last period especially has meant that we are no longer mutual strangers. In a way, we're having our own girl talk. Mainly though, we are predicting who in the history class is going to have a problem with us showing up.

"Do you think any of the girls will kick off about me? Ms Waverley might come and remove me herself if they cause enough fuss."

"Relax, girl! You'll be fine! Mrs Watson won't let them do that — you know she is one of the best teachers around."

"She's certainly up there. Her class is just so laid back."

"Exactly! Why should that change because we have decided to show up?"

"It really shouldn't, but has anything made sense today?"

Chloe warmly replies, "Everything we've done has been the best." It's an incredibly romantic thing to say to a friend. Again though, I believe girls are usually this affectionate towards their friends. I'm sure some even kiss each other on nights out. Try that with guy friends — it won't go well.

"Yeah, including throwing some shade back for a change!"

"You needed sunglasses for that. See when you told everyone about Stephen's messages? It's probably the coolest thing I've seen anyone do here."

"Yeah. I can't help but feel a little worried about what he's going to do."

"You're a girl now. He can't hit you, even if he so badly wants to."

"Oh yeah! Perks of the best sex!"

"Too right! Anyways, we best grab some lunch. The other girls aren't here quite yet, obviously so we can pick exactly where we want to sit. Always the same table, though. We're not going too crazy."

We grab some hot 'food' from the school canteen. To be fair, it's really not the worst. Some mediocre pasta with a tomato ragu and a tiny little bit of 'meat'. Unless you leave the school grounds at lunch, the pasta or the paninis are the safest option for a meal. And considering we have been kept in the same room all day, I seriously doubt that anyone would be thrilled with Molly outside of school grounds either.

As we take our seats, facing away from where the guys usually perch their ugly frames, we tuck into our lunch. The bell rings a minute later and the cafeteria swarms with miscreants of all shapes and sizes. It takes the other girls a few minutes to claw their way through the warzone that is the lunch queue.

"Hey, you two!"

"Hi, Holly! Where's the others?"

"Oh, they're taking a gamble on the mince and tatties that they're serving. I'm with you two though, the pasta is the least risky thing." We can all have a laugh and a joke about how we pretty much had the same chat while we were in the queue.

"One day, we have got to start going out for lunch! Our bodies will

268

thank us!"

"Hmm, I don't know. I'm not sure fast food is much better." Chloe's right, but I think I know what Holly means.

"We could go somewhere for a meal deal or something, though. Even a bakery or something."

"Oh, I never even thought about bakeries! Weird, 'cause I love cake!"

"Who doesn't?" Feels odd to be quoting an earlier conversation with the same girl but it has the same desired effect. We speak enthusiastically about cake for a couple of minutes when Sasha and Grace join us.

"Ugh, that damn queue. At least the food is hot." Sasha's not best pleased. Grace is much more upbeat though.

"Hey, gang!" It's weird that I don't feel like an outsider. I'm just part of the 'gang' she's talking to. Holly, Chloe and I all greet the girls simultaneously, though obviously with different words. If we all said the same thing at the same time, we'd appear like animatronics at a cheap kiddy diner.

"How's quarantine, anyways?"

"Oh, Sasha, it's the best. Truly thrilling."

"We can at least get some work done in peace. Well, when we aren't being interrupted by first-years or other morons."

"They didn't lock the library for you?"

"They can't lock it. People need books and laptops. We've been sat in the corner furthest from the door, just studying." The girls, who would likely start teasing Chloe if she had been working with a boy all morning, are totally fine with that detail. And why shouldn't they be? We're just two girls, working together.

Grace asks us if we've been doing history work. A natural assumption considering it is the one class Chloe and I are both in. It's also the only class that Grace is also in. You'll be wondering why I knew only her name up until now if I've been in the same class as her since we returned in August. It's the exact same reason why I only knew Chloe by name as well — what reason did that old, hideous husk have to speak to the girls? My social life will be better than his if it keeps trending this way.

"Yeah, we've got loads of notes. We'll share them in class." My kind offer is not met with the expected reaction.

Grace's eyes almost pop out of her skull, Sash's jaw about hits the table and Holly raises her brow. Oh yeah! They didn't know we were going to be back in a classroom next period.

"You'll be in history? Can you do that?"

"We'll find out. It's Chloe's idea."

Chloe swallows her mouthful of pasta before justifying this. "We need to start showing everyone that Molly is nothing to be afraid of. Sorry, she is no one to be afraid of. Being trans is nothing to fear."

"Well, we're just so uncertain. It's so new to everyone."

"New to most." Chloe replies. "In my group, I've been seeing it for a few years now." She turns to face me. "I didn't mean to call you a thing, there. Sorry that it came out wrong."

"Oh please, don't worry about that. It's far from the worst thing I've been called today."

Holly asks the dreaded question.

"What has anyone said to you?"

"Where do I begin, eh, Chlo?"

"Just about every insult you can think of times ten. She did absolutely wreck Stephen though."

"Stephen? Like in our year?"

I take this moment to indulge in my badass moment from earlier. No need to add any more dramatic details — the entire confrontation is like something from a film.

"The Higher Modern Studies class comes in to the library to get laptops while me and Chloe are working on history sources and that. Stephen, big 'hard man', walks in giving it all 'oi, oi fag boy' and that. The funny thing about that is that Stephen saw Molly before anyone else. On Friday, I came in to talk to the school about my transition. Stephen unknowingly saw me as I was leaving and that night, he was messaging the group chat. He said things like 'that new girl would get it.' Now that he knows who the new girl is, it seems his tune has changed."

"Oh my God! What did you say to him today then?" Sasha's eyes light up — she's clearly a fan of drama.

"I basically exposed his crush on me to the entire library. Our whole mods class now knows he had a thing for the 'tranny'."

"Ha! Brilliant! You're awesome! I hate that guy. I hate pretty much every guy."

Fair enough, Sasha. Just don't ask me about relationships and this conversation will be great.

"So, I know all about you three," she says, pointing individually to Grace, Chloe and Holly. "But what about you, Molly? Any crushes? Past loves?"

"Oh I'm about as boring as it gets. I genuinely never had a girlfriend before, and Molly isn't likely to have any affection thrown her way. Not here anyways."

"Pfft boring! Hang out with us more often, and we'll see if we can score you a hunk!" Well, that sounds horrible. I do want to get on with these girls though.

"No promises, there. But I'd love to be part of this group you have."

"You clearly hate the guys enough for me to be all right with that."

Chloe enthusiastically thanks Sasha for being so open and welcoming, then asks the other two how they feel.

Holly's voice wavers as she audibly weighs up her decision. Grace meanwhile has an answer right away.

"My one condition is that you are totally committed to this."

"Come on, Grace. Do you really still doubt her?" Chloe's tone sounds tired and a little annoyed.

"I don't doubt her at all! What I mean is that she better sit with us in history as well. And be available to hang out on weekends and after school sometimes. She needs to know that being girlfriends is much more than a group chat and gaming, with odd sports days thrown in. I know you're one of the girls, Molly. I want you to be one of our girls."

"Aww, I'm touched. Of course I'd like to spend time with you all!"

Holly finally has an answer. "Well even in a democracy, my vote doesn't even matter now. But I trust you, Molly. You're a good laugh so sure, let's see how this works out."

"Thanks, girls. You are all so kind. I'm happy to—"

"Well, look who it is."

Chloe locks eyes with the interrupter.

"What are you doing here?"

"I'm talking to the fag."

"I have nothing to say to you." I'm not lying, either. Why would I want to speak to Stephen?

"Well, I've spent the last forty minutes being laughed at over what you said. I know bitches like to kiss and make up all the time, but I'm not taking that shit. You better watch your back. If there weren't so many people here, I wouldn't think twice about killing you."

"And you're sure you don't mean kissing her?"

Hey! Nice one, Sasha!

"What did you say, slut?"

"Oh Stephen, just f*ck off."

Holly now joining in on the fun.

"Who asked you?"

"No one asked you to be here."

Grace joining in now means all the girls have wasted breath on this cretin. I'm going to end it again.

"Look, you have my number. If you want to flirt with me, practise on there first. Kay?" Undoubtedly the first time I've ever said 'kay' and the sassiest I've ever sounded.

"Ha, ha, hell yeah, Mols!" Chloe's seen me destroy the same guy twice in two hours. I'm glad she's enjoying the show. These conversations set all of my nerves off and I end up all breathless by the time Stephen gets the aggressive message and retreats to the table at the back — where the lads hang out.

"You're so cool! Wish I could insult guys like that!" Sasha's almost drooling at the thought of being so cutting.

I regain my composure a little faster than I anticipated.

"I'll gladly teach you all. It's just something I've picked up through years of emotional abuse from those guys." The mood dramatically drops, so a change of topic is needed. Luckily, Chloe's got it covered

"So how are the rest of the year group taking to Molly now? Still all upset over it?"

"Well, it won't surprise you that it's already on Facebook. Besides that, some teachers have been mentioning the importance of what you did this morning. They've been highlighting it as something unique and bold and inspirational. That's been getting dog's abuse in response, I'm afraid." Sasha's tone is like that of a news reporter. It really shows how keen she is to go into journalism. Something I've also thought of although my career plans have really been put to the back of my mind since last week.

"Ah, that's okay. I'm sure they will eventually accept me. Not everyone can be as amazing as you girls about it all."

The girls are all flattered by my praise of their progressive attitudes. We'd keep chatting like we've known each other for years but the bell ends any chance of that. Grace joins Chloe and I in our hike up to the third floor for history while Holly and Sasha go their separate ways. We take the stairs at the end of the corridor, beside P.E., on the ground floor and walk up all three flights (six flights if you count the spiralling staircases separately) and we pant as we reach the top.

"One of us needs to break a leg or something! We'd have a lift key!" Grace has a point, but it's a pretty crazy one.

We are the first students to arrive at the classroom. Being seniors, we are allowed to let ourselves in and start taking our books out and getting organised. We sit at the table nearest the front just as Chloe and Grace always have. I would always be sat behind them on any normal day. This is the furthest thing from it.

Clearly, the other girls don't expect Molly to be there either. Meghan walks in, and a minute later, Kendall and a couple of other girls who I might be able to name if we played a game of hangman over it follow suit. I've definitely heard them before — it's more like literally having no reason to care. Unfortunately, they know my name all too well.

"Oh look. It's the little girl who 'owned' Stephen in the library."

"You mean little *boy*, right?"

"Oh yeah, silly me. Little, pathetic, sissy, fag boy, 'Molly'."

"Oh cool it with your *Mean Girls* sh*t." Grace is definitely not somebody to mess with.

"Wow. I honestly didn't know you knew so many words!" It's a childish comeback, but their behaviour is just as immature, if not more so. "And I suppose Daddy let you use his big dictionary for grown-ups, huh?"

"Whatever, fag." The thing that's the worst here is that I don't even know this girl's name. The most hostile and unwelcoming of the bunch and she's so irrelevant that I can't even think of her name. Meghan actually hasn't said anything yet. She's confused, it's clear to see.

"You can sit with us, Meghan. She honestly doesn't bite."

Meghan sits at the end of the table beside Grace while I'm beside Chloe at the other end of it. I'm in that awkward position of wanting to say something to comfort her but knowing it could get worse if I do. So I don't say anything to her at all.

Mrs Watson walks in a minute later than that and sits straight down at her desk after just a quick glance at her class for the afternoon.

"OK, class. Time to do the register. Meghan?" Her eyes scan for Meghan's face and she marks her as present. See, Mrs Watson isn't a fan of the cringey way of taking the register. She finds it especially weird for seniors to be shouting 'Here!' like they are back in primary school.

"OK and I'll have to mark Molly and Chloe as here even though they're n—" I think that means that her eyes have caught a glimpse of Chloe's purple hair. "Oh, you're here? So is Molly down there all by herself?"

"Molly's right here. You just can't see her behind the screen."

Mrs Watson peers over to see the shocking truth. "OK, you're both marked as here then. Nice to see you both." And she continues the register as if nothing has changed. This is a true professional at work. None of this faux outrage of faux pride — a teacher doing her job.

She finishes the register and goes straight on to running through our tasks for the day. She wants us to start planning essay paragraphs. We can work together but we can't write the same thing, and chat and music is always allowed when you're in a class of eight. We all put one earphone in at the front table and I play my music very quietly. I want to try to involve myself in as much girl chat as possible. And it's not going to be hard based on how popular I've been today.

Mrs Watson always sounds so genuine. "Oh Molly, I've been hearing about you all day. The juniors were asking me all sorts of questions about it, the fourth years were a nightmare to settle down this morning. You must be exhausted."

"Yeah, that would be a word for it. But hey, it's a choice I made, and I'll leave it there."

"You seem to have a friend or two here now, though. And now, whenever the girls and I end up on one of our feminine tangents, you

274

won't feel left out by it all."

"That'll be nice!"

"Yep. Right, class! Books open and see what you all can come up with."

And that's it. That's all that Mrs Watson has to say on the matter. The girls on the other side of the room have nothing to add and for a fleeting moment, everything seems normal. That is until Ms Waverley pops in to see how we are getting on and finds her two isolated girls are back in class.

"Oh, girls! I wasn't expecting to see you two here!"

Mrs Watson continues to show why she is one of the very best.

"Oh, they asked me before the lesson. I said since it's just a class of eight and now all girls, I didn't see any issue with it."

"That's fair enough, then. Good practice for how the rest of the week will go. I'll leave you all to continue working hard on your history."

And then she vanished and that was it once more. No further chatting about Molly or having to justify my existence to everyone. The tension has evaporated, and now it just feels like history class. I love history class.

The odd tangents include chat about what was on TV last night (something I still have no idea or interest in but can at least try to understand) and then it's all about UCAS. That deadline is coming up in January. I really need to see Mr Francis about my applications, etc. But again, just nice to not have all of the conversation be about me. I've heard so much about myself today that I'm becoming white noise to my own brain.

One Week Down

Where do I begin with what's happened in my life since last Sunday?

Just eight days ago, I was an entirely different person on the surface — someone who lived completely at odds with my mind. He was hairy, he was gross, he dressed like he didn't care — more disgusting than anything, he was me. That sloth, that ugly creature, that horrid, gruesome monster — it was me. I was it. I was a monster. And every time I caught a glimpse at myself, be it in the mirror on in a shop window, I was served a bone-chilling reminder.

I'm not who I am. This thing that stared back at me stole the majority of my childhood. I was like a Disney child celebrity in just that sense and I only wish I could have had the immense wealth and worldwide fame to accompany the heartbreak. It would have really cushioned the blow on the overwhelming misery I felt day after day. It dragged me close to the edge once or twice. Not the edge that you'd think — I never wanted to hurt myself. What I wanted to do was almost even worse — I wanted to give up.

I wanted to just accept that my life would be wasted behind this husk of a boy. There's no other possible way for things to go, is there? There was no other choice, was there? Well, there was.

Like any other typical weekend, a former friend and I spent last Sunday together just wasting time for the thrill of doing so. Once he left, I was able to ditch the charade — or so I thought. Mum came home unexpectedly to catch me with high heels and a skirt on. I'd even used her lipstick, there was no other conceivable way to explain it. But just like that, I'd accidentally managed to do the one thing I longed to do on purposely for so long. I burst that fake bubble of a pretend boy and emerged in my true form as a girl.

To everyone else, I was disgusting. To everyone else, I was a freak.

But to me, I was finally happy. At long last, the weight of male expectation was off my feminine, soft shoulders. No longer would I have to live up to impossible standards that wouldn't even bring me a shred of joy had I reached them. No, now I could be myself. I could rewrite myself in my own image and really let the world see me for the first time.

Mum decided that I needed to take the week off school to work on this new beginning. My first steps were truly taken just last week, at the age of 16. My first word was contained within my first sentence. It was the first time I'd ever felt truly alive. We worked on feminine hygiene, we worked on makeup, we practiced walking and talking — in short, I rewired my brain to shake off all of that masculine mess and show off my feminine flair for the first time.

We went to see the doctor, the hairdresser and even managed to squeeze in a day of shopping for a new wardrobe. Not that we needed much though, since one of my neighbours donated her daughter's old clothes, not knowing exactly why my mum asked for them in the first place. I wonder what Courtney's going to say if she ever finds that out. Would I even want her to know? Is it creepy to even ask that question, even internally?

All of this practice and training was leading up to the pivotal meeting with the school's headteacher and the deputes. It was all riding on that one meeting. If I made a strong first impression, they would have to allow me to be myself. If it came off as nothing more than drag pageantry, it would have been laughed out of the building. Well, as there is now a part two to my story, I'm sure I don't need to tell you that the meeting was a success.

Come Monday — today — I was able to live my high school life as my real self. As Molly. I also came out to my older brothers just last weekend and they both seem to be all right with it. They have no real choice but they could hate me and disown me if they wanted to. They were actually pretty nice about it over the video call but let's see how they deal with me when I'm physically right in front of them.

Now, my old friends didn't appreciate the change of direction. They tried to laugh it off and they keep telling themselves that I'm only joking. Even now, the majority of the school doesn't want to believe in the girl who stands directly in front of them. The girl who stood on stage this morning and poured her heart out to everyone. I told my story. I confessed to the murder of my male mirage. I recounted my tale of sorrow and revelation in a bid to make the transition less turbulent but it was like a Boeing flying through a twister which caused a tsunami. Pretty much everyone at school hates me after today, some definitely more than others too. I do apparently have a few friends now, too. Only time will tell how genuine that all is but I like the girls, and they seem to at least not hate me.

I've spent the day in what is essentially quarantine today while the other students' and their toxic attitudes were free to roam the school. One girl, Chloe, decided to stay by my side all day and we did eventually break ourselves out and actually return to a classroom. That in itself had mixed results but then something odd happened. I wasn't the talking point. In that period of just over an hour, my identity faded from being the headline. I'm sure it was still the 'thème brûlant' everywhere else in the world.

Sorry, my French tick just came through. That term means 'burning issue.' Essentially, the French way of saying I was the major talking point. If Chloe's right, I'll be exactly that for a while to come yet. Parents don't even know yet. But they will. Everyone has to know eventually, and I'm more than through with concealing myself to keep other peoples' lives easier and less confrontational.

Anyways my Mum's car is outside to take me home after a busy first day of school. Where do I begin in recounting it?